Praise for *The Murder After the Night Before*

'What a ride! Unflinchingly rea[...]
also brilliantly funny at times, [...]
**Jesse Sutanto, author [...]
Unsolicited Advice [...]

'The horrors of going viral on social media
twinned with a twisty murder mystery –
contemporary fiction at its best, I loved it!'
Jackie Kabler, author of *The Perfect Couple*

'Funny, touching, horrifying and surprising almost in equal
measure with a brilliantly believable heroine… loved this book'
Catherine Cooper, author of *The Chalet*

'A fast-paced and satisfying read'
Charlotte Bigland, author of *It's Not Me It's You*

'*The Hangover* meets *Fleabag* in this ribald, twisted mystery'
PJ Ellis, author of *Love & Other Scams*

'Once again, Katy Brent has shown her immense talent at
writing dark humour with a thought-provoking core'
Sarah Clarke, author of *A Mother Never Lies*

'A flawlessly plotted murder mystery.
Devilishly brilliant. I loved it!'
Sarah Bonner, author of *Her Perfect Twin*

'*The Murder After the Night Before* is so page-turningly
compulsive Katy Brent may just be my new hero…
Feminist, funny and timely, it's everything I want in
a novel and then some. An absolute must-read'
Amy Beashel, author of *Spilt Milk*

'Totally addictive'
Hannah Tovey, author of *The Education of Ivy Edwards*

KATY BRENT is a freelance journalist and has been in the industry for over fifteen years. She started work in magazines back in 2005. In 2006, Katy won a PTA award for New Journalist of the Year. More recently she has focused on television journalism. Writing a book has always been her dream and lockdown finally gave the time she kept using as an excuse for not doing it.

Also by Katy Brent
How to Kill Men and Get Away With It

THE MURDER AFTER THE NIGHT BEFORE

KATY BRENT

HQ
An imprint of HarperCollins*Publishers* Ltd
1 London Bridge Street
London SE1 9GF

www.harpercollins.co.uk

HarperCollins*Publishers*
Macken House, 39/40 Mayor Street Upper,
Dublin 1, D01 C9W8, Ireland

This edition 2024

8

First published in Great Britain by
HQ, an imprint of HarperCollins*Publishers* Ltd 2024

Copyright © Katy Brent 2024

Katy Brent asserts the moral right to be
identified as the author of this work.
A catalogue record for this book is
available from the British Library.

ISBN: 9780008536718 (PB)
ISBN: 9780008665609 (TPB)

This book contains FSC™ certified paper and other controlled sources to ensure responsible forest management.

For more information visit: www.harpercollins.co.uk/green

This book is set in 11/16 pt. Sabon by Type-it AS, Norway

Printed and Bound in the UK using 100% Renewable Electricity at
CPI Group (UK) Ltd, Croydon, CR0 4YY

For Cherith, the brightest star in the sky

1

#IsMollyMonroeAwakeYet

*

From: SparkleMagazineGroup
To: All Staff
Subject: Staff Christmas Party
Date: 15 December
Time: 9.30

HEY YOU GUYS AND GALS!
Christmas is just around the corner and we're ready to celebrate tonight! Don't forget to collect your four drink tokens before the cars arrive to take us to the venue.

After a very difficult couple of years we know we are truly blessed to have such a dedicated and hardworking staff force. We really want to thank you for all your commitment and quality over this challenging time and hope to raise a glass with you later this evening as we look forward to the year ahead.

Your tremendous efforts have been hugely appreciated. This company remains a success because of each and every one of YOU!

You're all brilliant.

The HR Team x

PS: You need to be at Fire Meeting Point One at 6.30pm. ON THE DOT, guys, we're not waiting around for any stragglers. Cars are on the meter.

*

Oh.

My.

Dear.

God.

I know, before I even attempt to open my eyes, that this is more than just a hangover. It has to be, right? There is no way anyone can possibly feel this horrific and it be caused by alcohol alone. My poor head is pounding out a questionable drum and bass track while my throat feels like I've deep-throated a cheese grater.

I must have picked up a virus last night.

Yes. That has to be it.

Something dangerous and terminal.

Or.

Maybe I'm already dead.

That would explain why my eyes are burning and they're not even open. It must be the dazzling brightness of heaven.

Or.

The burning fires of hell. I think that's probably more likely.

Trust me to be so wholeheartedly agnostic only to find out that hell is real the hard way. I should've spent more time walking old ladies or whatever it is saints do. But, actually, this can't be hell because my poor dead head is resting on something really, really soft. And, actually, if I move my head a little bit to the right, there's a sweet spot where it's still cool. And I'm sure hell is neither cool nor soft. So. It's either a cloud or my pillow.

Okay. I'm pretty sure that I'm not dead and am actually just at home in my bed.

Dramatic bitch.

Still not convinced I'm not in the process of dying from a hangover though.

'You can't die from a hangover.'

A voice. A disembodied voice. An acousmêtre in (possibly) my bedroom.

I have a narrator now?

How very *Gossip Girl* of me.

I, very gingerly, open my eyes. Yay. It *is* my bedroom. I don't think I've ever been so happy to see my bedroom.

There is also a man in my bed.

A man I have never seen before in my life. Although obviously I must have seen him before because he presumably didn't simply materialise right here in my bed. I should probably be worried by his presence or at the very least slightly surprised, but the truth is, I am too hungover to care.

And I still do not recognise him.

Not one bit.

'You *do* realise you're saying these things out loud, don't you?' the man-stranger says.

Oh.

'Yeah. From "oh my dear God" right up until "oh". Just then.'

I twist my head on my pillow so I'm fully facing him. The world spins off its axis and my stomach flip-reverses like a Nineties R&B track. That's not me trying to explain how good-looking he is, by the way. Even though he is. The world *actually feels* like it has lurched into a different orbit. Am I still talking? The stranger in my bed (ooh that's a good title for my memoir, I must put it in my phone) doesn't reply so I assume my brain has finally caught up with my mouth.

He's definitely handsome.

Definitely someone I'd stare at, but lack the confidence to approach, in a bar.

Nice work, drunk me.

'Hi,' I say. I smile. Or it might be a grimace.

'Hi.' He smiles or grimaces back. Mirroring. This is good. I think.

'I'm Molly . . .'

He rolls his eyes.

Is it my breath? I try to surreptitiously check, but it's not the easiest thing to do when you're three inches from someone's face.

'I know. You're Molly Monroe, you're thirty-two and you work on a magazine for tween girls but you really want to write your memoir because apparently you've got *quite* the backstory. Although that was the *one* thing you didn't elaborate on. You share this flat with your best friend, Posey, who is also a journalist but a "proper" one. You don't believe in any god, but you're willing to hedge your bets when you're violently hungover. As demonstrated just moments ago.'

He pauses. Runs a hand over his face. Continues.

'And you never, *ever* usually do this kind of thing. Have I missed anything?'

'It would appear not.'

He studies me.

'Do you know *my* name, Molly Monroe?'

Of course I don't. I don't even remember his face let alone anything that needed auditory processing. I smile at him again. He smiles back. Again.

'I'm guessing that's a no then? By the way, Molly, you've got some lettuce in your—' He taps his front teeth.

'Lettuce?'

'From the kebab, I'd wager.'

'The kebab?'

'Yes. You owe me £4.20 for that by the way. And £19 for the cab.'

'I . . . I . . . do?' I don't remember a kebab. Or a cab.

'I'm kidding. I mean, it did cost that. But you don't have to pay me back.'

I'm so confused. Who is this person? Did we have sex? Why do I keep doing this sort of thing? I try to take a furtive look under the covers. I'm surprised to find that I'm still fully dressed. In last night's clothes. But that doesn't necessarily mean we didn't have sex. I do some kegels to assess the situation further. It doesn't feel like sex has happened. I mean, it's usually pretty obvious, right? Unless the guy is completely tiny. Or he couldn't get it up. But that doesn't mean stuff didn't happen. I wish I could just remember.

'You're talking again.'

Shit.

He props himself up on his elbow and looks at me. Kind of intensely, if I'm honest. Brown eyes. Like Galaxy Minstrels. Rudely attractive.

'We didn't have sex, Molly.' I can't work out if I'm pleased or mortally offended. 'You were insanely hammered. I mean, like ridiculously pissed. Absolutely all over the place.'

'Don't sugar-coat it or anything, please.' He has the decency to look sheepish.

'Sorry. I just wanted to make sure you got home safely. You didn't have a clue what was going on. I had to find your address from your driving licence and hoped it was up to date. And you kept leaving your bag everywhere. You were trying to put it in a bin at one point. You seemed to think it was a postbox and it would be sent back to you.' I'm horrified. Forget dying of a hangover, I now just want to die from utter humiliation. If there is a God, he/she can send a sinkhole to the Clapham Junction area, right now, so the ground can literally open up and swallow me. That would be ideal, really.

And he's still talking.

Great.

I can't get enough gut-wrenching embarrassment before

I've even had a coffee. 'You were sick in the Uber. Luckily you timed it pretty well and he kicked us out just up the road.'

'Yes. That sounds super lucky. Do you mind if I make a coffee before the next instalment?' I'm trying to hide how mortified I am with humour, but it's not landing and I just sound prickly. My man of mystery/knight in shining armour doesn't seem to notice though.

'Milk, no sugar, thanks. Have a go at remembering my name while you're in the kitchen.'

'All right, Rumpelstiltskin,' I mutter, scooting out of bed and wobbling to the door.

I hear him chuckling to himself as I stumble down the hallway to the kitchen, with all the coordination and grace of a newborn giraffe.

A really, *really* hungover one.

*

I drag myself through the lounge and into the kitchen where I give myself the speech about letting myself down with my carry-on and spot two things. The stinking remains of a kebab. And my phone. I scoop the kebab into the bin as I click the kettle on and reach for my phone. Hopefully it will give me some clues about the man in my bed. I pick it up and wobble it around a bit, waiting for the facial recognition to bring it to life. But it doesn't and I realise the battery has died and I was obviously too much of a drunken mess last night to plug it in to charge.

Of course.

This is standard practice for me. My dad even *insisted* I have a landline in the flat so he can at least get hold of me on that because my phone is never charged. Or it's lost. Plus he's super tight about calling mobiles as he doesn't have one. I take my annoyance at myself out on the phone and angrily scoot it across the worktop. I must remember to plug it in though or I'll have no music for the bus to work. I shudder at the idea of the forty-five-minute journey with only my thoughts to listen to. They're not being very kind to me right now.

As I wait for the kettle to boil (which is the most painful of sounds at the best of times) I try to recall something, *anything*, about last night. I can't have forgotten it all.

So, I know it was my work Christmas party. And we had it in some dingy pub basement and not a proper venue because it's like loads cheaper and cuts and all that stuff. And yes, it really was as depressing as it sounds. I'm pretty sure that's why Paloma – my work best friend – and I decided to make the most of the free drinks. It's very rare for us to get anything free from our company, so on the occasions they splash out – even for four drinks per person – we like to take full advantage. But the level of hangover I'm currently experiencing is substantially more than four drinks' worth. What happened last night? I never get blackout drunk. Well, hardly ever. Actually, it's something I do more regularly than I'd like to admit, even to myself.

As I'm pouring the hot water into the two mugs I've prepped with instant coffee, I have a sudden and unwelcome flashback of not-quite-cold white wine being poured into not-quite-clean plastic glasses and I feel that horrible vomit pre-cum gathering in my mouth. Knowing that a full-scale puke is only seconds away, I gather my hair up in one hand and rush to the sink just in time to watch half-digested kebab and salad – and chips by the look of things – saturated in a white wine and who-knows-what-else marinade clog up the drain.

I'm sick a total of three times before my stomach finally stops clenching and hating me. The sink is completely blocked and I know Posey, my flatmate who has the patience of a saint usually, is going to freak if she gets up and my regurgitated night out is the first thing she sees. My eyes are watering as I make a grab for the kitchen roll, to cover my hand while I pull the chunkiest bits out of the plughole. I'm so hungover and generally unable to get my brain and body working in harmony that I accidentally knock one of the mugs over with my elbow. It spills like an oil slick over the worktop, soaking everything in its wake. Tea towels, bills we've left after opening – and my phone. I reach for it, but it's too late. It's already a half-dead seal pup. I sigh heavily and swipe out the tub of rice which we keep especially for these moments and shove my phone in, hoping I've rescued it in time. I then have to take a few moments, letting my back slide down the wall, until I'm sitting on the floor. The temptation to lay my poor head on the cold, cold tiles is too much and I manoeuvre myself into a child's pose, letting my forehead rest on the soothing smoothness of parquet.

It only helps for about three seconds though and my head

starts swimming and pounding again. Miserably, I hoist myself onto my knees. Pain shoots through them. I'm too young to be getting joint pain, surely? I peek under the hem of the dress I'm still wearing from last night and spot a nasty graze on one knee. The skin around the wound is already darkening and I can tell there will be a bruise by lunchtime. Skirts will be out of the question for a week or so, then.

I shift myself onto my bum and inspect my other knee, which is in a similar state of ruin. I must've fallen over and landed on them. A flashback of me on my knees and drunk on some London street flickers in some part of my brain but I don't know if it's a memory, or if I'm imagining what could've caused my injuries. Anyway, it's gone before I can get a proper handle on it. I hoist myself up, quickly make another coffee to replace the one I spilled and head back down the hallway to my room.

'It's Jack,' he tells me as I hand him a mug, almost burning my hand off as I hold it towards him so he can take the handle. 'I thought I'd help you out as you're being such a gracious host.' He's out of bed and sitting on the edge of it now, also fully dressed. He's wearing a pair of black jeans and a black sweater, which looks like it could be cashmere. I want to rub my face against it. Instead, I sink down next to him on the bed and hold one of my hands to my aching head.

'Hi, Jack,' I say.

'No, no. I came here of my own accord.' He grins. I groan.

'Too early for dad jokes. Too hungover.'

He gives me a look of concern which may or may not be genuine. It's hard to tell when my vision is showing two of him.

'Do you have any painkillers or anything?' he asks. 'I think you should probably take something. You look like you're suffering.'

'I was sick in the kitchen,' I confess.

Jack eyes his mug and puts it down on the bedside table, gently pushing it away with his fingertips.

He rubs my back, almost tenderly, and for a moment I want to throw myself against his chest and wrap his arms around me, beg him to stroke my hair. I must be super hungover to be feeling this needy.

'Poor you,' he says. 'So from what I could gather, when I found you wandering around Vauxhall in tears, was that it was a big work night out?'

Oh Jesus. 'Tears?' Why was I crying?

'Yeah, you were pretty upset about something, but I couldn't work out what. Did you argue with someone?'

A flicker of something flashes in some neural pathway or another deep in my brain. But again, it dissolves into nothing before I can reach it.

'Maybe. And I was in Vauxhall? Alone?' This makes no sense. We were out in Soho. And I'd already agreed to go back to Paloma's with her. She lives in North London. We usually tag team like that on a night out so neither of us has to travel home alone. One of the many delights of being female in a big city. God, maybe I fell out with Paloma and that's why I'm here with a stranger instead of at her place, letting her feed me buttery toast. I rub my face. I don't want to go to work today. I wonder if I can call in sick but suspect it would be too obvious. Why do workplaces insist on having parties on weeknights?

'Yeah. Just sort of wandering around. Wailing. Near my house,' Jack says, giving me a weak smile, but the shame is already creeping up through my skin, coming out of my pores along with the alcohol. 'I couldn't just leave you like that. Anything could've happened. And you were actually quite delightful and charming once you'd forced me to buy you a kebab.'

'And chips,' I say.

'Oh, you remember the chips?'

I twist my head towards the kitchen. 'The clue was in the sick.'

BEEP BEEP BEEP BEEP BEEP

We both jump as the alarm on my Echo Spot goes off furiously. Well, Jack jumps. I cower like a wounded animal.

'Ah, I suppose that's your cue to get up?'

I shake my head miserably. 'That's my cue to leave the house or I'll be late. It's the cue that I slept through my phone alarms.'

He pulls a sympathetic face. 'And my cue to get going too in that case.'

I stand up to see him out but he waves me away. 'Don't worry about manners, Molly Monroe. Get ready. Get some paracetamol and get to work.' He makes his way to the door.

I stare after him, mutely, wishing I had the brain capacity

to think of something clever and/or funny to say. I can't. Then, just as I'm about to go and cry in the shower, he turns around.

'My number's in your phone by the way.' He smiles. 'Under Jack.'

2

*

I don't cry in the shower, as it turns out. Jack's smile and suggestion that I should call him – *I mean that's why his number is in my phone, right?* – have made me feel a bit better. Not *massively* better, I'm still horrendously hungover – possibly still drunk – but better enough to propel me into my en suite. And enough to make me smile a little as I rinse the soap, booze and shame down the drain.

I come out of the en suite – 'en suite' is *really* upselling what's basically a hose in a cupboard – dry my hair with a towel and look around for something vaguely clean to wear to work. As I'm grabbing a pair of leggings off the floor, I hear the front door close softly; Posey must have just left for work. It's quite late for her but I guess she might be interviewing someone or meeting a source or something. Whatever the reason I'm just thankful that I don't have to face her yet and have an awkward conversation with her about my drinking/the mess in the kitchen and/or bringing strange men back. I know, she's got a point and male violence against women blah blah blah, but she acts like she's never done anything like that in her life. And I can say as an on-the-ground eyewitness that she has. At uni she was probably worse than me. I've definitely had to scoop her off the floor a few times after too many £1 shots. You'd never think it to look at her now though. I can picture her disapproving face as she lectures me about keeping myself safe. I love Posey, and we've been friends for a long time. But she's not been the party girl I know and love since her big promotion a few months ago. Or maybe she's just finally behaving like a grown-up. Or maybe it's something to do with the fact that she didn't lose her mum at the age of twelve.

I look at my Echo. It's almost 9am. I'm supposed to be at my desk at 9.30. Even if my bus is running on time and traffic is good, it takes at least forty-five minutes door to foyer. I'm going to be late anyway and everyone else will be too, so I sit down in front of my dressing table to blow-dry my hair and put some make-up on. I might feel like something the dog coughed up, but I don't have to look it.

Twenty-five minutes later and I'm ready. I've even managed to run my GHD through my hair and give it a bit of bounce. There's not a great deal I can do about the shadows under my eyes or the very specific alcohol pallor I'm sporting, but whatever. I'm just going to be sat in the same office, seeing the same people I see every day. I feel a wave of anxiety roll around somewhere inside me as I remember Paloma and our probable argument.

I *need* to check my phone. I scream with frustration when, after five minutes of throwing pillows and clothes around in a panic at not being able to find it, I remember it's sitting in the rice box in the kitchen. I go and grab it, gritting my teeth as I realise it's still absolutely dead.

'For fuck's sake,' I hiss, reaching for my bag and my coat. I'll have to hope for the best when I get to the office. I slam the door behind me, silently cursing myself for not checking my keys are in my bag first – I've caught myself out like that many times before. I scrabble around in my bag for a moment, slight panic rising in my throat, until I feel the cool metal beneath my fingers and the reassuring weight of the novelty willy keyring Paloma 'Secret' Santa'd me. It's only then that I realise our next-door neighbour is standing outside his door, vacantly staring at me over the little wall that divides his house from ours. I jump slightly, spooked.

'Oh, morning, Patrick,' I say.

He doesn't reply though, just continues to stare in my direction, not actually at me, more through me. A few too many beats of silence pass before he says, 'Molly. Sorry, yes, good morning. I was miles away.' He smiles, suddenly, and his face settles into middle-aged laughter lines, but he has shadows under his eyes. He's one of those men who suit ageing, usually, but he looks pinched and strained this morning. Who am I to talk though? He's some sort of big-time lawyer and even though his face looks worn, his designer suit is immaculate.

'Were you up with the kids?' Patrick and his wife, Trudie, have a daughter who is about three and newborn twins but I'm not sure if they're boys or girls. They like to wake up early. Obscenely early. It's why I have earplugs. He frowns slightly at me, as if he can't make out what I'm saying and tugs his shirt collar. 'The kids?' I emphasise. 'Did they keep you awake?' God, this is hard work.

'The kids. Yes. They did. Sorry, I'm barely with it this morning. I need coffee, urgently. I'll let you get on.' He smiles apologetically before letting himself into his house and closing the door. Thank God he didn't want to hang around and chat. I like Patrick and Trudie, as much as anyone likes their neighbours in London, but my God they are dull. Trudie always has a look on her face that reminds me of a small prey mammal. She only ever talks about how tired she is or about the children. I got stuck next to her in the queue at Sainsbury's at the train station once and it was enough to make me swear never to have kids. Patrick's not much better. He isn't a great conversationalist, which makes me wonder how he's such a successful legal person. Don't they have to like give big speeches in court and stuff? I think Posey has a bit of a crush on him, but I can't see it myself. He's attractive in that successful older man way but he hardly oozes charisma. It's strange actually. On the surface they have it all. They're living the dream we're all sold. The big house in a nice area, two cars (which is just ridiculous in London because you don't even really need one), a litter of gorgeous kids, money, bifold doors. But they never seem to be very happy at all.

It's bitterly cold this morning so I shrug on my coat, pull the hood up and shove my hands deep into my pockets.

I shouldn't be too late if everything moves through town like it should. Although the ice which has made the ground slick doesn't bode well. Oh well. I blow out a cloud of air and start my trek to the bus stop.

It's not until I'm halfway down the road that I realise Patrick was going *into* his house in his suit. He doesn't work from home, that I know. And even if he did, why would he suit up for it? He probably just forgot something indoors, I decide. Being an adult doesn't make you immune to that kind of thing.

I should know.

*

It's so cold I find myself weirdly hoping that someone will sit next to me on the bus so I can siphon some body heat off them. I wish I could afford to get the train in. Even being squashed against someone else's armpit, but with proper heating, sounds luxurious right now. Or maybe I could be one of those super-fit people who cycle everywhere. There's zero chance of that ever happening though. I'm so accident prone, I'd last about two days before being mowed down and killed at a roundabout. The bus pulling into the stop breaks my thoughts up and the driver gives me a look which says, *Well, are you bloody getting on or not?* I step forward and wait for the doors to open and the heat from inside to warm me up.

I tap my card on the reader and look around. The bottom level is standing room only, so I drag myself up the stairs. If I get a seat up here I can maybe have a little snooze before I get to work. I sit down and pull my phone out of my bag before clicking my tongue loudly when I see the dead screen and remember – again – it's out of battery. Or drowned.

Never mind. I'm not really in the mood to scroll through social media and see that yet more of my friends are getting engaged, married or pregnant. Or promoted. I sound bitter. I'm not bitter. I know my time will come eventually and, until then, I'm quite happy to enjoy the last hurrah of my youth. Not many of my friends would be able to have a night like last night these days. Can't bring a fit man back when you've already got a partner/fiancé/spouse installed at home. And you can't roll into work late and hungover when you're head of a department. I'm just not ready for those responsibilities yet, or I'd have them. I firmly believe in divine timing.

I settle in my seat, propping myself up against the window and decide to daydream about Jack instead. I hope he's really as fit as I thought he was and I don't have some lingering beer goggles or something. It's also a very good sign that we didn't have sex. I've been in situations like that before where I've woken up knowing I've had sex, even though I can't remember it. So it shows he's a decent guy. Something gnaws at the back of my consciousness, reminding me that it's infinitely depressing considering a man *not* having sex with you when you're too drunk to consent as decent. The bar really is fucking low.

After about fifteen minutes the bus has filled up a bit

more upstairs and I can see a gaggle of teenage girls out of the corner of my eye. They all seem to be looking over at me and whispering, raising perfectly shaped eyebrows in my direction every so often. It's a particular type of hell being a teenage girl, but it's also quite disturbing being surrounded by them. I must look like an old mess. They're all in the plaid skirts and blazers which indicate they go to the expensive private school nearby. Urgh. I'd hate to be that age again. But I also hate that I can feel the weight of their stares and hear the occasional laugh. I really wish my phone was charged. I want nothing more now than to slip my earbuds in and sink into Spotify and oblivion. They're not *really* laughing at me anyway. It's just that horrible hungover anxiety. I'm feeling bad because I can't remember last night and can't access my phone to find out what happened which led to me being alone and in tears in Vauxhall.

I try to block out my paranoia by focusing on what I *can* remember. It's a grounding exercise I was taught by a therapist once, not long after Mum died and I was having regular panic attacks. What do I know for sure? What is fact? I remember arriving at the venue with Paloma, everything was fine then. We'd got ready in the office and then walked into Soho because we missed the bus that the company had provided. We stopped at a pub near Bond Street station for a quick drink because as Paloma said, 'The idea of walking into that viper nest stone-cold sober is enough to give me the runs.' We each downed a large glass of Sauvignon Blanc. And we got the rest of the bottle free, so we necked that as well. We were both tipsy when we arrived at the mock-Tudor pub whose basement function room our company had hired. Nothing says the season of goodwill quite like a pub basement, after all.

'Putting the fun in function room,' Paloma had murmured as we checked in our coats and collected our drinks vouchers.

'Dysfunction room more like,' I'd replied, staring at our co-workers out of situ and feeling a snaking sort of terror coil around my insides as I spotted middle-aged Carol from human resources spinning around on the dance floor, totally alone, in her flat, comfortable work shoes.

Paloma snorted. 'Putting the HR in HRT.'

I remember laughing at that. I remember swapping our drinks vouchers for those plastic glasses of not-quite-cold-enough white wine. There was a beautiful young bartender who made me feel frumpy and old.

But everything else is a blur. The memories are there, but like a bar of soap in a bath. Impossible to grasp. I hope Paloma and I didn't fall out. I want to tell her about finding a handsome man in my bed this morning. I want to tell her about Jack.

I squeeze my eyes shut, willing my brain to work a bit better as the bus grinds to a stop, stalled by a traffic jam.

'Urgh. *Come on*,' I hiss in frustration, which causes the teens to shriek with laughter. Grow up.

But the laughter dislodges something in my brain. A grain of a memory where there's laughing and bright lights, not the dysfunction room though. Hands on me. Shot glasses being clinked. The memory of sambuca is so sharp I can almost taste it.

And then it's gone. Back into the impenetrable depths of my psyche.

I huddle deeper into my seat, trying to make myself smaller, less.

The giggles and whispers of the girls are causing my anxiety to rise and fall so much I feel like I'm on a particularly turbulent flight and not the 137 bus.

I need to get off.

I stand up and stagger slightly in my rush to press the bell to make the bus stop.

As I half walk, half fall down the stairs, I swear I hear someone say: 'Slag.'

God, I need to stop drinking. I can't handle this morning-after paranoia.

I'm two stops from where I need to be, but I don't care. I get off the bus and greedily breathe in the smog of Central London in morning rush hour.

'Breathe, Molly,' I tell myself. 'Everything's fine.'

*

I spend the ten-minute walk to the office trying to remember other grounding CBT stuff I've been taught. What can I see? What can I hear? What can I smell? Buildings, cars and petrol. Probably not quite the holistic ideal behind the technique, but it keeps my mind occupied as I make my way to my office building. It's nestled away on an unremarkable side road near Hyde Park Corner between the goods entrance of a chain hotel and a bakery that claims to be French but produces a depressing amount of instant coffee and thick tea in polystyrene cups. There's always a smell of detergent and cooking outside. Our company, Sparkle Media, used to have all five floors but we've been reduced to just two over the past year. I'm not even sure what the other floors are used for now.

Nausea tumbles in my stomach as I rush into the building and swipe my security pass. I'm alone in the lift to the fourth floor – where *Girl Chat* lives – which I'm pleased about as I'm in no mood for small talk. I breathe deeply – in and out, in and out – like the app on my dead phone would tell me to if it could, in an attempt to calm the storm in my gut.

I have a weird feeling as I'm making my way through our semi-open-plan office to my desk, almost like I'm doing the walk of shame not just coming in to work on a normal, if slightly hungover, Thursday morning. It's more like I'm stumbling home, reeking of stale wine and disgrace, my knickers in my bag, while everyone else is still in bed.

I'm getting too old for this.

Paloma is already at her desk. Her eyes widen when she sees me and she immediately shuts down whatever she was doing on her computer. She looks up at me, guiltily. Was she talking about me with someone? Fuck. I wish I could remember if we fell out. And if so, what it was about.

'Hey,' I say, carefully, like pressing a bruise to check if it still hurts.

'Molly,' she says. I can't work out her tone. Is she being cold with me? She sounds more surprised than anything. 'I didn't think you'd be in today.'

I attempt a laugh but it comes out strangled. 'I was seriously drunk but it would have been too obvious to pull a sickie today.' I pull out my chair, trying to appear casual and nonchalant and not like my heart is punching its way out of my chest.

'No, it's not that, it's—'

'Listen.' I sit down and wheel myself over to her on my chair. 'I really can't remember anything. Like, total blackout. I'm really sorry if we argued. You know what I'm like. Can't keep my mouth shut when I've had too many wines.' I'm certain I hear a stifled laugh from somewhere in the bowels of the office. I look around but everyone's heads are down.

'We did argue a bit but it's not that—'

I wheel in even closer. Oh, God. Something in my core liquifies. 'I can't remember getting home,' I go on. 'And there was a strange guy in my bed this morning. Well, not strange, he was actually very nice. Hot, too.' I shake my head. 'Not that that's important. Nothing happened. He just made sure I got home. Which was really very nice of him . . .' I trail off, aware I am babbling.

'Shit, Molly.'

'What? What is it?'

'You don't know, do you? Seriously?'

I shake my head again, slower this time, dumbly. And for a few seconds I have that lost-footing lurching sensation deep down inside me, because I know something terrible has happened. Something that can't be undone. The terror that's been lurking inside me since I woke up takes its chance to get me fully in its grip and I'm beginning to spiral. What is it? A terror attack? Has someone died? Has some mad world leader pointed a nuke at us? I feel completely sick again and take some deep breaths. 'What's happened?' My voice is a whisper now.

'Haven't you seen your phone?' Paloma is looking at me like *I'm* a bomb.

'No.' I reach down and pull it out of my bag. 'I didn't charge it when I got in last night and then it got wet, so it's been in the rice box. Paloma, please. What's going on?'

She hands me her charger and I plug my phone in while she inhales slowly, bracing herself for something as we wait for my phone to come to life.

But she doesn't get the chance.

Just as my phone starts to come back from the brink of death, the door to Robyn's – she's the editor of *Girl Chat* – office swings open. Carol from HR is in there with her.

I gulp, involuntarily. Loudly.

'Molly. Can we have a quick word, please?' Oh, God. A 'quick word' is passive-aggressive office-speak for 'you're massively in the shit'. Or 'we're letting you go'. A thousand possibilities race through my mind at once. Am I in trouble for my too-many sick days? Robyn had wanted to talk to me about that. Or was I a complete mess at the party? I shouldn't mix alcohol with my anxiety meds.

Paloma's eyes are back on her computer and she doesn't look at me as I walk into Robyn's office, feeling like I'm heading for the gallows.

3

@anonymouse: How can you give a blow job
when you ain't got no lips?

*

Robyn doesn't look happy.

To be clear, she *never* looks happy. She's got one of those faces that always looks a bit pinched and pissed off. Resting chewing-on-a-wasp face, Paloma calls it. But this is different. The rage – and something else, something I can't place – is emanating from her and I desperately want to scurry back out and hide behind my computer. Or, better still, in the loos.

Meanwhile, Carol is looking down at her shoes – are they the same flats as last night? – and tapping her pen on her knee. Another fragment of memory comes back to me and it's something to do with Carol and she's turning her back on me. But then, like before, it's gone. Only this time I can feel its shameful residue bury snarly roots deep within me.

'Sit down please, Molly,' Robyn says, indicating the empty

chair in front of her desk. Carol's slightly to the right of it and still won't look at me directly. Like I'm the Medusa or something.

I sit down, right on the edge of the chair, tucking my feet underneath. Neatly. Like that will make any difference to whatever this situation is.

'I don't think I need to explain to you why you're in here, do I?' says Robyn, then kinder, adds, 'Molly, what were you thinking?'

I look at her. She's trying hard to keep her voice level. 'I don't know . . . I don't remember.' I look at my hands, which are wringing each other tightly in my lap.

'Molly. This is serious. I can't believe I'm having to tell you this.'

'I don't know what to say,' I tell her, not looking up. 'I'm guessing I was drunk and inappropriate and upset a lot of people?' I brave a look at Carol, who can't move her eyes from me now, her expression unreadable. 'Did I upset you, Carol? I'm so sorry.'

'Well, you were quite unkind at one point actually, Molly, but that's not what this is about.'

Oh. God.

Robyn perches on the edge of her desk and examines me for a moment, assessing. She sighs, deeply, and I think I hear her murmur 'fuck' under her breath but I'm not sure because the blood that is suddenly rushing into my ears is deafening.

'Okay, Molly,' she says. 'You need to brace yourself, because I'm going to show you something now. And it's not going to be very nice for you to see.' Robyn's initial fury has

27

dissipated and she's now looking at me with something like concern as she spins her computer screen around to face me.

At first, I don't know what I'm looking at.

It's a grainy video that looks like CCTV footage, but I can soon tell from some sniggering and dodgy camera work that it's been filmed on a phone. It's almost dark but I can make out the outside of a pub or bar. There are a few people milling around, smokers, stragglers, whatever. And then the camera zooms in and the image hits me like a fist.

A woman on her knees in a busy London street.

A woman kneeling in front of a man.

A woman with a man's hands on her head, in her hair, as she bobs backwards and forwards at his groin.

And that woman is clearly, unmistakably me.

My head spins and I clutch my stomach, feeling like my bowels might drop out of my body. And it's bile pumping through my veins now, not blood. I clutch Robyn's desk and try to remember my breathing exercises as I watch my knuckles turn white. But I can't even remember *how* to breathe and I'm gasping for air while Carol gently puts one of her hands over one of mine. I'm fascinated by it for a second, transfixed by her wedding band, a liver spot, nude manicured nails.

'Molly, come on. Breathe with me,' she's saying. 'You're having a panic attack. Breathe in and out slowly. Come on. It's okay. Could you get her some water?' She's talking to Robyn like *she's* the boss and Robyn is doing what Carol is telling her and it's all wrong. And there is a video of me giving someone a blow job on my boss's computer and my boss has seen it and so has Carol and who else and what is happening. 'Do you have a paper bag?' Carol is asking Robyn now and Robyn is staring at me like I'm dangerous, but she's also scrabbling around for a Pret bag that's on her desk. She shakes out what looks like a cheese and ham croissant but that's wrong too because Robyn doesn't eat carbs and maybe doesn't eat anything at all. But she must do because now Carol is turning the bag inside out 'so you don't inhale the crumbs' and she's holding it over my nose and mouth, so very gently. And she's nudging my right hand with her left one, encouraging me to hold the bag myself. 'Okay. Now Molly, breathe in for four and out for four. Slow that breathing right down. That's it.'

And it works. I remember how to breathe.

After a few moments, my heart isn't trying to bang its way out of my body through various pulse points and my thoughts aren't a mash of madness. Carol smiles gently and takes the bag away. She puts a glass of water into my hand, telling me to take little sips and I start crying. It's been so long since I've felt like someone has taken care of me. And it's taken a video of me on my knees performing drunken fellatio to make it happen. My head's hanging down and I can't seem to lift it. My own body is so ashamed of me that it won't let me be in control of it.

'Are you all right?' Robyn asks me after what feels like several decades.

'Not really.' I try a smile, but the muscles in my face aren't working properly so it comes out strained and twitchy. 'Where . . . where did you get that?'

Robyn and Carol exchange a look. Without words they

discuss who is going to deliver the bad news. Carol does a small nod and takes my hand again, which I'm sure isn't really allowed in HR-land. 'Molly. It came to our attention that this video has been posted online.' She squeezes my hand so so gently, like my bones are baby-bird fragile.

'Right.' Online. But what are we talking here? Social media? MailOnline? Or like page three of Google search? 'Where?'

Carol opens her mouth to say something, but it's Robyn who delivers the killer blow. Which is what I will probably call my memoir. Should I not die from mortification right here and now. Which I sort of hope I do.

'You're trending on Twitter!' It's not quite a shout, more a yelp. 'Have you not looked at *anything* this morning?'

I shake my head and my bottom lip starts to wobble. I can't stop it. 'I didn't charge my phone last night and then I was late so . . .' I trail off. 'Twitter?' I remember how shifty Paloma was acting when I came in. She must've been looking at it. Oh, God. OH, GOD. I'm whimpering.

'I'm going to make you a nice tea.' Carol pats my hand. 'It's going to be okay, Molly.'

Robyn's stare is stony as Carol lets the door click shut behind her. 'I wish I could say the same, but this is bad, Molly. You'd better have a look.'

I don't want to.

I don't want to.

I want to close my eyes and crawl under Robyn's desk and wait there until they call my mum to come and pick me up. But this isn't school and I'm not seven. And my mum is dead. The thought of Mum makes me start crying again. Who else has seen this?

'Molly. You need to face this. This is happening.' Robyn's voice is softer. She's not much older than me and, despite being my boss, is clearly very much out of her comfort zone. She clicks Twitter open and pushes the wireless mouse over to me.

There's a saying that goes something like, the thing you fear is never as bad as the fear itself, isn't there? Well, let me tell you this, that's a load of crap.

Because this is truly, truly beyond anything even my twisted brain could come up with.

I'm a hashtag.

#IsMollyMonroeAwakeYet

And I'm not just trending locally, oh no, Robyn's Twitter trend settings are national so she can keep an eye on the things the whole country is talking about.

And right now, one of those things is me.

I click on the hashtag and blink numbly as the tweets load. There's too many to read but I skim and scroll and get the gist of it. I've been tagged in a lot of the posts, by people I don't know falling over their cyber-selves to name me or call me a 'slag' and all the other versions of it.

Carol comes back in with a mug of tea and sets it down next to me but I barely register anything else as I keep scrolling.

From what I can piece together, the video was originally posted on Twitter around midnight. It's a recording of a TikTok live, broadcast at 11.35pm last night. The anonymous (shock) Twitter account has the audacity to ask: 'anyone know who this mess of a cocksucker is? Lolol. Someone's gonna have a sore head in the morning.'

The first few replies aren't so awful.

Look at the tinsel in her hair. Someone needs to tell that chick that the party is over.

Well it ain't for that dude lol

This has been retweeted over five thousand times. Lots of party popper GIFs and bottles of Champagne being uncorked.

Hideous, yes.

But ultimately harmless. And something I'd probably even laugh at. Or would have. Yesterday, when it wouldn't have been me.

It's a few hundred retweets later where it gets really unpleasant.

M8 though! Who is this dirrrrrty piece? Look at her just noshing off her man in public like that. No fucks given. What a slaaaaaaaaag.

Prolly not even her own man, dirty bitch

The retweet count is going up as I watch.

It's a few people who name me.

Looks like a girl I went to school with. Think she's called Molly. Haha. Didn't know she was such a bike. @gleesh69 this Molly?

That dirty piece is called Molly Monroe. She works in the same company as ma GF. Hey @MollyMonroeNotMunro. How ya doing? Bet she'll be taking a sickie.

And that was it.

Named.

Shamed.

No one asks who the man is.

Similar stuff follows. There's lots of comments talking about my oral sex technique, of course.

@MollyMonroeNotMunro blahdy hell sis. This is just a handy with a tongue on the end lololol. Tips babe, get that dick right down your throat, pet.

Someone else had found a photo of me from the magazine's website and posted it along with the caption: 'How can you give a blow job when you ain't got no lips?'

Again, hundreds of replies including one – bizarrely – from an aesthetics company asking if I would like a consultation for lip enhancement injections.

I made a promise to myself many years ago that I would never cry at work. I didn't want to be one of those women you see in the toilets, weeping or reapplying ruined mascara because of something that's happened in their personal life. Something they've let creep into their professional life.

Tears are not for work.

But, as I have limited control over my body at this moment, fat tears are spilling out, falling onto Robyn's desk, faster and faster.

And it's not just tears.

There are horrible noises coming out of me that I can't control either. Gasps and sobs and shudders that make Robyn and Carol look at each other like worried owners of a cat that's coughing up a fur ball.

'Maybe that's enough, pet?' Carol says and Robyn clearly thinks I've seen enough too, as she turns her computer screen away from me.

She hands me a tissue from a little packet on her desk and waits while I calm my breathing again. It's like I'm having an out-of-body experience. I can see myself sat, huddled on the chair in Robyn's office, but I can't feel myself here.

It's like I'm watching myself on a screen.

A video filmed on someone's phone.

Robyn looks at me, quizzical, puzzled. Like she doesn't know what to do with me. She's had girls in here crying before, of course. When someone has been dumped or been the victim of some baseline trolling about something they'd written, but this particular hysteria is definitely a first for her.

A first for all of us.

'I think it's probably for the best if you go home for now, Molly,' she says finally.

I look up at her, horrified.

'Am I being fired?'

'No,' Carol says firmly, before Robyn has a chance to open her mouth. 'Not at all. But we need to work out what's gone on here and there's obviously your mental health we need to consider as well as the reputation of the company and other things.'

The 'other things' are unsaid, but she means complaints that people will make or have already made about me. Staff and readers, advertisers etc. Urgh. It's clearly a minefield and not one they can keep a lid on now it's viral. *Girl Chat* is all about preteen innocence. I spend most of my professional life writing about baby animals. A video of me giving head in a London street isn't exactly on-brand.

'We've contacted Twitter and asked for the video to be

removed,' Robyn tells me. 'Although, it's going to be hard to keep a lid on now it's been shared so many times. But because it's a video involving a sex act, it could be seen as revenge porn so we're going to push for that angle. If we can find out who posted it and why. Do you have any idea who could have done this? Do you know who the man is? Is it a boyfriend? Someone you've been out with?'

I shake my head and whimper a no.

'Okay. The other thing we need to consider, and this might be tricky for you to think about, but you are clearly very drunk in the video. I think you should consider whether or not you were too drunk to consent to what happened. There's the very real possibility that you were sexually assaulted, Molly.'

The words are a sucker punch.

I feel Carol's hand gently touch my shoulder, but it makes me flinch.

'Sorry, sweetheart,' she says. 'I know it's a lot.' Then to Robyn. 'I'm going to call her a car, okay? She shouldn't be going home on the Tube.'

Robyn nods her agreement and Carol skulks out of the office again.

'You should go and get anything you need from your desk,' Robyn says. 'And think about what we've said. Call me anytime, okay? I mean it.'

I walk back into the main office and everyone is suddenly very busy looking at their screens or phones or cuticles. Anything that isn't me.

'Are you okay?' Paloma asks as I unplug my phone. Five

hundred and ninety-eight notifications. Thirty-eight missed calls including from my dad. My dad, who never calls my mobile. Shame runs its nails down my spine again.

I look at her. 'Not really.' I try to give an ironic laugh, but it comes out like I'm being choked.

Or like I'm gagging on a stranger's dick.

'I've been sent home.'

'Oh,' Paloma says. 'On full pay or what?'

I hadn't even thought of that. 'I . . . I don't know. I didn't ask.'

We both glance through the glass walls of Robyn's office, but she's got her chair swivelled the other way and is involved in a deep and important conversation on the phone, judging by her gesticulations. Now isn't the time to go back in there and ask about money, I'm guessing.

Paloma touches my arm. 'Call her later, you need to know where you stand.'

'Or kneel,' someone on the opposite desk says. I don't catch who it is, but Paloma clearly does as she stands up and starts shouting at Beulah, an art director who's been here about six months.

'Shut your mouth,' Paloma snarls.

'It's not *me* who needs to keep my mouth closed. Is it?' Beulah snipes back.

'You know what? It's women like you that make it harder for the rest of us,' Paloma says. 'What you're saying is fucking misogynistic.' She sits back down and mutters 'arsehole' under her breath. I can feel the fury radiating off her.

'Don't worry about it, Lo,' I say, giving Beulah a look my mum would have called 'daggers'.

'I do though. You shouldn't be having to put up with that shit at work. You should report her.'

'I've got bigger things to worry about at the moment.' We're keeping our voices low. I've been shocked out of my hangover but am still in that weird limbo out-of-body place. I look around my desk and grab a few things for no reason at all.

'Don't forget Duckie,' Paloma says, handing me the stuffed duck that sits between our computers. My mum gave him to me on my first day of school, for good luck. Well, thanks, Mum. That's worked out well for me. I blink back tears. Crying in front of Robyn and Carol is one thing. Bawling in the middle of the office is another.

'Molly pet, your car's here.' Carol appears from nowhere and picks up my jacket for me. 'Come on, love, get yourself home. Have a rest and we'll catch up later, okay?'

I give Paloma a small smile as Carol ushers me out of the office and into the lifts like she's a bodyguard. I feel terrible again that she's being so nice to me when I am almost certain I would have been a nasty, drunken bitch last night. Less than twelve hours ago. It's mad to think how much has changed since then.

Carol hands me my coat and tells the driver where to take me. 'I'll call you soon, love. Just have a rest for now and try to stay off that thing until I do.' She points at the phone, which has been pinging away like popcorn in my hand. She gives my shoulder a gentle squeeze before closing the door.

'Clapham then, love?' asks the driver and I nod, catching his eye briefly in the rear-view mirror. I wonder if he's seen the video. Or if he knows the reason I'm being sent home from work at – I look at the clock in the car – 10.34am.

'Yes please,' I say. 'Just off Lavender Hill.'

If he does know anything, he stays respectfully quiet as we make our way through the nicer parts of London. I press my forehead against the window of the car thinking how different this is to my journey in to work just an hour and a bit ago. All I was thinking about then was telling Paloma about Jack. And hoping that we'd not had some huge row.

Now I'm confused about everything.

The tiny charge my phone managed to pick up while plugged in at work has run out and it's a brick in my hands again. But maybe a brick with answers. I look at it thoughtfully as we drive, wondering if there might be some clues as to why I was in Vauxhall or why I was crying. And, who the man in the video might be. I try to make the pieces fit together, but they won't. Too many are missing. It's like a jigsaw bought from a car boot.

The street is painfully quiet as we pull up to the flat. We're the ground floor and basement of a Victorian (I think, I don't know, I'm not a historian) house. The other two floors are a maisonette, also owned by Jesse, our landlord. It's usually rented out but Jesse's living there at the moment. There's a story as to why but Posey knows more than me. She's good at that sort of stuff. A proper newspaper journalist. Posey can grill someone, get a hard news line *and* a touching personal story out of them before they even realise they're being interviewed. Not like me. I've been stuck at *Girl Chat* for the past five years writing for nine-year-old girls. I'm pretty much an expert on llamas and sloths but that's about it. I cringe into myself as I remember the image of me sucking off a random man.

No wonder Robyn doesn't want me in the office.

I thank the driver for the lift, noting that he's still avoiding eye contact with me, take a deep breath and scuttle out of the car. There's no one around, thank God. As I'm trying to get my key in the lock, I have a sudden flashback to my awkward encounter with Patrick this morning. Could he have seen the video? Is that why he was acting so weird? The thought of him seeing me like that makes me feel dirty and I scurry into the flat before anyone sees me.

4

@ScouseJim: PSA: Do Molly in the loo,
not on the streets.

*

Both of the flats are self-contained and I'm grateful I don't
have to worry about running into Jesse, as I shuffle miserably
through my front door. To the left is Posey's room. As she
pays the bulk of the rent, she gets the master bedroom with
the huge bay window, the en suite that is a proper bathroom
– complete with one of those gorgeous free-standing baths
with the claw feet – and enough space to swing a fairly large
cat. Maybe an ocelot.

She's also got a bit more privacy than me as I have to go
down three little steps before reaching my room. It means our
rooms aren't quite back to back and there's a good amount
of wall between them. Which is obviously a good thing when
two single women in their early thirties live together. The
thought of sex makes me shudder. It's a life of celibacy and
sobriety for me from now on.

Posey's door is firmly closed I notice as I take my shoes off and I shuffle down the three stairs, not even wanting to look into my own room as I walk by. I can still smell the vague hint of stale alcohol, manly aftershave and despair as I pass it. My stomach dips and rolls as my mind tries to rifle through the black hole of last night. Again, I have a half-memory of someone screaming at me, but it's gone before I can get a proper grasp on it. Was it a scream of anguish, terror or just absolute disgust?

I have no idea.

The flat has that weird middle-of-the-day feeling about it. It's quiet, no TV or radio white noise. No one moving around upstairs.

Like an illicit sick day.

I stalk past my room and into the lounge where I throw my bag down on the floor and glance at my dead phone. I know Carol *very specifically* told me not to look at anything, but I should at least charge it properly. Plus, how can she seriously expect me *not* to. Yes, part of me wants to crawl into the little cupboard where the boiler and our towels live, and stay there forever, having meals delivered to me by Deliveroo. But there's that other part of me that *needs* to know what's being said. That part of me that wants to keep poking my brain again and again asking, 'Does this hurt? What about this? What about this?'

I take in a lungful of air, noting that the bins need taking out, and plug my phone into the emergency charger which we always have next to the TV because one of us will not be able to find our *actual* charger. It's a good system that only fails when one of us takes the emergency one to work or something. And forgets it.

That's usually me.

As I wait for the charger to do its magic, I go into the kitchen to make myself a hot drink. I grimace as I pass the sink, remembering throwing up in it earlier. I quickly wipe it and throw some bleach down the drain before bits of my puke cause a blockage and we have to call in Jesse. My stomach does another flip of revolt as I realise Jesse has probably seen the video too. There's something grimy about him. I can picture him holed up in one of his 'investment properties', watching it, with the curtains closed.

Why am I picturing *that*?

What the fuck is wrong with me?

The thought of everyone I know and have ever known seeing the video fills me with another overwhelming surge of horror and I fall to the floor, gulping down big, shuddery sobs.

*

I stay there, crying, for about twenty minutes before I decide to look at my phone. I then spend another twenty minutes sobbing even more when I realise I hadn't switched it on at the wall. I want to speak to Posey so badly. I remember I can message her from my laptop and feel relief fill me up. Maybe she can even come home and we can watch movies on the sofa or something. Anything to take my mind off what's happening to me online. My laptop is in my bedroom so I have to brave the horrors from this morning. It strikes me, again, how odd it feels that only a few hours ago, I was a different person. One with a mammoth hangover, sure, but excited about the nice man in my bed, looking forward to a gossip with my work friends, a life still intact.

I tiptoe into my bedroom, closing my door behind me and clicking the light on. I hadn't bothered opening the curtains on the small, narrow window that looks out over the paved corridor between our back gate and the tiny back garden. Posey's tried to make the space look pretty with some potted plants but it's still mostly drab and damp. My room smells of alcohol-sweat and there's the lingering scent of vomit too. I suddenly recall someone holding my hair back. Was that here? Was that Jack? I try to grab the image: Are they male hands, are they friendly hands? Are they holding my hair back or pushing my head down? But the wisp of memory floats away as quickly as it came.

I open my laptop and switch it on. The last few websites I was looking at appear, showing the woman I was yesterday. The woman I was before last night. I'd been doing some fantasy holiday-ing. This is a particular favourite pastime of mine when I'm feeling low. I search for beach holidays I'd never in a million years be able to afford. It has the weird effect of making me feel simultaneously better and much, much worse. I'd inexplicably been reading about the Greek islands when really a day trip to Bognor is much more my reality.

I shut down the page, watching the ridiculously blue seas and the houses on stilts evaporate into pixels, before disappearing completely.

I'd also been optimistically looking at bikinis and beachwear, clearly forgetting that I live in a London flat-share, I have no savings and my family home has been sold. I click the little cross that shuts all the internet pages down. None of it is important anymore. That version of me doesn't exist.

I relaunch Chrome and open the iMessage app. I quickly tap out a message to Posey asking if she's seen what's happened. The message whooshes off into cyberspace but doesn't show as delivered. Weird. I resend but the same thing happens. *Please don't be off-grid on some story today, Posey. I really need you.* Ignoring Carol's advice I open Twitter. I've never been able to leave a wound alone.

My account, which is unlocked and had a couple of hundred followers last time I looked, now has over fifteen thousand. My last comment has become a long, long thread. Mostly of abuse, but there's an occasional offer from men I don't know, offering up their dicks for sucking. My DMs are currently at 909 unread. I dread to think what's in there. I can guarantee it's worse than what's being said on my public timeline. I've been tagged in reposts of the video over and over again, more times than I can count. Any hope I was clinging on to about it being deleted somehow evaporates.

Tomorrow's chip paper.

It's my mum's voice in my head. I picture her standing in our little kitchen in her kind-lecturer pose. Her hands on her hips and her head tilted to one side.

'It's not though, is it?' I wail out loud. 'It's online forever. Whenever someone searches for me, this is what they'll see.' Tears sting my eyes again and I wish my mum was with me right now.

I look at my cutesy Twitter page. I'm smiling in my profile pic. It's few years old now and I look young and happy. I can't *remember* being that young and happy and I get a weird, almost-homesick type of feeling when I enlarge it. It's not homesickness. I've never been homesick for anywhere. People sometimes. My mum, mostly. A pang of longing for her almost floors me and I shake it away. I'm a grown woman. I'm too old to be wanting my mum when things go wrong.

You're never too old to need your mum.

That's what she'd say to me if she were here. Then she'd probably clap her hands together, all business-like, and make me a cup of sugary tea. The cure-all for everything. I miss her. I wrap my arms around myself and take three deep breaths. I need to focus on the present.

I stare at the face of my twenty-seven-year-old self. I'm almost unrecognisable. Has life really pummelled me that much in a few years? The banner on my Twitter page is a childish illustration of non-existent animals like panda-corns, unicorns, bunnies with wings. My profile blurb is shouty and doesn't sound like a thirty-two-year-old woman.

@MollyMonroeNotMunro
Hi! I'm a writer on Girl Chat and love all things unicorn, alpaca and llama! I also love anything sparkly or glittery and long weekends with my friends! She/her

It's so at odds with the video that now covers my timeline that I actually have to move to my tiny bathroom and throw up in the loo until nothing comes out apart from a yellowy liquid. There's no way I won't get fired over this. No way at all.

There are hundreds and hundreds of comments which gradually get nastier. Sometimes the comments break off into their own threads. The rape threat one is pretty gruesome. There are even some death threats in there. I click 'report' on a few of the comments, then give up and slam my laptop closed again. I was hoping that there would be some clue as to either who posted it, or who the man I'm with could be.

Then I remember Jack.

He seemed so adamant that he had been the good guy who'd brought me home at the end of the night. What if he's lying? But no, he found me, inexplicably, in Vauxhall and the video, though grainy, is clearly Central London. Still, maybe he's remembered something else by now. He might be able to cast some light into the shadowy recesses of my mind.

I go back into the living room where my phone has now come alive and is vibrating every few seconds with notifications. I quickly change the settings, turn notifications off and scroll through my contacts until I find his name.

Before I even get the chance to hit the call button, the landline starts ringing. As usual, it makes me jump out of my skin. Posey and I always startle when it rings. It's such a rare event that we forget we even have one most of the time and it never fails to terrify us. Then we laugh at ourselves. Once our heart rates return to a normal level, of course. It's not very funny when you're having a panic attack.

'What the fuck is *that*?' I remember Posey hissing one night, eyes wide with confusion. 'Is it an alarm? Are we on fire? Are we dying of carbon monoxide?'

'I think it's ye olde landline,' I'd said as I stood up and walked over to where it sat in a cradle near the TV, my movements exaggerated, like those of a very old lady.

Only marketing companies and my dad ever call the landline. My dad never calls me – well, apart from today. My hands tremble as I pick up the cordless landline phone, knowing already it will be him.

'Molly?' His voice is gruff and I wonder if he's started smoking again. I hate that he doesn't look after himself properly anymore.

'Hi, Dad,' I say, 'how are you doing?'

'Never mind about me,' he says, not unkindly, then he waits.

What do I even say? *Hi, Dad! Guess you've seen a video of me doing the rounds on social media by now. Yeah, I'm annihilated drunk. Yes, that is me giving a bloke a blow job outside a pub.* No. I can't say any of that. But the unending silence is so painful.

'Are you calling just to let me know you're not speaking to me?' I finally ask.

'No,' comes the reply. 'What the hell were you thinking, Molly?'

I sigh. 'Well, I wasn't. Look, I can't remember to be honest. I can't remember a thing about it. I'm sorry.'

He sighs and it sounds tired and heavy. 'Jesus Christ, Molly, I thought you were meant to be smart? What would your mum say?'

I stay silent, shame burning any words off my tongue.

'Christ, Molly,' he says again. 'Everyone knows you're my daughter.' I prickle as I feel the weight of his second-hand shame, piled on top of my own.

'I'm so sorry,' I repeat. I don't have any other words.

'God, it's a bit late for that. Are you okay?'

I can't answer him this time because I'm concentrating too hard on holding back the silent sobs that are threatening to explode from me. Poor Dad. He has enough to deal with without having to comfort his adult daughter. His stupid *stupid* adult daughter.

'Look, Molly, I don't think it's a good idea for you to visit this weekend. Actually, you should probably not come for a while. Not until this has all died down anyway.'

My heart silently breaks but I manage a choked, 'Okay, I understand.'

'I'll call you soon, okay, Mols. I love you.'

I open my mouth to tell my dad that I love him too but I end up saying the words to a dead line.

*

Standing there, with the phone in my hand and my dad's words ringing in my ears, I've never felt more alone. My cheeks are clammy with tears and I just want to speak to my best friend so badly. I can't stop the sinking feeling that

Posey has seen the video and is so ashamed of me too that she can't even bear to talk to me. The messages I sent earlier still haven't been delivered. Has she blocked me? I take a deep breath and scroll through the stored contacts on the home handset until I find Posey's work number. I press the call button and wait. I need to hear my best friend's voice, even if she's cross with me.

But it's not Posey's voice on the other end of the line. It's a man's. 'Hello. *The Post*. Posey's phone.'

'Oh . . . hi . . . is Posey there at all?'

A pause. It's overly long.

'She's not available at this moment. Can I take a message?'

'Um . . . it's actually a personal call. I'm trying to get hold of her about something important and her mobile phone seems to be off. Is she out on a job?' There's another excruciatingly long pause and some muffled talking, like whoever answered has his hand over the mouthpiece. What's going on? My palms have started to sweat so much I'm scared I might lose my grip on the phone. Is Posey really avoiding talking to me? Has she told her workmates about the video? Oh my God, have they seen it? My mind races several furlongs ahead, picturing an entire newsroom watching me, laughing at me. But she's my friend, she wouldn't do that to me, would she?

The voice comes back on the line.

'Actually, Posey didn't show for work this morning. We've been trying to get hold of her too. When you speak to her could you get her to drop Oliver a line? We assumed she's just at home, sick or something.'

'Oh. That's odd. I'm actually her flatmate and she definitely left for work this morning.' I remember hearing the front door click shut and that flood of relief that I wouldn't have to face her yet.

'Weird. I guess she could be out on a job then, but I'd have thought Oliver would know. And why would her phone be off?' Posey's colleague sounds confused too. 'I'm sure she'll turn up. Can you pass the message on if you see her before we do?'

I say I will and after some goodbyes, hang up, feeling troubled. I check the messages on my computer again, still nothing from Posey. Still hanging undelivered in cyberspace. I walk back into the hall and look at her bedroom door. It's possible that she's just forgotten her phone and it's run out of battery. That's why no one can get hold of her. I decide to check and see if there are any other clues as to where she could be.

'Probably a doctor's appointment or something and she's just forgotten to tell work,' I tell myself as I push her door open. But even as I'm saying the words, something inside me is saying this isn't right. Posey's blinds are firmly closed and this alone sets off an internal alarm system. Posey is one of those annoyingly perky morning people – and I mean this in the most affectionate way – who throws open her windows before throwing herself into the day. She's a compulsive bedmaker and the bed is not made. Her sheets are a knotted tangle, the pillows haphazard. Wherever Posey went this morning, she went in a rush. I open the blinds and let the diluted winter sun into her room. I do a quick scan for her phone but there's no obvious sign of it and I don't want to root around in her stuff.

'Where are you, Pose?' I ask the empty room before stepping out and pulling her door closed behind me.

5

*

I wander back into the living room and remember that I was about to call Jack before I spoke to my dad. I look at my phone, still plugged into the charger and feel as drained as its battery. I'll try him later. What I need right now is a cup of tea and my bed. My eyes ache from crying and from the lack of quality sleep I had last night. The idea of sinking into my bed, closing my eyes and escaping for an hour or so feels like a holiday. Hopefully, by the time I wake up, Posey will be on-grid again and she'll be able to help me figure out what happened last night and what to do about the video. This is a wonderful plan so I head to the kitchen, screw my nose up at the smell of the bin, vow to take it out later and make myself a cup of tea. I leave my mobile charging, but pick up my laptop and crawl into bed with it. Once I'm there, I can't resist that temptation again to take a quick peek at Twitter. To press my fingers into the open wound once more.

Among the slew of new comments telling me what a 'stupid bitch' and 'slag' I am, some people have helpfully provided links to articles about me. So now I also know that I'm being talked about in the *actual* media as well as social media. Great. I check how many times the video's been shared. It's in the thousands now. I click on one of the links which takes me through to a gossip website that has posted a 'story' with the headline '20 Tweets Mucky Molly Monroe Probably Wishes She'd Deleted'. After a brief intro outlining who I am and what I've done to earn myself the nickname 'Mucky Molly', there's a list of old tweets where I've said something that sounds like innuendo out of context. Some examples are: 'Just taken an online personality quiz and it turns out I'm a people pleaser', 'Just impressed everyone in the office by fitting 22 marshmallows in my mouth' and, my favourite, 'Well, today absolutely blows'. Journalism at its finest. And Mucky Molly? *Mucky Molly?* Is that who I am now? There are also a few handy widgets at the bottom of the article so it can easily be shared on socials. I can see it's been shared over a thousand times. If I wasn't curling in on myself with shame and humiliation, I'd probably be amazed.

That wasn't the only one. Not by a long shot.

Someone else has written a long-form think piece about me, or rather about how the internet reacts when I'm filmed giving a random man a blow job in a London street. It's posted on a more serious site, aimed at millennial women with brains and careers. The sort of thing they're encouraged to scroll through on the way in to work. It's called *The Water Cooler*.

Molly Monroe – the Party Girl None of Us Want to Be
By
Sasha Ferrari/ @itsmeSashSash

One can't help but feel sorry for Molly Monroe. If you haven't been on Twitter in the last 24 hours, in fact if you haven't been on the net in the last 24 hours, then you might not know who I'm writing about. For the uninitiated, Molly Monroe – or 'Mucky Molly' as one tabloid site has dubbed her – has become the latest unwitting overnight social media sensation.

While we're all much more conscious of what we post publicly these days – none of us want a Justine Sacco–style public shaming – there's still very little control over what others can post about us, or who then shares that with their own followers. And while we're all trying to be hashtag kind, at least outwardly, the pack mentality of a public pile-on is a compulsion too tempting for many to ignore.

Monroe, who's 32 and works for a cutesy preteen magazine (think llamas, sloths and unicorns), had a normal life up until last night. Like most young professionals living and working in the capital do at some point, Monroe had a night out. And like many of us have done before her, ended up having one too many drinks. But while most of us can usually shrug any drunken shame off after a day in bed and some heavy carb consumption, Monroe hasn't been quite so fortunate. A short, less-than-ten-second video clip of her, on her knees in an unnamed London street, giving oral sex to an unidentifiable man has been circulating on Twitter, Facebook and TikTok. And while there are certain laws in place to stop this kind of content being posted without the subject's knowledge, what do these actually mean in real life? The sad truth is, not a great deal. The original poster of the clip has disappeared from social media without a trace and trying to take down every copy that's been downloaded and shared is like trying to get toothpaste back in the tube. And, because as we all know, what goes online stays online, this is something that will likely haunt Monroe for the rest of her life.

While most of us were still sleeping this morning, tabloid sites had already scoured her social media for photos before Monroe had the chance to shut them down.

Since the early hours of this morning, she's been called every conceivable version of every misogynistic slur imaginable. A witch hunt on social media, spurred on by a tabloid news site, named her within thirty minutes of the original TikTok going live. Interestingly, there has been no such public outcry to name and shame her male co-star. And whoever posted the video clearly didn't think he played an important enough role to even film his face. None of the passers-by in the clip have come forward to explain why they walked on and ignored what was going on, or laughed, rather than stepping in and politely stopping what was at best, a terrible drunken error of judgement and at worst, a sexual assault.

Now Monroe will become a cautionary tale told to our friends, girlfriends, daughters. She'll be the example used to remind women not to drink too much on a night out, not promiscuous, to amend our behaviour because other people – usually men, let's be honest – can't be trusted. Molly Monroe's name will forever be associated with this one night. Future employers will be able to see the story. Her future children, should she have any, will see it. She's another reminder that our society is still patriarchal. It's still built on misogyny. Women's sexuality is still used to shame us into submission and obedience.

And Molly Monroe has been made into the sacrificial lamb to remind us of that.

I read this a few times before humiliation and exhaustion get the better of me and I fall into a stressed sleep, dreaming fitfully of mobile phones and Twitter posts and Posey.

*

I sleep for about an hour before I jolt awake, unsure if something in the flat or something in my dreams has woken me. I wonder if it might've been Posey coming home, but as I pad out of my bedroom, I can tell that the flat is still as empty as it was earlier. I shuffle into the living room and unplug my phone, which is now proudly boasting a full charge. I quickly open my message app, but there's still nothing from Posey. I call her mobile, but it goes directly to voicemail. I leave a quick message, telling her to call me back as soon as she can, that I really need to speak to her. Then I flop down onto the sofa and scroll through my contacts until I find Jack's name. I take a deep, shuddery breath and hit the call button.

His phone rings five times before he answers.

'Hello?'

'Jack? It's Molly. Molly Monroe. Er, from this morning?' I stammer.

'Jesus, Molly.' His voice sounds genuinely concerned. 'I've been hoping you'd call. I don't have your number. Are you okay?'

'You've seen it then?' My heart plunges to my feet.

'Yes. I'm so sorry this is happening to you. Is there anything I can do?'

'Yes, maybe, just be honest. It wasn't you, was it? I mean, I don't really think it was but everything is just chaos in my head and I don't remember so I need to ask . . .' I'm rambling.

'Sorry, you've lost me. What do you mean?'

'The guy in the video. Is it you?'

'Christ, Molly, no. *No.* I told you what happened. I told you I'm not like that, I'd never . . . do *that*.' He sounds mortified and I feel terrible for making him feel that way.

'Promise?'

Jack sighs down the phone. I imagine him rubbing his hand over his face in exasperation too. 'Molly. If I was that sort of a guy, don't you think we might have woken up with our clothes off? If you think I'd let a drunken girl do that in public, do you not think that, if I ended up in her bed, I'd try to take things further there? It's not me. I promise. I found you hysterical in Vauxhall when I was on my way home and I made sure you got back safely. I stayed to make sure you didn't choke on your own sick or something.'

I believe him. 'Okay. I'm sorry, it's just—'

He cuts me off. 'You have nothing to be sorry for. I can't even imagine what you're going through right now. But, it's nothing to do with me. I promise you that. I made sure you were safe, okay?'

'Okay.'

'I need to get back to work, but I'll check in on you later, all right? Are you at home?'

'Yes, work sent me back. I think they're trying to figure out what to do with me. I don't think it's very on-brand to have your chief narwhal reporter's amateur porno all over the net.'

Jack laughs darkly. 'I'm sorry,' he says. 'But that was pretty funny. Look, try and get some rest. Stick Netflix on or something. Have a bath. It will die down. And there are ways to clean up internet searches too. I work in IT as I told you last night but I'm guessing that's not information you retained?'

'I'm sorry. I hope your job is nice.' I pause for a moment. 'So, it's not the worst thing in the world? Even though it absolutely feels like it and I could die of shame.'

Jack's voice seems very sombre when he replies. 'No, Molly. It's not. Nowhere near.' A couple of beats of silence. 'I'll check on you later. We'll work it out. Try not to worry.'

He ends the call and all I can think of is his voice.

We'll work it out.

We. A team.

I wipe my eyes, feeling a little bit less alone in this.

*

The Twitter app on my phone has a little red circle telling me that I have over five hundred new notifications. I'm tempted to open it and continue to torture myself, but instead I press down on the icon and delete the app. Hopefully that will give me some peace at least until, as Jack said, it blows over.

Which I realise is a very bad turn of phrase right now.

Then I check again to see if Posey has resurfaced. But she hasn't. I call her mobile again but it's still off. I feel a knot of worry begin to loop in on itself in my chest.

Posey is never incommunicado.

Not for this long and definitely not without warning me.

Maybe she's working out how to ask me to move out. Or maybe she's checked into a hotel or something because she can't bear to face me.

I sit down on the sofa and pull one of the throws around me. It smells of Posey's perfume, something sweet and floral. Where *is* she? It's only late afternoon but the weak winter sunlight has already faded, making it feel like it's much later. Anxiety gnaws at my brain.

I decide to check Posey's room again. If she's gone away without telling me, she'll have taken her toothbrush and her make-up from her bathroom. Her bathroom is the most luxurious room in this place. In the absence of a hot tub or the space for one, we've often both sat in her huge bathtub in our bikinis, drinking Prosecco with half a bottle of Radox poured in. Into the bath, not into the Prosecco.

I pad back over the bare floorboards in the living room and hallway to Posey's room, smiling at the memory of us drunkenly sliding around on socked feet, pretending we'd nailed moonwalking, a few weeks ago. I really hope she hasn't gone away, even if it's just for work and not because she's avoiding me. I need to see her. I need her to soothe me back to normality and remind me that, this too shall pass. I go straight to the bathroom, clumsily groping around for the light switch on the outside wall, hoping that I see her Sonicare toothbrush in its charging socket near the sink. But when I flick it on, I wish I hadn't. I wish I'd never come into Posey's bathroom at all because now I'm on the floor and I'm screaming.

I'm screaming so loudly and I wonder if I will ever stop.

Posey's been here all along, in the bath.

Floating, waxy-skinned and very definitely dead.

6

*

Posey is dead.

Posey is dead in the bath.

She didn't go to work.

She didn't go to work because she's dead.

I can't drag my eyes away from what's in front of me. Instead, I realise I'm blinking almost manically, as if the scene will change if I open and close my eyes enough.

She's dead.

Everything else looks so normal and I keep blinking, maybe in the vain hope that when I open my eyes again, Posey's dead body will no longer be there. Her toothbrush is neatly tucked into the holder on the sink. The lid is on her toothpaste, unlike mine which seems to go missing the moment I take it off. The fluffy towels she bought from Selfridges in the summer are neatly lined up on the heated towel rail and there's an empty bottle of Twin Oaks Sauvignon Blanc at the side of the bath.

I don't know what to do or remember how to stand up.

I need to call someone.

I take some deep breaths and manoeuvre myself into a standing position, willing my feet and my trembling legs to move, to work with me. Steadily, holding onto the wall, I half walk, half drag myself to the living room and take the landline phone out of its cradle. I notice there's a smudge of my foundation on it. It's never seen as much action as today. I take another gulp of air and dial 999, moving to the sofa, once again certain my legs will give way if I stay standing.

Someone answers immediately.

'Nine-nine-nine. Which service please?'

'I . . . I . . . I don't know?' I stammer. I'm hoarse from the screaming. 'My flatmate is dead.'

'Okay, connecting you to the ambulance service.'

Ambulance? But she's dead. Why an ambulance? Before I have a chance to make the operator understand that Posey's dead and she doesn't need an ambulance, I'm speaking to someone else.

'Hello, caller, can I take your name please?'

'It's Molly.'

'Okay, Molly, what's happened?'

'I . . . I . . . don't know. My flatmate is dead. In the bath. I think she drowned.'

'Okay, love. Is she definitely dead? No signs of life? I can talk you through CPR?'

'I'm sure. She's floating and blue and her eyes are just staring. I think she's probably been there all night. And day.' My voice cracks, saying words my brain hasn't even processed yet.

'Okay, I've dispatched an ambulance. They'll be there as soon as they can, okay? I'll stay on the line with you. Are you in any danger? Is there anyone else there with you?'

'No, I don't think so. I'm sorry, I think I'm in shock.'

'It's all right, Molly. Some police will probably arrive too, but it's nothing to worry about. They just need to have a look around, okay? Have you got someone with you?'

'N-no,' I stutter.

'No neighbours or friends nearby?'

My mind pulls up an image of the Twitter hashtag about me. 'No. No one.'

'Okay, love. Well just sit tight then and there will be a crew with you as quickly as possible. What's your flatmate's name, Molly?'

'Posey.' I sniffle. 'Posey Porter. She's a journalist.'

'That's a very cool name for a journalist.'

'Yes,' I agree. 'She hated it though. She was teased about it at work. Everyone called her Nosey or The Nose. But it was good-natured, you know?'

'That's funny. Do you want to make yourself a cup of tea or something, Molly? I know tea always helps me when I've had a shock. Throw some extra sugar in there.' My mum used to swear by sugary tea too. Something hard and lumpy forms in my chest.

She continues to talk to me as I make a mug of tea and pile spoons of sugar into the liquid. The normality of the actions along with her soothing voice keep me calm and weirdly grounded while inside I'm still screaming.

'The ambulance crew will be with you shortly, Molly.

They're just a few minutes away now. Do you want me to stay on the line or are you okay?'

'I think I'm okay now,' I tell her. 'Thank you. Thank you so much.'

'No trouble at all, Molly. You look after yourself, okay? The ambulance will be there really soon. And the police. But like I said, it's nothing to worry about, okay?'

We say goodbye and the line goes dead. For a horrible moment I feel completely untethered and like I'm going to be sick again. I think about the operator asking if there's anyone who can be with me and wonder if I can call Jack. I can't think of anyone else at all. Since this morning and the horrible viral video, Jack is the only person who has been on my side. Well, apart from Paloma but I still have a sinking feeling of shame in my stomach when I think of her and how she mentioned we had a falling out. I suddenly feel the ache of loneliness as I realise this. No one else was there for me, not my friends, my colleagues or even my own family. I literally have no one else to turn to apart from a man I don't know at all. I sit down with the tea I've just made and tears fall into my lap. I can't be alone right now. I really can't. I pick my phone up from where I threw it earlier and call Jack's number before I can talk myself out of it.

He answers immediately this time.

'Molly? Are you okay?' My reply is just sobs. 'Molly? What is it? What's happened?'

'It's Posey,' I manage to say. 'My flatmate. She's dead. I just found her.' The silence that follows is so long I think we've been cut off. But then I hear a breathed 'fuck' down the line.

'Molly. I'm just so sorry. What . . . Do you know what happened?'

'No. I'm just waiting for an ambulance. I called them and they asked if I had anyone to be with me and the only person I could think of was you which I know is insane because I only met you last night. Well, this morning as far as my conscious mind knows but I just . . .' I trail off and take some long breaths, aware I'm beginning to sound on the verge of hysteria.

'I'm on my way, okay? I'll cycle over and be there as quick as I can, Molly. Try to stay calm, okay? I'm coming.'

I nod into the phone before the call disconnects and I allow myself to give in to the tears.

*

Jack arrives thirty minutes later, about the same time as a police car carrying two uniformed officers. The paramedics were already here. They knocked on the door just moments after I spoke to Jack. There was a man and a woman, who made more tea and confirmed that Posey had died. I didn't need the confirmation, but it made me collapse anyway. The flat is suddenly full of people, more people than have ever been here at one time. Apart from the party when we moved in, but yeah, different vibe. It's making me feel anxious and I'm about to call for Posey to come through for moral support before I remember that's *why* all these people are here.

I can't do this.

I can't do this without Posey.

The police ask Jack and me to sit in the lounge while, along with the paramedics, they remove Posey's body and take pictures of her bathroom and bedroom. They are taking approximately four hundred hours to do this. Jack turns on Netflix and makes even more tea while we wait. I think I have flushed any remaining alcohol from my system with tea by this point.

'You look like you could do with something stronger?' Jack says, but I shake my head vehemently.

'No. Just pile sugar in the tea, please.' I can never see myself drinking again to be quite honest. The shock has pushed the remnants of hangover away too and I'm shivering on the sofa, hunched over myself. He looks at me for a second and then grabs one of the many throws Posey and I have collected over the years and gently drapes it over my shoulders. 'You're shaking,' he says, eyes wide with concern. How did I get here? How did it get to the point where Posey is dead, I'm a scarlet woman all over the internet and the only person I can turn to for comfort is a man I just met? I can feel the tears begin to build up again and this time they come out in noisy sobs that echo around the lounge. Jack hands me a mug of tea and looks horrified at the noises I'm making.

'I can't believe you've known me less than twenty-four hours and you've already seen me vomit, ugly cry and fellate a stranger on the internet,' I say, although 'wail' would be a better attribution.

'Yes,' Jack agrees, solemnly. 'None of those were on my Molly Monroe bingo card.'

'You should go.' I sniff. 'I'm clearly some sort of harbinger of doom. You should go before something terrible happens to you.'

Jack reaches for my hands and holds them in his own. They feel big and warm.

'And if I go, who will be here for you, Molly?' he asks.

'I'll be okay.' Although, actually, his words scratch me on the inside. No one else would come. I'm truly alone.

'I'm not going anywhere. So just get that thought out of your head right now.'

I smile, weakly, and he pulls me into him, rubbing my arms like a parent trying to warm up a cold toddler. He holds my gaze and I feel safe. For the first time today.

Our tender moment is cut short by someone crashing in through the front door shouting, 'What the fucking hell is going on here?' The voice belongs to Jesse Keyes. As in my landlord Jesse.

'Who's that?' Jack whispers as Jesse makes his way up the hall, heading towards the lounge.

'Our landlord.' I sigh. 'This is exactly why I didn't want a neighbour to be with me.'

*

'Sir!' A police officer is calling after Jesse, who seems to have no intention of stopping and listening. 'We really need you not to be here at the moment,' she says. 'We're still assessing the scene.'

A chill of fear scuttles down my spine at her words. *Assessing the scene?* What does this mean?

I look up at Jack, who shakes his head.

'I'm sure it's just something they say until they can establish the cause of death,' he soothes.

Then Jesse's voice. 'Assessing the scene? For what? This is my bloody flat, love. If something dodgy's happened in here, then don't you think I should know about it?'

We can't see him yet but I can already picture him looming over the petite officer I'd opened the door to four hundred hours ago. There's silence for a moment and she must've backed down as we hear Jesse's footsteps approaching the lounge.

'What the fuck is going on?' he bellows at me. 'And who the fuck are you?' he bellows at Jack.

'I'm Jack, a friend of Molly's. I'm supporting her. She's had some upsetting news.'

Jesse eyeballs me and I feel myself wither. I've never really warmed to our landlord and I'm fairly certain the feeling is mutual. Jesse always treated Posey like the adult and went to her with any grumbles or concerns. He's always treated me like an annoying child Posey was looking after. Which I suppose is a pretty fair analogy. He's not an unattractive man, not by any means. In fact I'm sure there's a certain type of woman – and a good few men – who would appreciate Jesse's gym-honed physique and year-round tan. He's always dressed in athleisure wear, today grey joggers and white T-shirt with the sports brand logo pushed out a full inch by his left pec.

'What upsetting news?' he barks. 'I've come over to talk to you about all that stuff on the internet. I've seen the address on there. What the fuck, Molly? You wanna get a brick through the window? Who's going to pay for that?'

I can feel Jack tense up as Jesse continues to snarl at me.

'Could you ease up a bit please?' Jack says. 'Molly is very upset. There's a bit of a situation going on here. In case you hadn't realised.'

Jesse shoots Jack a look that would make the undead go scuttling back to their graves.

'Well? What?' Jesse turns to me. 'Have you had a break-in or something?'

'No,' I choke. 'It's Posey.'

'Posey? What's *she* done?'

'Nothing, Jesse. She's . . . she's died.'

'Died? What? What are you talking about?' He stares at me for a full minute before crouching into a squat. 'Shit.'

'We're just waiting for the police to come and talk to me, Jesse, so if you don't mind.'

'What happened?' His voice softens.

'I don't know. That's what they're trying to find out,' I say. 'I went in there earlier and found her in the bath. But I don't know. I don't know.'

Jesse stares at me for a moment and it looks like he hates me. 'I've seen your video,' he says eventually. 'I really don't need *this* in one of my properties too.' He looks like a bull and I imagine angry steam coming out of his nose.

Jack stands up. 'Look, you're clearly upset but this really isn't the time, mate. I think you should go and calm down.'

'And I don't think you should be telling me what to do in my own property. *Mate*.' The men look like they're about to square up to each other and this is a terrible idea even without two police officers just centimetres away.

'Can you just go please, Jesse?' I say through my tears. 'I've got enough to deal with without you being angry at me right now.'

'Okay. But we *are* going to talk, Molly. Soon.' He gives me a withering look as he strides out of the room towards where the emergency responders are doing their stuff. 'Be careful with that. I'll bill you for any damage to the paintwork,' we hear him snap before the front door slams shut.

'He seems nice,' says Jack.

'Oh, his bark is worse than his bite. He probably just wanted the police to know who's boss. He's the sort of man who refers to them as pigs.'

'Like I said, he seems nice.'

*

The police are ready to talk to me soon after Jesse leaves. It's horrible. I feel like I'm being interrogated. Two more have arrived and they're *not* wearing uniforms. I know from watching *Line of Duty* that this means they're higher up. A woman and a man. They introduce themselves as Detective Inspector Tom Wolfe and Detective Sergeant Iris Freeman. They're in my living room, asking me about finding my best friend's dead body. It's completely surreal. And today has already been peak-surreal in many ways.

The man speaks first. He looks like he could be a very tired dad of young kids. He's what Posey would call a Silver

Fox, but I suspect he's younger than he looks. Perk of the job, I guess.

'We won't keep you for long, Miss Monroe,' DS Freeman is saying. 'We're aware this has been a traumatic day for you.'

'That's okay,' I reply and offer them both a weak smile, which I immediately regret because why would I be smiling right now?

'So, we just want to ask you a few questions about the deceased, how you found her and that sort of thing. Is that okay?' DI Wolfe asks.

I nod.

'Okay,' he continues. 'So, we know that today has been a bit of a . . . er . . . tough one for you, Miss Monroe.' He doesn't need to tell me he's seen the stuff online. The weight of his words says it all. They're thick with it. 'But let's try to focus on what happened when you found Miss Porter for now, okay?'

I nod again but I now can't get it out of my head that the police officers sitting opposite me have seen me giving a stranger a blow job.

Brilliant.

'So just tell us in your words what happened.'

I take a deep breath. 'It's like I said on the phone, I went into her bathroom and she was just there in the bath. I could tell she was dead because her eyes were open and around her mouth was blue. Then I sort of cried for a bit.'

'Right. And this was tonight?'

'Yes, right before I called the ambulance. Posey didn't turn up for work today and I was checking to see if she'd taken her toothbrush, I thought maybe she'd gone away or something? But I just saw . . .'

'Okay, Miss Monroe. Why did you think she'd gone away?'

'I don't know. I was trying to find out where she was. I hadn't been able to get hold of her all day and I wanted to talk to her about . . . the thing.'

Wolfe and Freeman nod in unison as if choreographed.

'I called her at work and they said she hadn't turned up but I thought I heard her leave this morning, and then I got all paranoid that she'd seen the stuff online and hated me and thought maybe she'd decided to go away so I went to check if her stuff was in her bathroom and then . . .' A bubble of grief chokes me up and I go mute.

'It's okay, Miss Monroe. Take your time,' says Freeman.

'Miss Monroe, when did you last see Miss Porter?' Wolfe asks.

'Just then, before they took her away.'

'Alive. When did you last see her alive?'

'Oh.' Of course. When *was* the last time I saw Posey alive? I *thought* I heard her leaving the flat earlier today, but I didn't actually see her. I went straight to my Christmas party from work yesterday – a small wave of shame rolls in my stomach – so it must've been the night before that. Posey had convinced me to help her put up our Christmas tree.

'If your company is having its Christmas party then we might as well fully embrace Christmas ourselves,' she'd said, throwing me a bag of tree decorations. 'Alexa, play Christmas songs.' I'd rolled my eyes as Mariah Carey began blaring out of the little speaker. 'Don't think I didn't see that eye-roll,

Monroe. Wait there!' She skipped into the kitchen, singing badly along to Mariah on the way. She appeared two minutes later holding two mugs. 'Here,' she passed one to me, 'Baileys! It might be a little bit dusty as I think it's from last Christmas. Or maybe even the one before, but yay.' She clinked her mug against mine. 'Now it's properly Christmas, bitch. Drink up and get decorating. And at least try to do a decent job. If I have to redo your half like I did last year then I'm not getting you a present.'

We'd spent the rest of the evening drinking the dusty Baileys, decorating the tree before sinking into the sofa with tinsel wrapped around our ponytails.

'Are you sure you won't come to mine this year, Mols?' Posey had asked me. 'It won't be the same without you. Mum has said she might even come and drag you down.' I'd spent the past few Christmases with Posey and her extended family in Surrey. It was better than sitting at a table across from my dad, which is how I'd spent most Christmases since my mum died twenty years ago. But I'd turned down Posey's mum's offer this year. I'd had an idea that I'd stay in the flat by myself and embrace my grief, feel my feelings and do other stuff recommended by self-help books about loss. It doesn't sound like a whole load of fun but I figured there would come a time when I'd need to stand on my own two feet and not try to fill the hole in my heart by borrowing other people's joy. Or drinking until I could no longer feel it.

'I have big plans,' I'd told her. 'And they don't involve getting dressed at all.' Posey had stared at me for a longer amount of time than felt comfortable, her eyes searching mine for any sign that I wasn't being honest with her. And I wasn't. Not totally. A huge part of me wanted nothing more than to travel down to Godalming with Posey on Christmas Eve and fall asleep on the trundle bed in her childhood bedroom. Her mother, Tina, and stepdad are like the parents in books and her old room has been kept exactly as she left it before she went to uni. She has two half-sisters and one half-brother, all younger, all as cute as baby animals. Their home is detached and has five bedrooms and *grounds*. It's lovely and perfect. But it's so lovely and perfect, it also has the effect of making me so very, very sad. And while Tina goes above and beyond to make me feel like part of the family, the hole caused by grief continuously reminds me that I'm not. Worst of all, I'd started to feel that my being there, cocooned in my sadness, was making everyone else sad too. I hadn't wanted that for them this year. It was time to keep my melancholy to myself.

I become aware of the two officers and Jack looking at me expectantly.

'Sorry,' I say. 'I think the last time was the night before last.' I gesture at the tree. 'We decorated the tree together.'

The man, DI Wolfe, scribbles something in a notepad. 'So you didn't see Miss Porter yesterday at all?'

'I . . . I don't know,' I say, my voice is small with shame.

'You don't know?' DS Freeman has blue eyes and they are looking at me and probably judging me even though her face remains passive. I think she must be about the same age as me, which is hard to believe when she is all proper and I am just an absolute mess.

'I was pretty drunk last night,' I say, as if they weren't aware. 'I don't remember if I saw her when I came in. But I can't really remember what happened. I just don't know.'

'We didn't,' Jack interjects. I'd totally forgotten he was with me last night. I stare at him, almost in wonder. Maybe he *can* help fill in some blanks after all. 'I found Molly wandering around in Vauxhall late last night. It was after midnight, probably closer to one. I was on my way home from seeing friends locally. She was extremely distressed about something and seemed disorientated. So I called her an Uber and brought her back here.'

The two officers exchange a look.

'Nothing untoward,' Jack says. He's so calm it transfixes me. 'There are still some gentlemen around, believe it or not.'

'Sounds like Miss Monroe was very lucky to run into one of them,' DS Freeman says pointedly. 'And what happened when you came into the flat, Mr . . . ?'

'Mayhew. Jack Mayhew.'

DS Freeman scribbles something down in her notebook and shows it to DI Wolfe, who gives one nod, quick and precise. Then he leans forward, closer to Jack, urging him to continue.

'Er, so I had to let us in because Molly couldn't get the key in the lock. And it was dark, no lights were on. I couldn't see a thing and I ended up crashing into a console table by the door. It made quite a bit of noise actually and then I had to feel along the walls for a light switch. But no one came out or shouted to be quiet. I'd had a few drinks myself so things are a bit hazy after that. Molly sort of stumbled off to her room saying she was going to be sick. And I followed her.'

A horrible memory of being on the floor, head hanging over the toilet bowl, someone holding my hair out of my face, crashes back into my consciousness.

'You held my hair back while I was being sick,' I say to Jack. Shame permeates me, but I announce it like a revelation. Maybe my memories aren't lost forever. Maybe Jack will help dislodge them from whatever part of my brain has gathered them up and locked them away.

'Yeah, I did. I wanted to make sure you didn't pass out in the loo and give yourself a head injury, to be honest.'

'And then what happened?' Wolfe asks.

'Then I helped Molly into bed. She fell asleep and I went to sleep next to her.'

'Not gentleman enough to take the sofa?' Wolfe says.

Jack stares at him very hard. 'She could have choked on her vomit,' he says as if it's obvious that I would have, indeed, choked on my vomit. 'She wasn't safe to be left alone. I was really worried about her actually. With good reason, considering what's happened to her online today.' I shrink into myself.

'Okay.' Wolfe blinks slowly and turns his attention back to me. 'Did Miss Porter have any mental health issues? Was she depressed?' The thought of Posey as depressive almost makes me laugh.

'No, not at all. She was very happy. She'd just got a promotion she'd been wanting for ages. A pay rise. She was excited about her career, about the future. You're not suggesting she . . . ?'

'No. We're just trying to establish facts. Tick off some boxes. Was there anything that was causing her to be more stressed or anxious than usual?'

'No, not at all. She was fine. She was happy.'

'Did she regularly get extremely drunk? Was she a problematic or binge drinker, would you say?'

I think about Posey and our regular wine nights, either at home or in local bars. I can't remember a single time in the last few years where I'd seen her sloppy drunk. I think about the Twin Oaks next to her dead body in the bathroom. It was weird actually. Out of character. But maybe she'd had a hard day. Who am I to judge?

'No, not at all. I mean, she drank, yes, but she never got fall-down-embarrass-yourself drunk.' I have to avert my eyes from both detectives. I can see the words *Not like you, then?* hovering above their heads. 'I haven't seen her like that since university, really. She wasn't like that. She was responsible. That's why this is so weird.' Wolfe is scribbling something again. I wonder why he doesn't just record everything on his phone. Or maybe he is. Then the thought of being recorded without my knowledge makes the room spin again and even though I'm sitting down, I find I have to grab the arm of the sofa to steady myself.

'Had you and Miss Porter had an argument, Miss Monroe? Were you on good terms the last time you saw her?'

And suddenly that creeping horror I felt this morning is back, snaking through my veins. Only this time it's nothing to do with Paloma or the strange man in my bed or the fact that I'd been sick in the kitchen. Because I have a very clear memory from last night. Of me standing in front of Posey in a bar, loudly shouting at her.

I feel like I'm falling and gasping for air when there is none. 'I don't know,' I say. 'I don't know.'

I don't want to eat.

I am completely numb.

I look at Jack, the awareness that I barely know him striking me again. 'Posey is dead,' I say. 'My best friend is dead. And everyone thinks I'm a horrible slut. And probably an alcoholic.'

Jack drops his phone onto the lone wingback armchair Posey bought as a 'statement piece' and sits down next to me. Slow, measured movements like I might bolt.

'I know it feels like that right now, but it won't be like this forever,' he says.

'I don't know what to do,' I say and as the words leave my mouth it feels as though they were the very last things inside me. I am hollow. I wait for tears or anger or *something* to come. But it doesn't and the hole inside me swells larger, sucking everything into its void.

'Is there someone I can call for you? Your parents?'

I shake my head. 'No, not really. My mum . . . well, she died when I was little and my dad . . .' I trail off, thinking about the awkwardness of our phone conversation earlier.

'Oh God, Molly. I'm so sorry,' Jack says and I try to shrug it off – *it's nothing, just a dead paren*t – but tears are already pooling in my eyes and the bags under them. 'How about a hug instead?' He gives me a sad little smile that makes my heart ache like a new bruise.

'Yes. Yes, please. Very please.'

'Big or small?'

'Big, please. Big bear hug.' He wraps his arms around me and pulls me into his chest. I let my head rest against the bit where his heart is and am comforted by the warmth and the rhythm. But then I remember that Posey has a heart in her chest that will never ever beat again and I still feel nothing and I want to feel something so I lift my head up and press my lips on Jack's not caring how I smell or taste. I need to feel something.

He pulls away. Too quickly. It winds me.

'No. No, Molly,' he says softly and puts my head back on his chest. And I wither in my shame, my grief, my despair, getting smaller and emptier until I disappear.

8

@britbrat: I'm gonna kill you, dirty cunt

*

I must've fallen asleep after that – apparently it's a typical reaction to trauma and probably mortifying shame – because the next thing I know I'm waking up alone on the sofa with a blanket tucked over me. I don't even know what time it is. Or what day it is. Or what time of day it is. Weak sunlight is nudging its way into the living room through the French windows that lead outside to the small, paved yard which we call 'the garden' but is really not much more than a patio. It's morning. The morning after.

Muscle memory makes me grab for my phone. I'm surprised to see it's 11am and I've slept through the whole night. There's a missed call and a voicemail from the HR department at work, but that's not something I can deal with right now. I delete them both. Against my better judgement, I reinstall the Twitter app. Maybe it will distract me from the pain of finding Posey's body. I *need* to know what's being said about me. If it's died down at all. My mouth feels like I've been licking sawdust for eight hours and I can already feel my heart racing at levels that surely must be tachycardic, but I open the app anyway. My racing heart sinks. The video has now been shared over 25k times. The comments are still rolling in. I know I could choose not to look, or I could mute it all, delete my entire account, pretend it didn't happen. But it's like I'm being compelled to read all the horrible things that are being said about me. Like it's some kind of penance. If I hadn't been so bloody drunk that I was dishing out blow jobs to strangers, maybe Posey wouldn't be dead. If I'd just behaved like a normal person instead of getting so stupidly, unforgivably drunk. I'd wanted to let my hair down. But I ended up letting everyone down.

I slump back down into the sofa, feeling tears prick at my eyes. What sort of a person gets into the kind of state that they can't remember something like a public sex act, I ask myself for what feels like the billionth time.

What happened? What the hell happened?

I need some water and probably some painkillers.

In the kitchen, I find a scribbled Post-it from Jack stuck on the kettle.

Hey you, I had to go to work and didn't want to wake you. Will check in on you later. Drink some water and eat some toast before you end up in hospital. Jack x

I notice he's thoughtfully popped two pieces of bread in the toaster and left a clean glass on the kitchen counter, which

I fill with water that I swallow with some paracetamol. Then I make a cup of tea using the last dribble of milk and head back into the lounge. My thoughts turn again to Jack and how kind he's been. I guess there's no precedent for picking up a drunk girl who becomes a meme and then finds her flatmate's body, hours after meeting her. My clumsy and desperate attempt at kissing him also flashes before my eyes and I feel a fresh sting of humiliation. With everything else that's going on, is it weird that I keep thinking about him rejecting me? Twice.

Do I secretly enjoy shame?

Is this a breakdown?

I need to make some sort of plan about what to do next. Everything feels so very, very unreal at the moment. I can't believe that Posey's gone. I know everyone says that when they lose someone close to them, but I mean it literally. My mind actually cannot process the fact that my best friend, my funny, beautiful best friend is dead. And the increasing conviction that I could have prevented it makes me want to throw up.

I'm certain Posey wouldn't have been so stupid as to get in the bath late at night after drinking. That's the sort of idiot move I'd make, not her. But the ghost of a memory of me shouting at her somewhere keeps niggling and prodding at my mind. Did we argue so badly that she came back here and drank herself into oblivion? Did I not only fail to prevent Posey from dying, did I somehow also cause it?

I haven't wanted to face what's on my phone. Not properly.

But it's the only way I'll be able to get some answers about what happened that night.

The only way I'll know if I did something terrible. Well, something *else* terrible.

I take a huge sip of tea that's still too hot, but who cares, I deserve pain.

My phone starts vibrating in my hand. I'm so on edge that I spill tea on my lap. It burns the tops of my thighs but, again, I don't do anything about it. Jack's name is flashing on my screen.

No photo. No last name. I hesitate for a second before I answer, shame paralysing me momentarily.

'Hi.'

'Hi. How are you doing over there?' he asks.

'I'm okay,' I say. I mean it's half true. I'm not lying on a mortuary slab like Posey.

'Good. Did you find my advice slip?'

'I did. I'm eating toast and drinking tea as we speak.'

'Good,' he says again. Then a pause. Long. Awkward. 'Look about last night. Things are hard for you right now. I don't want you feeling bad because I pulled away.'

I snort.

'No, really. I don't. Because I don't want to take advantage, Molly. You're going through hell right now and it wouldn't have been fair. I'm not like that. I'm not an arsehole.'

'This is a weird and morbid version of It's Not You, It's Me,' I say.

'Not exactly. And, to be honest, it *is* you. You're vulnerable. And I'm not a piece of shit. I care about you, Molly.

I know we've only known each other for . . . about thirty-six hours, but I feel responsible for you. Okay? So please don't use the fact I pulled away as another stick to beat yourself with.' His voice is gentle, soothing.

'Okay,' I say.

'Promise?'

'I promise.'

'Okay. I need to get back to work, but I'll check in on you later.' He hangs up.

I stare at my phone for a bit, before taking a deep breath and opening the email app. It's my personal account. I have never had my work email on my phone, an attempt at some sort of work/life balance in theory, but the reality is that I just don't care enough to be available 24/7 for my job. I scan through the dozens of emails that have come in since Wednesday night, not totally sure what I'm looking for, but hoping there is something that might dislodge a memory or something. And then I see it. An email from Posey sent on Wednesday night. My fingers begin to tremble as I open it.

From: PPorter@gmail.com
To: Mollymoo@gmail.com
Subject: Don't want to fall out
Date: 15 December
Time: 23.37

Mols,
I don't want to fall out with you. Hopefully, you'll see this when you've sobered up a bit. You were really out of order

tonight and I need to say something because it wasn't fair. You agreed to meet me. I've had a bastard of a day, well a bastard of a week tbh, and there's some stuff I needed to talk to you about. I get you had your Christmas party but you should've just said no instead of leaving me hanging around Soho like a dick. Then you turned up with a gaggle of drunk dickheads you picked up fuck knows where. Those guys were sleazes. I feel super bad about leaving you with them but JFC Molly, you weren't a nice drunk tonight. Just let me know you're safe please. I won't sleep until I hear from you, so now I'm worrying about you on top of everything else.

The way you spoke to me in the bar tonight was really not okay. I'm not your enemy, Molly, I'm your best friend. I only wanted to know who the guys you were draped all over were. You didn't need to go off at me like you did. That's why I left. I'm sorry I didn't wait for you. I hope you went home with Paloma.

I know you're hurting and I want to help you, but I can only do that if you want to help yourself too. You have to realise you're still grieving for your mum. I think your relationship with your dad too. You have to give yourself time to grieve. I know you think that ignoring it all is your way of coping, but it's not healthy. These things are happening, Molly, nothing is going to change that, but I'm here to help you through it. I want my best friend back. I feel like I've been living with a stranger these past few months. I don't know what's triggered you as you were doing so much better. But now it's like you're back at square one. Maybe you should think about seeing a therapist again? I've got so much I want to tell you about. I know what happened to Lulu Lawrence! I know that sounds mad, but I really, really would like to show you some stuff and get your opinion. It's weird. And quite scary. I don't want to say too much over email though. Maybe we can talk tomorrow night when you get home from work? I'll buy us a takeaway. We haven't done that for ages.

Look, I know this is super paranoid, but I'm worried about something happening to me. I'll explain tomorrow. But I want you to know that I've put together a file. It's in The Place. Just in case anything happens to me. Haha, what do I sound like? I've been watching too many Netflix crime docs before bed.

I just think—

Oh, hang on, I think I can hear you coming in haha. I'll just come and tell you myself.

Love you lots. Hate arguing.

Posey Xxxx

I'm crying again by the time I get to the end of the email. I *did* see Posey that night. And I was horrible to her. I pull a blanket tightly around my shoulders, finding the pressure soothing as I sob. She's right. The last few months have been difficult for me. Ever since Posey got her big promotion. I've tried to pretend I wasn't seething with jealousy, but I was. I was full of anger because I felt like Posey was leaving me behind. She had this great new job and it would only be a matter of time before she got a great new man and then bought a great new house and where would that leave me? Because since my mum died, I've been in this horrible purgatory where I've been looking for someone else to take care of me. I couldn't bear the thought of Posey leaving me. My tears are so violent, they physically shake my body. I didn't think I could feel any worse than I did yesterday. I thought *that* had to be rock bottom. But it turns out rock bottom was really a false bottom and there are several more layers of shame hiding underneath it. My darling girl was trying, willing to help me. And I constantly threw it back in her face. I'm the worst. I'm the absolute worst.

I cry tears of self-loathing and self-pity for a while, before I sternly tell myself to get a grip. This behaviour is exactly the kind of thing that Posey was talking about in the email. I read it again and other things jump out at me. I've been so worried that I'd been so appalling to Posey that she'd come home and got so drunk she fell asleep in the bath. But this email wasn't the rantings of a drunken person. Posey didn't sound drunk, not at all. So that was something of a relief. I don't understand what she means by The Place either. It makes no sense at all. She says it like it's something I should know, but I think and think and I still don't know what or where she means.

Then there was the Lulu Lawrence stuff. What did she mean she knows 'what happened to Lulu Lawrence'? I rack my brains, trying to recall what I can about Lulu Lawrence's story. She was a teenage girl who seemingly disappeared off the face of the earth last Christmas. It was a huge story for a couple of days but then got buried under the twenty-four-hour rolling news. I assumed she'd either been found or the police had discovered she'd run off with a boyfriend or something. Whatever had happened to her, it wasn't enough to be newsworthy, which was strange because Lulu was the kind of missing girl the media loves. She was white and blonde, ridiculously pretty and from a Very Good Family, i.e., two married, middle-class parents, no shady relatives. She didn't have a boyfriend, was popular at school and even had a semi-large TikTok and YouTube presence. That was mostly why she was on my radar at all. Robyn had asked me to do some research when we'd gone back to the office after Christmas.

'Why does a girl like that, with everything going for her, just disappear?' she'd wondered.

'There's definitely more to this,' Lexi, our deputy editor had said.

'Maybe she's done a runner because she's ashamed about something,' Zack, another writer, offered. I could certainly relate to that now. But then the headlines about Lulu had dried up, some despot dropped some missiles that killed civilians, a freak storm buried half of America in snow, another young woman went missing and her body was found days later – all the usual stuff – and no one was talking about Lulu Lawrence anymore.

So why was Posey?

I read her email again and something else strikes me. Hard.

She sent the email at 11.37pm.

She said she heard me coming in at 11.37pm.

I quickly scroll on my phone and open Twitter, almost dropping it in my hurry to confirm what I already know.

I open the notifications and am taken straight to one of the retweeted TikTok clips of my transgression that night. And I'm right. I knew I was.

It wasn't me coming in when Posey sent that email. It couldn't have been.

Because at 11.37pm I was on my knees in front of an unknown London venue, giving a random man a blow job.

There was someone else in our flat that night.

I read the email again and again and each time it becomes more screamingly obvious to me. Posey's death was not a tragic accident. My hands are shaking as I pace back and forth across the living room trying to calm my thoughts and arrange them into an order that makes sense.

Hadn't I thought there was something very strange about Posey dying like that? It didn't seem like the kind of accident Posey would have. It was so sloppy and careless and Posey was neither of those things. Not ever. I am the sloppy and careless one. That's why I'm still working in the same job, the same position I've had for the past six years, while Posey was a rising star. She'd just had that big promotion and was too busy bringing home expensive bottles of wine to celebrate with, not drinking alone in a bathtub. Something else tugs at my brain. That empty bottle by the side of the bath when I found her had been a cheap bottle of plonk. The cheapest. I'm hit by another memory, this one from earlier this year. It was around May, just after Posey had found out about her promotion. We'd been in the newsagent at the end of our road and I'd picked up the usual brand of Sauvignon Blanc we drank, which cost less than ten pounds, less than seven when it was on offer. Posey had snatched it out of my hand with a tinkling laugh.

'I think the days of drinking the cheapest wine we can find are finally behind us, Molly,' she'd said, squeezing past me to look at the bottles we usually walked past.

'They might be behind *you*, but they're still very much my reality,' I'd said, reaching for the plonk again. She'd lightly slapped my hand away.

'As if I'm going to leave you drinking that loo cleaner. Now put it back and be quiet.'

I did as I was told and then we went home and drank our 'posh wine' in the back garden, talking in exaggerated public school pronunciation and getting 'really rather blotto'.

There's no way Posey would, even on a very bad day, take a bottle of loo cleaner wine into the bath with her.

Before I know where they're taking me, my feet pick up pace and stride out of the lounge and through Posey's bedroom, towards her en suite. I pause at the door, my hand lightly grasping the cold handle, then I take a breath and open it. The image of Posey lying blue and bloated and bruised in the tub where I found her bursts into my brain. The bottle is still there; I guess tidying the scene isn't in the attending officers' job description. I feel panic begin to swish around in my stomach and run back into the lounge, trying to shake the vision from my head.

I collapse on the sofa and put my head between my legs, trying to still the room which seems to be both expanding and closing in on me at the same time. It's at that moment something else hits me.

Bruised.

Posey was bruised.

I screw my eyes shut and pull back the memory I'd been trying to shake away. I freeze it like a screenshot in my mind. Bruises. Yellow and purple around her neck, on her chest and around her wrists. I sit up dead straight. Suddenly my head is clear and calm as I realise what my gut has been screaming at me all this time.

Posey's death wasn't an accident.

Someone killed her.

9

*

Posey was murdered.

It is now glaringly obvious to me. The wine, the bruises,
the fact she was so scared she needed to tell me why, the fact
that *someone was here that night.* The realisation hits me so
hard it physically winds me, leaves me gasping for breath.
I need to call the police. I need to tell those detectives, Wolfe
and Freeman, who were here yesterday.

My fingers are so shaky that I can barely hold my phone,
let alone jab out the number from the card DS Freeman gave
to me before they left yesterday. I eventually manage it.

It rings four times before someone answers.

'Wolfe,' he barks.

I suddenly can't breathe. The room starts to fall away
from me and I drop the phone, having to grab onto the arm
of the sofa to stop myself hitting the floor alongside it. I can

97

hear Wolfe's voice saying something I can't make out. By the time I've sunk to my knees, trying to stop my breathing from spiralling into hyperventilation, the line has gone dead. I close my eyes and force myself to take slow breaths in through my nose and out through my mouth. I just about manage it when my phone starts vibrating on the floor.

It's Wolfe calling me back.

I answer.

'Who is this?' His voice still comes out as a bark and I feel a rush of terror flood me. There's a beat before he snaps: 'Come on, I haven't got time for this dicking around.'

'It's Molly,' I manage. 'Molly Monroe.'

'Right. Hold on.' I hear some muted voices as Wolfe must've put his hand over the phone's mouthpiece. It's followed by some frantic-sounding scrabbling around before I hear a door closing and Wolfe's voice become clear again. 'Miss Monroe. Sorry about that. How can I help you?'

I don't know what comes over me but I burst into tears again. Full-pelt sobs I have no control over. Wolfe waits for a few moments, letting me calm down, before he says, 'Miss Monroe. Has something happened? I'm going to need you to talk to me.' His voice has lost every drop of its previous irritation. It's gentle, soothing. Suddenly I want to talk to him. I need to talk to him.

'I found some stuff,' I say. He waits for me to go on. 'I've got an email Posey sent me that night. She was scared about something. We argued. I . . . I don't think her death was an accident—'

'Miss Monroe.' He cuts me off, not unkindly. 'We've been over this and we have no reason to think that Miss Porter's death, as shocking as it must be for you, is anything other than a tragic accident.'

'Someone was here!' I blurt it out like an exhale.

'I'm sorry? What . . . ?'

'In the flat. Someone was here in the flat that night. Before I got home. The email . . .'

Wolfe sighs. Again, it's not unkindly, but I get the sense that he's now trying to settle a spooked animal. 'Miss Monroe. Molly. You really need to drop this. Miss Porter's death was an unfortunate accident. Nothing more.' DI Wolfe's voice is patient, but I can sense the underlying irritation. This isn't a case as far as he's concerned and he's bored of talking to me about it. 'There is nothing to suggest that Miss Porter was in any danger. Nothing points to her being killed,' he says. 'Believe it or not, we *do* know what we're doing over here.'

'She was scared of something. She sent me an email. She told me to look for a file.'

'Did she say what she was scared of? Did she specify that she was afraid of someone in particular?'

'No, but she wanted to talk to me. And why would she make a file if there was nothing to be scared of? It's like she knew something was going to happen to her.'

There's a silence on the other end of the line. I almost ask Wolfe if he's still there but I can hear him breathing. He's weighing up what to say to me, how to fob me off.

'Miss Monroe,' he eventually says. 'There's no easy way

to put this. Our first responders firmly believe Miss Porter's death was an accident—'

'But,' I interrupt.

'Let me finish.' He returns the favour. 'In the nicest possible way, Miss Monroe, the only person who thinks this was anything other than misadventure is you. I've spoken personally with Miss Porter's mother and she accepts what the officers on the scene have said. With all due respect, you're not in the most reliable of mental states at the moment. You've admitted yourself that you were so drunk that night you can't remember if you'd even seen your flatmate or not. We really don't think there is anything nefarious about her death. I'm sorry.'

The shame. It burns through me again. Reminding me it's still there and will only ever need the slightest of prods to awaken. Reminding me that I will always be Mucky Molly, the girl in the video, the drunk, the slut, not someone who can be taken seriously.

'I understand this must be excruciating for you,' he goes on. 'The shock of finding Miss Porter, the online stuff and your history, it's no wonder you're struggling. I would recommend talking to a medical professional about some sort of trauma therapy.'

'Trauma?'

'Miss Monroe, you've been through some extremely traumatic events. It's not surprising that you're reacting like this. But it's something you can get help with.'

'Don't you even want to see the email?'

Wolfe sighs. 'Sure, send it over. I'll take a look. But don't hold high hopes for yourself, okay? I'm just looking at it. Bye, Miss Monroe.'

I don't say anything as I end the call.

Something I can get help with?

I stare at the phone in my hand like it bit me, cold venom snaking through my veins.

He thinks it's all in my head.

He thinks I'm hysterical and making it up.

But I'm not.

I'm not.

*

As I sit, digesting DI Wolfe's complete dismissal of me, my phone begins to ring again in my hand. The caller ID tells me Tina is trying to reach me. I know I need to talk to Posey's mum at some point. It may as well be now. Maybe she'll take my concerns seriously, even if the actual police won't.

'Hi, Tina,' I say as the call connects, my voice a wobble. She doesn't answer me right away but I know she's there because I can hear her noises of despair down the line. Noises I've been making myself over the past twenty-four hours. I wait. A few moments pass and then I hear her take a shuddering breath inwards. She's trying to breathe, to hold herself together while she's falling apart inside.

'Oh God, Molly.' Tina's voice is small and shaky. The voice of a broken person.

'I'm so sorry,' I say. It's trite. It's trying to plug a torn hull with kitchen towel. But I don't know what else I can say. I don't know what to do with someone else's despair. Her sobs get louder.

'I won't keep you,' she says eventually, when the gaps in between her tears become long enough for her to speak. This is oddly formal for Posey's mum, whom I've always thought of as strong and dynamic. I know as well as anyone how we can fall away from ourselves as we flail against grief. How sometimes all we can cling to are the formal conventions that are imprinted into us. My heart aches for her. 'I just wanted to talk to you about coming up to sort through her stuff.' She can't say her name, I realise. It hits me like a slap.

'So soon?'

'Jesse called. He said there's no need to wait.' We're dancing around the things we really want to say to each other. Tina wants to come here. She wants to be close to her daughter. She will know that Posey's bed still smells like her, that fragments of her very being are still floating around in her room. I don't want her to take those things away. She's accepting the police assumption that Posey's death was an accident. I know that her taking Posey's things, clearing her room out will mean any potential DNA evidence is gone. It is on the tip of my tongue to tell her about the email, to share my thoughts with her that Posey was killed by someone. But I can't do it. They stay stuck in my mouth, coating my tongue with their bitterness. I've lost my best friend, my rock, but Tina's lost her child. Her pain dwarfs mine. I can't add to it. I just can't.

'Okay,' I say instead. 'When?'

'Is Sunday okay?'

No. 'Of course. Just let me know what time.' There's a long pause and I wonder if she's just dropped the phone and crawled into a corner to cry.

'Will you help me?' she says eventually. My heart finally gives way.

'Of course.'

'Molly, could you do something else for me, do you think? I'm sorry to ask you, darling, but I just can't face speaking to her boss and sorting out picking her stuff up from the office.'

'I'll call Oliver,' I tell her. 'It's really the least I can do.'

'Thank you, Molly. Thank you so much.'

*

After Tina hangs up, I sit chewing my lip for a while. The police don't believe me and I can't talk to Tina about what I think has happened, but Oliver, he's bound to know something about the Lulu Lawrence story Posey was apparently working on. And I know he'll help me. Like everyone else, he adored Posey. He might even be able to help me decipher where this mysterious place Posey mentioned in her email is. Maybe she even meant somewhere at work. That would make sense.

Oliver's number is scribbled down on the calendar in our kitchen, so I walk through and tap the number into my phone.

'Oliver Valentine,' he answers right away.

'Oliver? It's Molly. Molly Monroe.'

'Molly, Jesus. How are you doing, love? God, I am just so bloody shocked about Posey. I just can't believe it. Are you okay? Are you coping?' I wonder for a second who told Oliver, but then I remember that the police would probably have issued a press statement after finding the body. She wouldn't have been named publicly yet, but it wouldn't have taken Oliver too many phone calls to find out that it was Posey.

'I'm as well as can be expected,' I tell him, truthfully. 'It's just so very hard. But I don't think it's fully sunk in yet. My brain hasn't accepted it. I think it thinks she's just on a work trip or something.'

'Yeah, I expect you're still in shock, aren't you? You found her, right?'

'Yes. I did. It was horrible. Have you spoken to the police?'

'I called them yesterday when we had the presser in. God, I just had this awful feeling, like I *knew* it was Posey, you know. Because we hadn't heard from her. The press alert said the deceased was a woman in her thirties who lived near Clapham Junction.' His voice cracks a little and I picture strong, capable Oliver, an unflappable newspaper editor, broken with sadness. 'I'm gutted,' he says. 'That girl, that woman, was something very special.' His words break my heart open.

'Yes. She really was,' I say. 'Um . . . her mum, Tina, called me just now. She wondered if it would be okay for me to come in and sort through her stuff over there? Is that all right with you?'

'Molly, of course it is. I'll get her personal bits and bobs boxed up for you. I don't think there's a massive amount here though. You know what a neat freak she is. Was.' He pauses and takes a big breath. 'It would be good to see you anyway. I won't skirt around the issue. I've seen the online stuff. You poor thing. You've really been through it, haven't you?'

'Yeah, it's been a pretty horrendous couple of days,' I say. 'There's actually something I'd like to pick your brains about anyway. To do with Posey,' I add, before he gets any ideas about trying to interview me for *The Post*. Oliver may be in shock and grief-stricken for his colleague and good friend, but he didn't get to be the youngest national newspaper editor in the country for nothing. He's a journalist right down to his toenails. And I've seen just how ruthless he can be. I've always liked Oliver and we get on well, but I'm acutely aware that he is definitely someone you want on your team, not against you.

'Intriguing. When were you thinking? It's quiet this afternoon if you feel up to it?' This afternoon feels both too soon and like it's a million years away. I remember this feeling of being outside of the normal concept of time that grief brings from when Mum died. The thought of actually going outside of the flat fills me with abject terror. I remember the girls on the bus to work yesterday morning, certain now that they'd been laughing about me. I felt anxious enough then and that was before I knew the whole world had seen that video. I don't know if I can do it. But then I think of Posey, how my beautiful friend is dead, possibly murdered, and I know I have to push through this fear. I have to do it for her. Because she was fearless and would absolutely have done it for me.

'Sure,' I tell Oliver hoping I sound braver than I feel. 'This afternoon is great. Around two?'

'Perfect, Molly. I'll see you then.'

10

*

I haven't been to Posey's office before, well, not inside anyway. I've met her in the foyer a couple of times and I've had occasional drinks with Oliver and some other staffers she worked with. She'd tried to bring up the idea of me coming in and doing some freelance trial shifts once or twice but I'd always batted her away.

'You need to get out of your comfort zone, Mols,' she'd tell me, eyeing me disapprovingly over a porn star martini.

'I love my job,' I'd reply firmly like we were actors rehearsing a scene.

'You hate your job.'

'I like my job.'

'Your job bores you. Your job doesn't challenge you.'

'I don't *want* to be challenged. I *like* alpacas.' Then Posey would drop the subject for a few months and we'd have the same conversation all over again. Sadness stings me in the throat as I realise my head is the only place this conversation will ever take place in now. Grief really doesn't get any easier, no matter how much of it you experience. After my mum died, a lot of people talked around me about the first year being the hardest. So when that first anniversary came and went, I expected the grief to go too. But it clung on as stubbornly as a stain. And this time there was no end in sight. Once I'd got through the 'first Christmas' and the 'first Mother's Day' all there was left was an endless stream of Christmases and Mother's Days without her. Grief isn't a thing. It's a *nothing*. It's a universe before creation.

'Miss? I asked you if you have an appointment?'

I snap out of my reverie and realise a young man behind the reception desk has been talking to me.

'Gosh, I'm so sorry, I'm in a world of my own,' I say. 'I'm here to see Oliver Valentine on *The Post*? It's Molly. Molly Monroe.' I watch his face for a flinch, a glimmer of a reaction to my name. Nothing. He's obviously very good at his job. Or maybe he's one of those social media puritans.

'Take a seat, I'll let him know you're here.'

I smile at him, probably more gratefully than necessary, and take a seat. The foyer alone puts *Girl Chat*'s shared office space to shame. Everything is made from either glass or marble and every surface is shiny. When Oliver descends from an escalator in the heavens to swipe me through the airport-level security entrance, he too is shiny. I remember marvelling at how other people's lives just kept going while voice could be right though. I decide to stay quiet for now. Instead I give Oliver a grateful smile as he softly pulls the office door closed behind him, making me promise to call him if I need anything, anything at all. He's right that she hasn't left much behind. There's a laptop that I assume isn't her company-issued one because they would've taken it back, a few notebooks with some shorthand scribbles and a framed photograph of Posey and me taken on a beach in Santorini a few years ago. I pick it up and look at our smiling, tanned faces. Someone snuffed the life out of that beautiful young woman.

'I'm going to find out what happened to you, Posey,' I say. 'I promise.'

And with that, I pick up the box and march out of the office.

*

I'm still fired up by the time I get home, determined that I can find out what happened to Posey. I'm hoping that her laptop has some answers. There's half a bottle of white wine, an expensive Sancerre, in the fridge when I look. I'm tempted to pour myself a large glass to sip while I have a look through Posey's stuff.

You need a clear head for this, Molly.

Posey's voice is strong and clear again. And right, again. I pour the wine down the sink, it's probably stale anyway, and make myself a tea instead. Then I take it through to the living room, make myself a little nest on the sofa with the blankets

'Thanks. So what happened with the Lulu Lawrence story? Why was Posey so keen to tell me she'd found her if she wasn't even missing?'

'I don't know,' Oliver says. 'I told Posey to drop it, that there was no story. Lulu's mum, Marilyn, has unfortunately got some mental health problems. She'd contacted us in the past with some rather fanciful stuff. That was it as far as I was concerned. Posey wasn't very happy with me. I even suggested that maybe the pressure of the promotion was a bit much for her and that she should speak to HR about stress in the workplace. You can imagine how well that conversation went.'

'Ouch.' I grimace.

'Yeah. Exactly. Anyway.' He claps his hands together, back to business. 'Look, thanks for coming in, Molly. There's not a huge amount of stuff Posey left, as I said on the phone, but there's a few bits. Take anything you want and I'll sort the rest.' He hands me a crate. 'I'll give you a few minutes, okay? Do you want a vending-machine coffee? It's a bit of a delicacy round here.'

'I'm fine. Thank you.' I know I should say something to him now, mention what I know about Posey leaving something for me to find in The Place, how I think she was murdered in our home, but something inside me is telling me not to.

That's your journalistic instinct. I hear Posey's voice so loudly, I actually turn around expecting her to be there. She's not, of course, and I haven't really heard her voice, it's my traumatised mind playing tricks on me. I wonder if the mine had ground to a shuddering halt after Mum's death. It felt inconceivable, even to my twelve-year-old mind, how the world could possibly keep on spinning. The feeling hits me now as the smell of Oliver's shower gel wafts around us. Life doesn't care about death. It doesn't give a shit.

'How you doing, Molly?' Oliver gives my shoulder an awkward pat. 'Come up.'

I follow him, in silence, back up the escalator, through a set of doors he has to swipe something to open and into a large, open-plan office.

'We're all the way back here,' he says, walking ahead of me, cutting through rows of desks and journalists who are typing and swearing and drinking machine-coffee. Oliver leads me into a glass room with a glass door which I assume is his office. He sits behind the desk and gestures for me to take the chair in front of it. I do. 'You didn't answer,' he says, and I must look puzzled because he adds, 'when I asked how you're doing?'

'Oh,' I say. 'No, I didn't.' Oliver raises one shoulder as if to ask, so? 'I don't know, really. It just feels so weird. I don't think I'm feeling anything at the moment. Just waiting for it to hit me.'

Oliver nods. 'Yeah, same here. I keep waiting for her to burst into the office with some mad lead on a story.' Now is the time to bring it up.

Do it, Molly.

'She actually sent me a weird email before she died,' I say, searching Oliver's dark eyes for something although I'm not sure what. 'She seemed to be scared about something she was working on. She said she knows what happened to Lulu

Lawrence?' I see Oliver flinch slightly at the mention of Lulu's name. 'What did she mean?' Oliver sighs and lets his head drop into his hands, weary. After a couple of beats, he looks back up at me. I notice his eyes are glistening.

'Posey had got a bee in her bonnet about Lulu's disappearance. She reckoned she'd been in contact with Lulu's mother and knew what happened to her. She wanted *The Post* to run a big story on it.'

'But?'

Oliver sighs again, heavier this time. 'There is no story. The missing person report originally filed by Lulu's parents was withdrawn. If there's no missing person, there's no story about a missing person being found.'

'Why wasn't any of this reported though? Lulu's disappearance was big news.'

'It *was*. But no one made a big deal about it. Publishers and police were embarrassed as you can imagine, leading with a missing girl story one day and then saying "oops, our bad" a few days later wouldn't look great. So it was sort of glossed over. You know what news is like these days, it doesn't stop. It wasn't long before something else came along and Lulu's story was chip paper.'

'Nothing is ever really chip paper with the internet though,' I say.

Oliver nods. 'No, but people find other things to talk about.' He reaches across the desk and pats my hand gently. 'It *will* die down, Molly. I know it's difficult for you right now, but even the internet will get bored.' My soul dies a little more even though Oliver is trying to be kind.

7

*

The police eventually leave after grilling me for approximately a month, telling me they'll be in touch if they need anything else from me.

'We're not treating this as a suspicious death,' I vaguely register DI Wolfe telling me as he makes his way to leave. 'From everything we can see, it's a very tragic accident.'

'Accident?'

'Miss Porter fell asleep in the bath and sadly drowned. The alcohol would have meant her body didn't respond when she couldn't breathe. It's possible she was already unconscious when she went under. It happens more than you'd think. Obviously, there will be a standard autopsy and toxicology blood tests. But yes, just a very sad accident.' He looks at me

79

for a second. My paranoia kicks up a notch. 'We'll let Miss Porter's next of kin know what's happened.'

I nod mutely. Miserably.

'Do you have somewhere you can stay tonight?' DS Freeman looks at me with sad doe eyes.

'No . . . I . . . do I have to?'

She shakes her head. 'No, no. We're done here. I just don't think you should be alone, Miss Monroe. It's been quite a day for you. Any family nearby or anything?'

I shake my head.

'I can stay with her,' Jack says. 'If that's what Molly wants?'

'Yes please,' I say.

'I think that's a good idea,' DS Freeman says. 'You're probably in shock and I'd sleep a bit better knowing you're not here by yourself. You're going through a lot.' She's probably even younger than me, I realise on closer inspection, and I feel suitably pathetic as she gives my arm a rub. 'If there's anything you'd like to talk about, regarding the video, you can talk to me, okay?' I think back to what Carol said about sexual assault.

'Thanks,' I say. 'I'll think about it.'

'Call anytime and ask for me, okay? Please don't feel you're alone. I have some good contacts who might be able to help you. Or I can put you in touch with victim support?'

I smile gratefully, but I can't even begin to consider the fact that I've, maybe, been the victim of a crime. DS Freeman gives my arm a final squeeze before heading down the path to the unmarked car her partner is already unlocking.

'Thanks for your time, Miss Monroe,' DI Wolfe calls to me. Under the streetlamp I see his gaze move to the house next door, the Goldmans, and he briefly nods a greeting to whoever is standing on their porch, also watching the detectives get into their car.

*

I stand by the front door and watch as the detectives pull away. The ambulance and squad car have already left and I think about Posey's final journey to the hospital mortuary. It feels surreal and I can't stop thinking how much she hated being cold. The thought chills me and I feel myself shiver, the coldness deep in the marrow of my bones. I'm completely numb. I guess this must be shock. I turn to the Goldmans, expecting to see Patrick there, briefly wondering if he's the ambulance-chaser type of lawyer. I'm surprised to see Trudie standing there. Her eyes slowly move to meet mine. She's holding one of their new babies in her arms, the light from their hallway making her blonde hair glow like a halo. She looks like a painting of the Virgin Mary. Beautiful and serene. She pulls the bundle of baby closer to her chest when our eyes meet. Hers are glacial and make me shiver again. Her toddler daughter arrives at the door, her breath making little puffs of white cloud as she tugs on her mother's sleeve, trying to get her attention.

'Go and play with your dollies,' she tells the little one but her eyes don't leave mine. It's unnerving, actually.

'Posey's dead,' I say, the words tumbling out of my mouth

before I can stop them. 'My flatmate. I found her. In the bath.' Trudie doesn't say anything but I see her nostrils flare slightly as she takes a sharp breath in.

'Just the one slut living next door now then?' she says.

I'm not sure I've heard her properly. 'What?'

Her lip curls up into a snarl and for a moment I don't think I've ever seen her look quite so ugly. I don't think I've seen *anyone* look quite so ugly.

'I said, just the one *slut* living next door now then,' she repeats slowly, each word a sharp, cutting staccato. She looks me up and down with a hatred that chills me before turning and closing her front door. I recoil into my own doorway, shocked and shaken by her vitriol. I can, kind of, understand why she'd say something so hurtful to me, I mean it's quite tame compared with what's been said online today, but not why she'd speak about poor, dead Posey with such hatred.

I can sense Jack behind me before I feel him lightly touch my shoulder.

'I only caught the end of that,' he says. 'Are you okay?'

I laugh darkly. 'I don't think my video debut has won me any fans in middle-class London.'

'Ignore it. Which I know is easy for me to say. But you really don't need to be thinking about stuff like that right now. Come on, come inside. It's far too cold to be standing out here.'

I nod and close the door and let Jack lead me back down the hallway into the lounge. 'Have you eaten anything today?' he asks, depositing me on the sofa and handing me a blanket.

'I can't even remember,' I say. 'I don't think so.'

and open Posey's MacBook Air, hoping it has some charge. Miraculously, it does. I'm quietly shocked because I'm very much the sort of person who consistently opens the wrong end of the paracetamol and nothing I turn on is ever charged. My lucky streak lasts for only two seconds though as the laptop is password protected. Of course it is. Posey wasn't an idiot like me. I half-heartedly try a couple of obvious things like 'Password' and 'PoseyPorter1', but unsurprisingly, they don't work. So much for that. I momentarily regret pouring the Sancerre away.

Look in the notebooks.

Of course! I grab the small pile of jotters and pile them on my lap. I'd initially dismissed them as being full of a version of shorthand I didn't understand, but on closer inspection I realise that there are some actual words and notes scribbled in them too. Nothing that really makes much sense, notes Posey had probably been taking while she was on the phone to an interviewee, a couple of reminders about things she needed to do, but, right in the middle of one of the notebooks I spot a carefully handwritten page.

6 $ 4 queen WALMART (YELP ` jack ; korean 9 fruit TOKYO music 8

Could this be it? It's such a random selection of words and weird punctuation that I don't think it can be anything else. I type it into the password box, without the spaces, and hit enter, mentally crossing my fingers. But it doesn't work. I growl in frustration at the computer. I try again, with the spaces, but still nothing. It must be something though. A reason some of the words are in ALL CAPS and some aren't. I try again, this time removing the spaces and only using the first initial of each word. I then spend a full minute blinking in wonder as the laptop lights up, alive and unlocked. I can't believe it and let out a burst of laughter which I then think is totally inappropriate given the circumstances and immediately start feeling bad about.

Stop punishing yourself, Molly. You really need to stop this.

To be clear, I don't *actually* think that my dead friend is communicating with me from beyond the grave. I had a similar experience after my mum died where I could hear her talking to me in my head. I thought I was going mad, but a very lovely child psychologist helped me understand that this is something a grieving brain will sometimes do, especially if the person you've lost was very close to you. Especially if the grieving brain is only twelve years old. It's a self-protection technique; you know them so well and what they'd say to you in certain situations that your brain suggests what they might say to you. I know there's a scientific explanation which makes absolute sense. But I still like to believe that a part of my brain is keeping a part of Posey alive. And this is exactly what she'd say to me if she knew what a hard time I mentally give myself. With Mum, it became less frequent over time, as I processed and came to terms with the loss. Although every now and again, she still pipes up and surprises me. I'm glad she didn't go away completely. I hope Posey is the same.

I greedily inspect Posey's home screen. It's bizarrely sparse, although, I realise that's just bizarre for me. My home screen is a horror show, Posey's *would* be clean and tidy. That's just who she was. There's just one folder on there and it's labelled LL. Even with my limited investigative journalism skills, I can work out it must stand for Lulu Lawrence. Posey must've been working on the story in her own time after Oliver shot her down.

I hover the cursor over the folder for a few seconds, letting an internal battle with my conscience play out. This is something so very personal to Posey that it feels intrusive. Even though she's dead. I don't think I'd like someone going through my private thoughts after I'm gone.

Of course you wouldn't like it. You wouldn't have an opinion on it at all. Because you'd be dead.

I click on the folder and open it.

*

I'm not sure exactly what I'd been expecting to find here. A folder titled YES I WAS MURDERED AND THIS IS WHO DID IT AND WHY would've been helpful but, unsurprisingly, it's not there. Instead there is a very neat cluster of folders with titles I don't understand. They're just sequences of letters and numbers that have no meaning to me, but must've meant something to Posey. I try to open one but a box pops up telling me the file is password protected and asking me to enter the password to continue. Obviously I don't know the password.

'Urgh!' I hiss at the computer, in frustration. I briefly consider slamming it shut, going to the little shop on the corner and buying a bottle of wine with the intention of drinking it all, or at least enough to knock me out. But the impulse passes quickly and I find myself staring at the computer screen again. The fact that I can't easily get into these files convinces me that there's something super important in them. And that makes me even more determined to get in. 'Come on, Molly,' I tell myself. 'Think. What would Posey have as her password?'

I try the obvious things like her date of birth, her half-siblings' dates of birth, their names, a combination of their names and birthdays. Nothing. Then I try her mum's and stepdad's names. Nope. Her real dad. Nada. Desperately, I try my own details too. Now, if this were a movie or Netflix show, that would've worked, and I'd be staring at the unlocked files in misty-eyed surprise. But it doesn't. I growl at the computer, my mind wandering to that bottle of wine again. I shake the thought away, gritting my teeth. 'Think harder, Molly.'

I think back to our university days and try a combination of Posey's favourite bands, books and films from then. The files remain, almost defiantly, locked. 'Fuck's sake!' I slam the lid down, tears of frustration threatening. I stand up and pace around the room. I won't give up. I won't! There must be a way of getting into those files. If Posey was really as scared of something happening to her as her email suggested, then she would have made sure I could open them. I sit down again and open the laptop. The desktop comes awake and I click on one of the files again. The password box pops up and I type in 'The_Place'.

And then I have my Netflix moment.

I actually can't believe it worked and I *am* staring at the unlocked files with misty-eyed surprise.

See, Molly. You really can do it.

Mum's voice resonates with pride in my head. I did it. I really did it.

My hand trembles as I click on one of the blue files and open it. Despite the neatness of her desktop, the contents of the folders are something of a mess. There are subfolders, random screenshots and other things that don't make any sense to me. I don't even know where to begin. And then I see it. A folder called 'Marilyn'. Lulu Lawrence's mother. I click it open and the first thing I come across is a screenshot of an email from Marilyn to Posey, dated earlier this year. It's confused and slightly rambling, but very obviously the writing of an extremely distressed mother, desperate for answers about her child, not being listened to.

From: MLawrence@gmail.com
To: PPorter@thepost.co.uk
Date: 18 May
Time: 21.08

Dear Ms Porter,
I'm hoping you can help me. I'm the mother of Lulu Lawrence who you may remember went missing at Christmas last year. Despite reports to the contrary, Lulu has never been

found and has not returned home. Her case has been closed, but never solved. My daughter is still missing.

I'm on anti-depressants. Who wouldn't be when their 16-year-old daughter has been missing for almost a year and whatever I do, it's shut down. The police are saying she's 16 now and even if she is missing, which they refuse to believe, she can leave home whenever she likes. She's not vulnerable, they say, but she's 16. Of course she's vulnerable. When I try to tell them this, they tell me that I told them she wasn't missing in the first place. When I tell them I didn't say this, they point out I'm on meds and am clearly a bit confused. I'm not confused. Why would I tell them she isn't missing when she is?

I've tried to start my own website, I've tried to make groups on Facebook and a @WheresLuluLawrence on Twitter but they were all gone in days. I've tried leaving comments on news articles but then they were all closed down. Even her YouTube and TikTok channels have been shut. It's like she never even existed. I know this sounds mad and a bit paranoid, but my girl is missing and something is going on, Posey. Please help me. You're my only real hope.

I read Marilyn's desperate words several times over, physically feeling her fear and confusion. Of course Posey could never have ignored an email as plaintive and pleading as this. She may have been a tough cookie when she needed to, but Posey's sense of justice had never wavered in the fourteen years I'd known her. Posey's reply is brief, she asks Marilyn for a phone number, says it's better to speak over the phone, and Marilyn supplies one.

From: MLawrence@gmail.com
To: PPorter@thepost.co.uk
Date: 2 June
Time: 20.38

Hi Posey

Thanks for your visit at the weekend. It was great to finally meet you. I hope that by seeing Lulu's home and her things you got a real sense of who she is and what a huge space she's left in my life.

I called the police again today to ask about why they're not letting the media write anything about Lu. This time they told me that they prefer to keep their investigation low-key at the moment. They agreed that it's out of character for Lulu to be missing for so long, but they also have no reason to believe it's anything other than a teen runaway. They've suggested she may be with someone she met online (like we've not been saying this for weeks) but putting it in the public eye could spook them and make them react so they want to keep it quiet. They've also said that because Lulu's 16 now, she's perfectly entitled to leave home if she wants to. It was only her birthday today, for God's sake! It's like they've been waiting for this to throw a new line at me.

I'm so sorry, Posey. I know this isn't your fault but I can't help feeling we're being let down by everyone while my beautiful, funny daughter is out there somewhere. And she could be hurt or being kept somewhere against her will. Why is no one taking this seriously? I'm just absolutely at the end of my tether. How long am I supposed to carry on like this for?

Mx

There are a few more emails, all in a similar vein. Poor Marilyn sounding more and more frantic as she comes up against more closed doors and dead ends. But there are so many things here that don't quite add up. Why would Oliver tell Posey that he can't report on the story because of restrictions due to Lulu's age? It's been over ten years since I studied media law as part of my journalism degree and a lot of things have no doubt changed, but even I'm fairly sure that this isn't the case when the child is a missing person. In fact the media plays a huge role in helping to find missing kids. And why are the police fobbing Marilyn off, when they're also saying that the original missing person report had been rescinded?

None of it makes any sense.

You need to speak to Marilyn.

Of course, I do. It's so obvious. One of the emails mentions that Posey had even visited the Lawrences' home.

When? I've been so blind.

Marilyn had given her number to Posey, so I add it to my own phone, creating a new contact, ML.

Call her. Do it now.

Yes. There's nothing else to do. I have to. I may not be able to talk to Posey, but I can do the next best thing and speak to Marilyn. I press the call button before I have the time to talk myself out of it. *Please answer, please answer.* But the phone rings until it clicks onto voicemail.

'Hi, this is Marilyn. Please leave a message after the tone and I'll get back to you as soon as I can.'

I sigh. Loudly. And just as the beep sounds, so that will be the first thing Marilyn hears from me. Fabulous.

'Hi, Marilyn,' I say, not quite sure where I'm going with this at all. I can't tell her about Posey's death on a bloody voicemail. 'My name is Molly Monroe and I'm a close friend of Posey. I know Posey's been helping you look for Lulu. I've got some information you should know. Please call me back as soon as you can.' I leave my own number and say sorry for some reason, before hanging up and hating myself for a moment. Should I really be getting involved in this? If it was something big enough to leave Posey terrified then it must be dangerous. She wasn't dramatic or neurotic, despite what Oliver has insinuated. But then I think of my own name trending on social media, on every platform despite my company's best efforts to get it taken down. I thought when something was online, it was there forever, but that doesn't seem to be the case with Lulu Lawrence. Posey was right. There is something seriously amiss here. I feel a familiar stirring deep inside me, it's the hunger to know the truth. I need to do this, For Lulu. For Posey.

For me.

*

While I wait for Marilyn to get back to me, I decide to refresh myself on Lulu Lawrence and the weirdness around her disappearance.

I type her name into Google and am immediately presented with a page of search results. They're mostly newspaper sites or news agencies and most have a headline along the lines of,

Police ask public for information
about missing teenager

I click on one of the top hits and read through what I already know, a story from almost exactly one year ago.

LONDON (12 December)—Police this evening have asked the public for any information about a missing teenage girl. Lulu Lawrence, 15, was last seen three days ago, when she went missing from a Christmas market in Manchester, which she was visiting with her parents. She went to get herself food from a vendor but didn't come back. Lulu was last seen wearing a pair of light jogging bottoms, white trainers and a dark green puffa-style jacket. She is five feet and four inches tall and has waist-length blonde hair, which was tied in a ponytail at the time she went missing. Marilyn Lawrence, Lulu's mother, said, 'If anyone has seen Lulu or knows where she might be, please call the police helpline, even if you think it's not important. We miss our little girl and want her home for Christmas. Lulu, if you see this, you're not in any trouble, baby, please get in touch with myself or Daddy.' Christopher Lawrence, the father, added, 'If anyone can help us find our daughter, then we beg you to do so. Lulu, the house isn't home without you.'

A couple of nationals, including *The Post,* had gone big on the story for a couple of days. I remember Posey talking about it at the time.

'It's one of those stories that seem to come ready-made for media,' she'd mused as we'd eaten pasta in one of the cheaper restaurants near Clapham Junction after work. 'She's blonde, pretty, middle-class. Nothing dark lurking in her background. The family will probably offer a nice reward for information and the media will fall over themselves to get her home. Right before Christmas as well.' She'd raised an eyebrow then. 'Perfect timing, right?'

We'd agreed that it would likely be a big story but after that initial flurry, Lulu Lawrence seemed to disappear again. Only this time it was from public consciousness rather than a Christmas market. I chew my lip as I think back to this time last year and how I'd not even thought about Lulu since that conversation. I scroll through the next few pages of search results, but there's nothing else. I try adding a few more words 'Lulu Lawrence found', 'Lulu Lawrence suspect', 'Lulu Lawrence search', but there was still nothing.

Weird.

Even if Lulu had been found safe and well, even if it had all been a big misunderstanding and she'd sequestered herself away at a friend's house, there would usually be a follow-up story saying this. Especially around Christmas.

Everyone loves a happy ending to stories like this, don't they? A Christmas miracle.

But there's nothing.

I open Facebook and ignore the notifications, probably all from people I hadn't spoken to in years wanting to know what happened to Posey or with something to say about my porn debut, instead going straight to the search bar and typing in 'Find Lulu Lawrence'. Surely there would be some group or something here sharing ideas and theories about the fate of Lulu Lawrence. Facebook exists for this sort of stuff. But, again, I come up with nothing. No groups, no people, no pages. I click open a new tab and search for the national Missing People website and tap Lulu's name into the search bar.

Zero results.

I try again with 'Louise Lawrence' and 'Louise Laurence' but nothing.

Beyond bizarre. Surely there would be some record of Lulu's disappearance on here, even if she'd been found.

Next, I open Twitter and type Lulu's name in. There are a couple of random comments. One from just after Christmas last year,

Does anyone know what happened with that Lulu Lawrence girl? News has gone quiet. She been found?

And another from earlier this year, summer.

Someone saying that Lulu Lawrence who went missing at Xmas didn't turn up for any of her GCSEs. Anyone know anything?

Neither of the users has a profile picture or any followers

to speak of. Neither comment has any replies or likes either. And both accounts stopped tweeting immediately after posting their respective questions about Lulu. It doesn't make sense. Absolutely no one is talking about Lulu Lawrence, she doesn't even seem to exist let alone be missing. Yet, Posey was convinced she'd found out what had happened to her. So convinced that she wanted to talk to me about it face to face and not over messages. It just doesn't add up. I taste blood and realise my lip has started bleeding from where I've been chewing it. I dab it with my finger as I try to balance out what I know about Posey and Lulu Lawrence. Did she find something out about the missing teenager that put her life in danger? And if so has the truth about Lulu Lawrence died along with my friend? Or am I having some sort of massive trauma-induced delusion brought on by finding my best friend dead in the bath on the same day a sexually explicit video of myself went viral? I should probably just go to bed and stop being hysterical.

You're not being hysterical. That's the patriarchy trying to silence you.

And now I'm hearing voices. Posey's voice to be specific. Definitely time for bed.

11

@MissDemiNah: I don't know how you all can be Rt-ing this crap and laughing at that poor girl. She's obviously too drunk to consent. You're all laughing at a sexual assault.

*

I wake up the next morning surprised at how well I've slept. For the first time in days, I don't grab my phone as soon as I open my eyes. I resist the urge to doom-scroll social media, looking for new ways I'm being picked to pieces by people who don't know me. Instead, I open my curtains, letting the watery winter sunlight in. The ground outside is white with frost and I shiver, wrapping a blanket around my shoulders before padding through to the kitchen to make a hot drink. I drum my nails impatiently on the worktop while the kettle boils, eager to get back to Posey's laptop and its secrets.

I open one of the blue files which I didn't get around to last night. It's a collection of screenshots from a Reddit subthread. A subthread dedicated to Lulu Lawrence. There seems to be a community, albeit a small one, also convinced that all is not what it seems with the official story about her disappearance. I click open the first one.

r/WhatHappenedtoLuluLawrence?

We are a small subreddit community dedicated to finding out what happened to missing schoolgirl Lulu Lawrence. Lulu Lawrence was a regular teenager. Until she suddenly wasn't. Her parents and school friends have tried speaking out about her vanishing just before Christmas last year, but they keep being shut down.

We want to know where she is.

———

by u/CBA123

Why is no one talking about this?

I know we've said it before, but I still can't get over why no one is talking about Lulu. I've been searching online for hours and there is literally nothing about her going missing apart from this sub and a few comments on Twitter which will probably get taken down. If I was Marilyn, I'd be posting everywhere, trying to get attention for my missing child. It doesn't make sense.

Replies:
u/LeoTheLion

Marilyn *has* been posting everywhere about Lulu, of course she has. There have been screenshots and other evidence that Marilyn has tried to set up online groups on social media and even a webpage, but they've been removed almost immediately. It's a media conspiracy.

u/CBA123

I just don't understand how there is such a media blackout of this. It's like total, surely something would have sneaked through?

u/WeAreAllBeingLiedTo

I found this, it's still a live link but was buried on p.12 of Google search. It's a report from a local news agency saying that 15-year-old Lulu Lawrence has not been seen in 48 hours and anyone with any information should contact Greater Manchester police.

u/LeoTheLion

Quick, screenshot it and add to the case files. Now you've flagged it on here, it will be gone within hours, if not sooner! I betchya.

u/WeAreAllBeingLiedTo

Haha. I've already done it.

u/CBA123

Has anyone mentioned that we wouldn't be having this conversation if it was a girl of colour who was missing? The media 'blackout' on missing kids who aren't white is a fucking disgrace.

u/LeoTheLion

CBA123, yes that's one of the reasons why we believe something really bad has happened to Lulu. Ordinarily, she would be the poster girl for missing kids. She's everything the media loves – blonde hair, blue eyes, nice MC family. That's what makes the lack of any coverage so baffling. It reeks of conspiracy. We all know the media coverage of missing kids who don't fit Lulu's profile is twisted, but that isn't what this sub is about. The inequality in coverage actually gives us a clue that something isn't right here.

u/KpopfanUK

Lulu is definitely still missing. I'm her friend. A close friend. We're all so worried about her. There's no way she'd have just gone off on her own. She wasn't street-wise at all. She never got in trouble. It's completely out of character. We're all so worried that something bad has happened to her.

u/IntoTheUnknown

Something bad HAS happened to Lulu. I know this for a fact. Look on the dark web. Your answers are all there.

u/PPorter

IntoTheUnknown, what do you know about Lulu? I'm a journalist and I'm working on a story about her disappearance. But it's so hard to find anything at all. Can you help me?

u/IntoTheUnknown

No, I can't. Too dangerous. I've probably said too much already. But there is a group like this one you should see. Dark web. Search TruthSeekers. It's all there.

u/IntoTheUnknown

THIS USER HAS DELETED THEIR ACCOUNT

u/LeoTheLion

PPorter – I have sent you a DM.

I flick through the other screenshots. They all say the same sort of thing, concerns about Lulu from people claiming to know her, speculation that there was a media cover-up and the occasional troll saying some derogatory things about Lulu. I ignore these. There are no more posts from LeoTheLion and I wonder what he said in his DM to Posey. I click through some of the other files, looking for a screen-shot of the message. But I find something else, something that chills me, despite the blanket I've wrapped tightly around myself. It chills me from the inside of my bones. Another email.

From: AnonX@hushmail.com
To: PPorter@gmail.com
Subject: You fucking stupid bitch
Date: 19 June
Time: 22.34

How many times Posey? How many fucking times have you been told to drop this fucking missing girl case? We warned you of the consequences if you carried on. You'd better be prepared to face them. You've not listened and now you're going to pay. Better tell that pretty flatmate of yours to watch her back too. We *will* silence you, Posey. Any way we have to.

There it is, right there in front of my own eyes, proof that Posey was in danger and that she was afraid. Not just that, but whoever this person was had threatened me too. Why hadn't Posey told me this? Fear is forcing the blood around my body faster and more urgently and I'm on my feet, checking the locks on the windows and doors. What had she stumbled into and why hadn't she warned me? If I'd had half a clue what was going on, there would be no way I'd have been carrying on with my life like normal. I stop pacing, rooted to the spot. I wouldn't have gone to the Christmas party, or if I had, there's no way I would've let myself get so drunk that my memories of the night were wiped. It wasn't just irresponsible of Posey to keep something like this to herself, it's fucking negligent. I sink to the floor and let myself cry hot, angry tears.

When I eventually manage to stop, I check my phone. There are messages from Paloma, Jack and Robyn, all asking me if I'm okay, all wondering if there is anything they can do. I only reply to Jack.

I'm okay. Everything is still very weird and upsetting. But I'm okay.

His reply comes quickly.

Do you need anything? I'm working but I can come over later? xx

No. Thank you. I think I just need to be alone with everything right now. X

Okay. I'll check in on you later. Please take care Molly xx

I turn back to Posey's laptop and click on the web browser. I type Reddit into the search bar and am surprised to see that her login details have been stored. I hesitate for a moment, is this going too far? Going through her personal DMs? This is something so very personal to Posey that it feels intrusive.

I click on the login button and head straight to Posey's direct messages.

*

The user calling themselves LeoTheLion did indeed message Posey. They told her that they had some information about Lulu but were only willing to disclose it in person. Posey agreed to meet them on the condition that it was in a very public place. They agreed to both have copies of *The Anglian Times* so they would recognise each other. Clever Posey. *Everyone* would be carrying a copy of *Metro* or *Evening Standard*. LeoTheLion asked for Posey's reassurance that anything they tell her would be off the record. They said, 'It's not just my job that would be at stake if it got out I've told a journalist this stuff.' Posey promised. And then the messages stop. I can only assume she met up with this person and they gave her some lead on Lulu. Another secret she'd been keeping from me. I sigh, considering sending a message to this LeoTheLion. Instead, I think about one of the other comments on Reddit about the dark web. I text Jack.

Hey. You know you said you were here for me if I need anything?

Hey you. Yes, I did say that. What's up?

Can you teach me about the workings of the dark web?

He doesn't reply right away, but when he does, I can almost hear the sigh in his voice.

If I say no, I guess you'll keep going until you find someone who will, right?

Correct.

In that case, it's better it's me. I'll call you tomorrow when I'm free. Jx

*

I fall into an uneasy sleep on the sofa, wrapped in my blanket. I wonder if I'm coming down with something as when I wake up, I realise I've spent the entire night here. The morning sun is making a lukewarm attempt at lighting the room. I hold a hand to my head, but don't feel overly warm. There's a banging on the door and I wonder if that's what woke me. Icy panic floods my veins as Posey's warning comes back to me. Who's here? Am I in danger? I'm frozen for a moment, then I grab my phone, ready to call for help if I need to.

I rub the remaining sleep from my eyes and stumble towards the door, which is being hammered again.

'Coming,' I grumble. 'Hang on.'

Behind the door waits a creature from nightmares. Pale and haunted. I can feel the grief dripping from every pore. It's so there, so palpable I can smell it on her. The broken woman who stands in front of me. Her eyes seem enormous in the whiteness of her face. She somehow looks like a very old woman and a very young girl at the same time. She falls towards me and I have to step quickly to stop her collapsing on the floor. In my arms she howls like a feral thing.

This is Posey's mother.

It takes some time for me to softly coax Tina Porter past her dead daughter's bedroom, into the lounge. She is both light as a baby bird and heavy with the weight of grief. She stumbles every few steps, falling to the ground like she'll never get up again. I eventually manage to settle her on the sofa and bring her a cup of sweet tea, strangely mirroring what Jack did for me a few days earlier.

'What happened, Molly?' She looks at me with pleading, baleful eyes. 'What happened to my baby?' Her voice cracks on the last word and she dissolves once again into tears, clutching a raggedy tissue that has taken on a grotesque form. A ghost's comfort blanket. How can I ever tell her that I don't think her daughter's death was an accident, and I think she was murdered?

'You've spoken to the police?'

She nods.

'So, they think it was an accident. That Posey fell asleep in the bath. She'd been drinking.'

Tina is shaking her head now. 'That's not Posey. That's not Posey.'

I don't know what to say. Instead, I sit down next to her, wondering how I can possibly comfort a woman in pieces. I reach for her hand, the one still holding the remains of a tissue, but Tina pulls away. And of course, she's right, it's what I suspected all along.

'Oh God, Molly, I'm sorry.' Tina's voice is a whisper. 'I can only imagine how hard this is for you.'

'It's okay,' I tell her, although I don't know if I'm reassuring her or myself.

'I had a call from the police this morning,' she continues. 'The autopsy and toxicology confirm that Posey's death was an accident. That she drowned in the bath after drinking. She was twice over the drink-drive limit according to the blood results.' Tina sighs heavily, as if she can breathe her grief out. 'I didn't think Posey would be so reckless.'

I don't know what to do apart from offer her more tea, which she accepts. I perch awkwardly next to her. 'It gets easier,' I say. She gives a little shrug at my platitude. 'I know everyone says it, but it does.' I pause. 'Well, maybe not easier. That's not right. But less—' I don't even know what I'm trying to say. 'Less like this, I guess.' I gesture at the two of us, tear stained and stricken from loss and shock.

Tina manages a small smile and places a hand on my lap. I notice her fingernails are freshly manicured, a deep coral colour. She could only have had them done in the last few days, they're new, shiny. Sadness ploughs into me as I think of Tina sitting patiently, blissfully ignorant of the torment on its way, while someone buffed and polished her nails. She sees me looking and pulls away like a dart. Slides

her hands underneath her thighs as if she's ashamed of her pre-grief self.

'I need to sort through her things,' she's saying now, looking at the floor. Then she lifts her gaze up to me. Her eyes are wells of sorrow and confusion. She knows she's breaking apart, but her mind hasn't fully accepted why. I know this feeling. I know she'll be trapped in this limbo long enough to push her through the funeral arrangements and the other death admin before it hits her. And when it does, it will be a tsunami that will leave her crushed. I hate the journey she has ahead of her. 'Will you help me?'

'Yes, of course. Anything you need, just tell me.'

'I want to take most of her stuff home, you know her personal things. But clothes and that stuff. You'll know better than me what's what? She'd want you to have first pick of her clothes and shoes anyway.' Tina makes a strangled noise. I think she was going for a laugh but it gets stuck in her throat. 'She was always moaning about you pinching her stuff.' I must look horrified as she quickly adds, 'You know, in a funny way. Posey's way.'

I smile. 'Posey's way.'

We finish the tea. 'I'm drinking more tea than a vicar at the moment, everyone thinks I need tea,' Tina tells me, and goes through to Posey's bedroom.

I follow her and, again, the memory of finding Posey in here just three days ago is like slamming into a wall. I breathe slowly and steadily, trying to quell the panic that's bubbling away like lava just under my surface.

'Where should we start?' Tina asks and I'm as clueless as

she is. How does one even begin to put the life of their child into bags and boxes?

We decide to start with clothes and I help her carefully fold them into three piles: keep, charity, bin. In the end I keep very little. A leather AllSaints jacket, which Tina insists I must have, and a couple of dresses that still have the tags in. I can't bear the thought of keeping something Posey has actually worn. Of wearing it myself while there are still bits of her, her DNA, her scent on them. All shoes end up on the charity pile. Posey had tiny, delicate little feet. I'd be like one of the ugly stepsisters in a Grimm's fairy tale trying to squash my feet into her shoes.

Then Tina starts to go through Posey's other bits and pieces. Her dressing table, the drawers next to her bed. The boxes underneath it. I cringe when she opens a shoe box which contains an assortment of vibrators and other things parents really shouldn't see.

'Oh God, Molly.' She pushes the box across the wooden floor towards me. 'Can you deal with this? I just don't need to know about that.' There's a tiny ghost of a smile on her face and I see a hint of Posey dancing on Tina's lips.

'I'm not sure I do either.' But I take the box anyway and put it in my room, underneath my bed.

When I go back to Tina, she's sitting in a puddle of clothes and bags on Posey's bed.

'I don't think I can do this all today, Molly.' She sighs. 'I don't know what I was thinking. My husband told me not to push myself but I needed to be doing something, you know?'

'It's up to you, of course, but I'll help you. You don't have to face this alone.' I mean it, but I also need to know if there are any clues in here. I feel less guilty about going through Posey's belongings if Tina is with me.

She smiles at me, kindly now. 'She loved you so much.'

'It was very mutual.'

'Shall we just do what we can, do you think? Take it slowly? I can always come back, can't I? It's not like we need to rush?'

I think of Jesse upstairs probably wondering if he can post the vacancy on SpareRoom yet, but I say, 'No. No rush at all.'

We spend most of the afternoon working alongside each other in a companionable silence punctuated by rounds of tea and the occasional memory of Posey. There are a lot of tears, a few laughs and, thankfully, no body buried under the floorboards. Posey's room doesn't even hint at her secrets. I'm pleased more than disappointed. We've managed to get through most of it by the time the light starts to fade. Tina blinks away tears as she stares at the boxes and bags.

'I'll come back with Peter and pick everything up after the funeral,' she says. 'Is that okay? There's more stuff here than I thought. So many books! I don't know where she gets it from. I was never a reader.'

'That's fine, of course it is, just let me know when so I can be here to let you in and give you a hand. I wouldn't want you having to deal with Jesse after that.'

Tina smiles. 'He called me actually. Asked me if I needed any help with anything. Asked about funeral arrangements

too. He actually seemed very sweet.' I stare at her, aware my mouth is hanging open. 'Don't look so shocked, Molly. He thinks the world of you girls.' She squeezes my arm and again I can only picture Jesse wanting to know anything because he's working out how quickly he can start advertising the room so he doesn't lose any rent. 'I suppose we need to start thinking about that now the body will be released.' Tina looks like she might collapse again and I wrap my arms around her. She is tiny, like a Barbie doll.

'Let me know if you need me to do anything,' I tell her. She smiles but it doesn't reach her eyes. I wonder if it ever will again.

'We're only going to have a low-key Christmas this year and it's only really for the little ones,' she tells me. 'But please come. I know you said you wanted to be independent this year but I think we need you probably more than you need us. At least think about it, Mols?' The thought of spending Christmas with Posey's family while she's lying in a grave makes the bile in my empty stomach swish around, a stormy sea deep in my core.

'I'll think about it,' I say.

'Promise me, Molly,' she says, holding the tops of my arms like a stern mother and looking right into my eyes. 'You'll stay in touch? Even when it's all over.' She kisses me on the cheek and smooths my unwashed hair behind my ears before visibly bracing herself to step back into a world her daughter is no longer a part of. 'She always thought you needed to have more confidence in yourself, you know? She told me what a brilliant writer you are and that you're wasted on that kiddie magazine. You need to believe in yourself like Posey did. Promise me, you'll try?'

I nod, too choked up to say anything.

When Tina is gone, I feel a horrible rush of sad emotions crash around inside me. There's the grief of course, that's going to be omnipresent for many months to come. I know, from experience, that eventually grief won't try to tug me down so low that I feel like I'm drowning in my own body. It will fade and become not quite bearable but something you can live alongside. If it behaves itself. But I also know that it can pounce on you and have you by the throat at the most unexpected times. For me, it's always smells that bring that pang of memory. That specific component of emotional pain that can feel like a very old wound and a searing fresh one at the exact same time. That never goes away completely. I'm prepared for that. What I'm not prepared for is the sadness I feel when Tina's words play over and over again in my mind.

You need to believe in yourself like Posey did.
You need to believe in yourself like Posey did.
You need to believe in yourself like Posey did.
She believed in me.

It's hard for me to process this, especially when I stopped believing in myself so long ago. After she started working at *The Post* as a reporter three years ago, she took me to a Mexican restaurant we loved on Clapham High Street to mark the occasion. It was her celebration but she made the whole night about me, about what her new job could mean for me. I'd been at *Girl Chat* for a couple of years at this point and had already written the same article – Which Middle School Girl Are You? – about a hundred times.

'This job could be so great for you as well, Mols,' she'd enthused as we sucked down tequila between courses. 'Think about it – you can pitch me ideas! You can even come in and do a bit of secret freelancing on your days off. Get some experience in a proper newsroom to put on your CV. You'd love it. It's so exciting. And you actually get to leave the office to follow up leads and speak to people.' She knew this would appeal to me. I frequently complained that my job had become more and more like an office job – all our interviews were done on the phone, rather than travelling anywhere, in the interests of saving money.

I promised I'd pitch her some ideas. But I never got around to it. She gave me a few little nudges and even sat down with me one night to come up with some, but I told her she was nagging me. She didn't bring it up again after that. I was a horrible, ungrateful friend. I can't believe she still wanted to help me so much when I'd been such a pain in the arse. Her words make me think about what Robyn said to me the other day, before she'd seen me on my knees after the Christmas party.

She'd caught me looking at job ads at my desk and called me into her office. I thought I was going to be fired on the spot. It came after a particularly unpleasant features conference where Robyn practically breathed fire at me when I presented my ideas.

'Christ, I hate this shit,' Paloma had murmured to me as we shuffled into Robyn's office for the monthly agony. It really doesn't have space for five of us, but Robyn doesn't like to leave her office. In fact, since she stopped smoking, she has absolutely no need to. Her assistant even gets her lunches and her coffees and goes to the post room for her so Robyn just sits behind her desk all day. She didn't move from behind it when we filed in squeezing our own chairs in. We were packed in, close enough to feel each other's breath. Lexi, her deputy, sat at Robyn's side so it felt like Paloma, Zack and I were being interrogated.

'Okay, what have we got then? Well done on last month by the way. We had some really good feedback from readers about the differences between llamas and alpacas.' She smiled warmly at Zack, her second favourite to Lexi. Even though the story had been my idea.

Sort of.

I'd confessed that I thought alpacas were made up.

'Think about it though,' I remember saying. 'Old MacDonald never had an alpaca when I was little.'

'The great conspiracies of the twenty-first century, Flat Earth, pandemics and *alpacas*,' Zack had said.

The others laughed, but I was being deadly serious.

And I told them so. 'I mean it. Never heard of one until about five years ago, despite being dragged to various farms where we could hand-feed goats and sheep. Now they're everywhere. Total designer animal. Llamas are too spitty and vicious, so alpacas have been genetically created as a toddler-friendly version.'

It took them a while to stop laughing, but eventually we came up with the definitive guide to llamas versus alpacas. Which had been given to Zack to write.

Lexi started, 'We've got the ultimate guide to tie-dyeing, how to knot your oversize T-shirt into the perfect crop, the baby bunny versus kitten vox pops. What else?'

There was silence as Robyn stared at us, her face open and expectant.

'Do you have anything, Molly?'

I'd looked at my notes. They were flimsy and that's being generous. 'Erm, I thought maybe we could do what it would be like to *really* have a unicorn. If they existed. So a funny piece. Like, watch that magical horn when you're doing the bits ponies don't love so much, like changing their shoes. They might just give you a little jab of their own. Or if you're trotting about the same place again and again, expect yourself to be magicked away to a more exciting place.' I pause. 'There's also some research that unicorns really did exist at one point, fossils have been found. They're not as pretty as the ones we think of though, so maybe something along those lines? Unicorn reality versus fantasy?'

'Hmm. There's something there,' Robyn said. She'd turned to Lexi. 'Could you ask someone in the art department to mock up a picture of what this *real* unicorn could look like? Last thing I want is us printing something that could belong on a horror movie poster, leaving all the nine-year-olds shitting their pants.' Lexi nodded and scribbled something down in her notebook.

'How about a guide to who is your actual friend and who is a middle-grade mean girl?' Zack had offered. Hmm. Ideal for him, I'd thought.

The next half an hour had been exceptionally painful and ended with Robyn looking at us like a disappointed dog-owner whose pooch had come in and shat in her shoes.

I must've looked super crestfallen as Lexi took us to the pub after. And that rarely happens these days. We munched crisps, drank wine and Lexi shared pregnancy horror stories, like the varicose veins she'd found days earlier.

Paloma had scoffed. 'That is nothing. I've had varicose veins since I was about ten.'

'No.' Lexi had dropped her voice to a whisper. 'Varicose veins on my vulva.' We sipped our drinks in a stunned silence after that. Paloma and I, with our legs tightly crossed.

On the way back to the office, Paloma had linked her arm through mine.

'Don't let Robyn upset you,' she said. 'She's probably going through menopause or something.' I smiled even though Robyn is only four years older than me and certainly *not* menopausal.

I'd tried to take Paloma's advice but after the meeting my confidence and love for my job had reached a low I'd never known before. I'd started looking at jobs the minute I was back at my desk.

'Um, Molly?' Fuck. It was Robyn. Of course, it was Robyn.

I closed the tab down but her voice had come from right behind, so there was no chance she hadn't seen what I'd been looking at.

'Could you pop into my office for a quick word, please?'

'Sit down,' she'd said, remarkably not sounding like she

wanted my head on a stick. 'Were you just looking at jobs, Molly?' There was no point denying it.

'Yes,' I said. 'Just having a look.'

'Anything take your fancy?'

'No, not really. Everything seems to be web based and I really love print.'

She'd nodded. 'I agree. Feels a bit like selling out, doesn't it? Print jobs are rarer than unicorn tears right now. I have a browse every now and then. Aren't you happy here, Molly?'

I hadn't known how to answer that. 'Oh, it's not that. I was just having a look.'

Robyn stared at me hard. 'You think I'm too harsh on you, don't you?'

'I . . .' She'd waved her hand at me, indicating I should stop talking.

'I am. It wasn't a question.' I was slightly surprised by her frank admission. 'I push you, Molly, because I know you can do better. Much better. I happen to think you are a great writer. I think you could go far. But I think you're scared of who you can be. That's why I try to push you harder. So you don't become complacent and forget that potential. You're too talented to be stuck here forever, Molly. But you need to pull it back. And I know you can do it. You *can*.' I'd thought I might cry. Robyn hadn't been this nice to me since I started. 'Shall I tell you a secret about me?'

I'd nodded, not trusting myself to talk sans tears.

'I hate it here. I'd love to leave. But I'm locked into a mortgage and a marriage. A life I've never wanted. So I'm stuck here. Don't make the same mistakes as me.'

I was surprised.

'You'd better get back out there. Have fun at the party tonight,' she'd said, smiling.

'You're not coming?'

'No, sadly not. I have a prior engagement with our marriage counsellor. Oops, that's another secret. Shh, yeah?' I'd nodded. 'I don't want anyone else thinking I am an actual human.' She grinned at me then.

'My lips are sealed,' I said as I'd pulled the door closed behind me.

Posey wasn't the only one who believed in me.

Why can't I just believe in myself?

I ask myself this question over and over as I climb into bed later and let exhaustion carry me.

12

*

I wake up the next morning feeling inexplicably sick. I keep thinking about my conversation with Oliver on Friday. Something about it just doesn't add up. I know Posey wouldn't go to him without solid evidence. Whatever this LeoTheLion person told her was enough to keep her pushing forward with her investigation. So why wouldn't Oliver run it? Why was he trying to paint this picture of Posey being overstressed and hysterical? We both knew full well that she wasn't. Suddenly, I'm sure that Oliver hasn't been completely honest with me. The churning feeling in my stomach is my intuition, my journalism instinct that I thought had been savaged by alpacas and narwhals. It's still there and it's telling me it's time to pay him another visit. Only this time, I'm not going to give him the luxury of being able to plan what he's going to say to get rid of me. This visit would be a surprise.

I leave the flat feeling a shot of invigoration I've not felt in months, maybe years. The snow has turned to a wet sleet and I have my hood pulled up, but this time it's purely to keep dry, not to hide my face from a world obsessed with my sexual misdemeanours. When I reach *The Post*'s building thirty minutes later, I look like I swam here. The panel of receptionists regard me like a stray dog as I drip a dirty puddle onto the pristine floor. But I refuse to let them intimidate me.

'I need to see Oliver Valentine,' I say.

They continue to stare at me for a few moments before one, a man with platinum-bleached hair, seems to come out of whatever trance my bedraggled appearance had put him under. 'Do you have an appointment?'

'No,' I admit, 'but I need to see him.'

'I'm afraid you can't see Mr Valentine without an appointment.'

'It isn't a request,' I say, keeping my voice level. 'I need to see him. Now.'

'I'm sorry, miss, but as I said—'

'It's fine. Let her through.'

I turn to see Oliver standing on the mezzanine just before the escalator, peering down at us. The guy on the reception desk shrugs and presses something which opens the glass security gates and allows me into the main part of the building.

'That was good timing,' I say to Oliver as I reach him at the top of the escalator.

'I was just about to grab something for lunch, but don't worry. I'll get my assistant to get us some sandwiches.' He doesn't even ask if I'm hungry or anything and it strikes me how much men assume.

'So what can I do for you today, Molly? Do you want to sell me your story?' He gives me an exaggerated wink. 'Mucky Molly breaks her silence.' His use of the tabloid nickname for me makes bile rise up in my throat, but I swallow it down. I'm here for Posey, not my bruised ego.

'No, I haven't changed my mind. I wanted to ask you some things about Posey, actually.'

Oliver nods. 'Two ticks.' He picks up the phone on his desk and calls his assistant into the room. She's a pretty brunette who doesn't look dissimilar to Posey. 'Leah, would you be able to grab some sushi. Is that okay with you?' he asks me. I can't bear sushi but nod anyway. 'Great. Thanks, Leah.' Then he reaches under his desk and pulls out two glass bottles of sparkling water and hands me one. It's ice cold.

'Do you have a mini fridge under there?' I ask.

'It's more of a mini bar.' He grins. 'You don't really think I can survive this job with that disgusting coffee alone?' I think of Robyn hiding miniature bottles of wine in a fridge under her desk and the thought is so ludicrous, it almost makes me laugh out loud. 'So tell me, Molly Monroe, how can I help you today?'

Just say it, Molly.

'I don't think Posey's death was an accident, Oliver. I think someone killed her.' I wasn't sure how I'd been expecting him to react but it certainly wasn't with the calm detachment he's showing. His face, which is usually open and smiley, shuts down immediately. And while his eyes don't quite turn cold, they definitely cool a few degrees.

'Why would you think that? I thought the police were very clear that it was an accident and nothing more. Have you said anything to them?'

'I tried to,' I say. 'But they weren't interested in what I've found out.'

'And what *have* you found out?'

'Well, there was that email for a start. I told you she was scared about something. And why would she say she knew what happened to Lulu Lawrence if it wasn't important? There were loads of scribbles and notes in those notebooks you gave me about her. She wanted to meet up with me that night to talk to me about something. I'm sure it was something to do with Lulu.'

'It's a shame you got so hammered that you ended up giving someone a blow job in public then, isn't it?' There's no mistaking the coldness in Oliver's eyes now. 'Honestly, Molly, you can't really be surprised that the police wouldn't take you seriously when you're all over the internet in that state.' His words cut through me in a way I've never felt before. 'I told you before that there's no story about Lulu Lawrence. Just like I told your friend.' *Your friend?* 'And I'll tell you the same thing I told her. Drop it.' He slams his hand on the table so heavily it makes me jump. 'Did you know that I had to refer Posey to the health and wellness manager because she wouldn't let this bloody non-story go?' He sees in my face that this is news to me. Posey was the sanest person I've ever met. Why would he do that?

'Why?'

'Because she wouldn't drop it. She was borderline obsessed. It wasn't healthy. She was acting like a mad bitch.' Oliver's misogynistic language cuts me again.

'But you *know* Posey,' I say, trying to keep the tremor out of my voice. 'You know she's not like that at all. She was a brilliant journalist. If she was "borderline obsessed" as you say, it would've been because she knew she was onto something. Christ, Oliver, you've known Posey for years. You know how much integrity she had.'

'Yes I knew her. Maybe you didn't know her as well as you think you did. Have you considered that?'

'I knew Posey better than anyone.'

'Really? So you know she was fucking your neighbour then?'

What? *What?*

'What are you talking about? What neighbour?'

'The lawyer. That Patrick Goldman. The one with a wife and kids. So maybe her moral compass and *integrity* aren't what you thought.' Oliver looks almost smug as he delivers this news and sees the look of incomprehension on my face. Posey and Patrick? *Posey and Patrick?* This can't be right. It can't. Oliver must have his wires crossed or he's trying to get a rise out of me because there's no way this is true. There's no way my beautiful, clever best friend was having an affair with a married man. And definitely not the married man who lives next door to us with his family-holiday-brochure perfect family. No.

'I don't believe you,' I tell him, because I don't.

He shrugs. 'Believe me or not, I don't care. But it's true. She told me herself.'

'So, you listened to her when she talked to you about her sex life, but not about a missing girl and a desperate family? You were supposed to be her friend, Oliver.'

'I *was* her friend. That's exactly why I had told her to leave the Lulu Lawrence story alone. She was making a mistake and I was trying to dig her out of a hole.' I can't listen to Oliver anymore. I push my chair back and stand up.

'It doesn't sound to me like you've been a very good friend to her at all.'

Oliver sighs deeply. 'Think what you like, Molly. But you really need to drop this. The police have said it was an accident. Move on.' He turns towards his computer, then adds, 'And stop fucking drinking.'

I shake my head at him, stunned and disappointed, before making my way out of his office and out of the building. It's freezing outside but it's stopped sleeting. I pull my coat tightly around me as I walk. I don't know where I'm going. There's so much for me to get my head around and I'm reeling from the way Oliver spoke to me. Posey and Patrick? How could that be true? Surely I'd know if Posey was seeing someone. There's just no way she wouldn't tell me if she was sleeping with our married neighbour. We were closer than that. Then I remember the other night, standing on the doorstep as the paramedics took away the body of my best friend. What was it that Trudie had muttered? Something about there being only one slut living in our flat now. What else could she have meant by that? If they were having an affair then Trudie must have known about it. Could one of them have killed Posey? I pull my coat even tighter at the thought. They both definitely have a motive. But what hurts more than anything is the fact that Posey didn't tell me. I can't understand why. I thought we told each other everything. Why would she confide in bloody Oliver of all people, but not me? My heart feels like it's been cracked completely open. Could he be right? Did I not know my best friend at all?

13

*

I walk and walk. I walk until I no longer feel the cold. Probably, because I'm so cold. Is this how hypothermia starts? Thoughts whirl around my head, out of control. Posey and Patrick. Posey and Patrick. Oliver's cold stare. *And stop fucking drinking.* Half memories of that night out too. And then another comment from someone I love shoots into my brain. *We're not that close. We're not that close.* Paloma. I double back and sit on a bench I just passed, winded as the memories rush back all at once. That night. *That night.*

*

From: mollymonoroe@sparklemedia.co.uk
To: palomalumbsdale@sparklemedia.co.uk
Subject: Fwd: Staff Christmas Party
Date: 15 December
Time: 18.01

Just to check, we're <u>really</u> not even going to try to make the Party Bus?

Paloma comes over to my desk with a smirk on her face.

'You're not seriously asking me that, Monroe?'

I laugh. 'Just checking. Of course, I don't want to be herded like cattle in the back of a souped-up transit van. I'd much rather make my own way there. Even if my shoes try to kill me in the process.' I look doubtfully at my feet. A lifetime spent in flip-flops and Converse is making my three-inch heels look perilous. My ankles are already crying for help.

'Well come on, chop chop,' Paloma says, slicking a final coat of red lipstick over her mouth. 'If we leave now, we can stop for a drink on the way. Don't know about you, but walking into a basement containing Robyn and a load of HR people sober doesn't appeal to me at all.'

'I'm ready.' I click my computer to shut it down. 'And yes. Walking into a basement with Robyn seems like a terrible idea. If this were a horror movie, I'd definitely advise against it. She's not coming though.'

Paloma looks at me. 'No?'

I shake my head. 'No. She told me earlier when she called

155

me in. Something to do with . . .' I break off. I'm desperate to tell Paloma about Robyn's marriage counselling session but it wouldn't be fair. I have no idea why Robyn confided something so personal in me and, as much as I don't like her, I'm not going to start spreading personal gossip. Not even to Paloma.

'With what?' she asks.

'You know what? I can't even remember what she said. So it must've been something super dull and married.'

'Well, there's still HR to contend with,' Paloma continues, having lost interest in our boss. 'The idea of walking into that viper nest stone-cold sober is enough to give me the runs.'

'Don't forget the women from Catwalk Magazine,' *I say. 'They always look so hungry. Do you think they might eat us?'*

'God, I hope so.' Paloma gives a devilish laugh. 'It's been so long since I've got laid.'

I roll my eyes. 'Trust you to make this into an erotic horror. Are you ready? Shall we go?'

We grab our bags, stuffing our heels in them for later. Over a decade in London has taught us that having two pairs of shoes for a night out is virtually essential. The Party shoes, which are the heels, and the practical shoes, which are a pair of foldable ballet flats for walking to and from the venues. They're also essential for moving around in once inebriated and keeping ankles intact. Paloma spent six weeks in a moon boot a couple of years ago after taking a particularly nasty stumble down the escalator at Old

Street. Typically, Paloma had managed to make even an NHS foot-brace look stylish.

'Shall we go to the Crown?' I ask when we're outside. It's a very cold night. But even so I'm not looking forward to being cooped up in an underground function room, which will be clammy and damp from all the bodies and all the breathing. Fingers inside my stomach begin to work themselves into a knot of unease.

Paloma pulls a face. 'Nah, let's walk up a bit and stop in a bar that looks like it has some life in it. Somewhere with an outdoor area. We should try to fill our lungs with as much fresh air as we can.'

I laugh and link my arm through hers as we make our way along Oxford Street, dodging tourists, prams and the insane.

'Don't let me drink too much,' I say.

Paloma barks out a laugh. 'Like I have any control over you, Miss Monroe, you wild child.'

'Really though, no lap dancing. If I look like I'm about to start gyrating, you drag me away. Kicking and screaming if you must.'

'Molly-moo, I intend to be drunk as a fucking skunk myself so you're on your own, girl. Besides, I think it's going to be a bit too much of a fish market for you.'

I look at her, blankly. 'A what?'

'With the exception of Farty Barry, it's about ninety-eight per cent women.'

'Well, that can only be a good thing. I'm hardly about to start sliding around on HR Carol's lap.'

Paloma laughs again. 'Let's just see what the night brings, young padawan. Let's just see.'

We stop in a bar near Bond Street station where we share a bottle of wine and Paloma forces me to eat two packets of crisps to line my stomach. Then we make our way to the pub where the party is being held. It's a mock-Tudor cry for help situated between Soho and Oxford Street. The main bar is lively and people spill out onto the pedestrianised streets, hands full of plastic pint glasses and vapes. We push our way inside and are horrified to the point of laughter at signs which read, 'SPARKLE MEDIA CHRISTMAS PARTY THIS WAY', complete with arrows showing us where to go.

'It's like something from London Dungeon.' Paloma shudders.

'BEWARE THE POINT OF NO RETURN,' I say as we clamber down too many steps to the function room.

*

The party is every bit as grim as we expected. The basement is dank and dark and very probably the only space our company were willing to 'splash out' on.

'Not even a fucking beer garden,' Paloma murmurs, almost in awe. 'We will suffocate down here.'

I give a bark of laughter. 'We'd better go and get our drinks vouchers then, before we are absolutely parched.' We link arms and walk to what appears to be a sign-in desk, manned by an unknown person presumably from the HR or Operations departments.

There's a clipboard.

It's all very organised.

'Name and publication, please,' the person, white and male, says.

'Paloma Lumsdale and Molly Monroe from Girl Chat,' I say.

He runs his eyes suspiciously over us, like we might be trying to gate-crash. For four free drinks and a few hours in a cramped basement. Finally, appearing to be satisfied that we are ourselves and not interlopers, he runs his finger down the clipboard and finds our names, before ticking them off with a Biro.

Such extreme organisation can never be fun, surely?

He hands over our drinks vouchers as if they were fifties.

Paloma and I make our way into the fray.

'Jesus Christ,' Paloma mutters under her breath as she clocks some of the women from HR throwing questionable shapes in an area that appears to be a dance floor. 'Putting the HR in HRT.'

I laugh and pull her towards the bar.

'Let's make use of these. Think we're in for a long night.'

Behind the bar is a woman who immediately makes me feel like I need to drink. She is young and tall and thin. A complicated tattoo sleeve covers her right arm. Her hair is a light pink colour which she's swept up into a messy bun. It's like candyfloss. She has a hoop in her left nostril and both her ears are more earring than flesh. She's absolutely beautiful and the kind of cool that intimidates me. Paloma has noticed her as well.

'Wow,' she says. 'Wouldn't mind waking up to that face tomorrow.'

I look at her. 'I thought it was intellect that turned you on, not just someone's looks.'

She shrugs. 'I'm fluid.'

'I don't want to hear about your fluids tonight, Paloma.'

She snorts. 'I'll save it for the debrief tomorrow morning.'

Bar Goddess turns to us. 'Yes?'

'Two large white wines, please,' Paloma says, holding her hand out for one of my tokens. Bar Goddess stares at them.

'You know these can be exchanged for anything, yeah? You're not limited to house white.'

'What do you recommend then?' Paloma has entered flirt mode. I almost feel sorry for Bar Goddess. She doesn't stand a chance.

We end up having two Jägerbombs each, which I know is a terrible idea on top of the wine I've already drunk, but everything is already so much more fun. I even join some of the revellers on the dance floor when the DJ – someone's brother in a pop-up booth – puts on retro Britney. I'm not a dancer usually but there is something about throwing my arms in the air that just feels so joyous right now.

It's probably the Red Bull.

We spend a half hour on the dance floor laughing at ourselves as much as the HR crew. Then I strike gold and find a clutch of unused drink tokens abandoned on a table.

'Paloma!' I shriek, my delight only semi-sardonic. 'More

drinks!' And it's back to the bar but we are grown-ups this time and Paloma asks the Bar Goddess if she can make any explicitly named cocktails. Bar Goddess smiles enigmatically and offers Paloma something called Sex on My Face, which delights Paloma.

'I'm in there.' She laughs in my ear as we gulp down the whisky, Malibu, Southern Comfort concoction.

'We must have food!' I announce urgently as someone dressed all in black waves a platter of prawn tempura in front of us. Paloma scoops about ten into a napkin and we plonk ourselves down at a table. There's a woman I know is called Carol who works in HR already sitting there. She doesn't seem to have got changed out of her work clothes and there are dark, damp patches forming under the arms of her work shirt.

'Hot flush, Carol?' I ask her.

She stares at me. 'I think I'll just go and get some water,' she says, not laughing. She scoops up the wine glass she's been nursing and stomps away.

'Mols, that was a bit rude.' I look at Paloma, who is also staring at me.

'What? You made the HRT joke!'

'Yeah, but not to her face. Jesus.'

'I wasn't meaning to be rude,' I stammer. I hate it when Paloma disapproves of me. 'I was trying to be funny.'

'It didn't land.' Paloma sighs and I begin to feel the glee of the night ebbing away from me. There's an unhappy silence between us now and I take my phone out of my bag. Posey's texted me asking where I am. I'm sure I told her it was my work party tonight. I have a vague recollection of promising to meet her later.

Mols, where are you? I'm going to head into Soho. Tell me where you are and I'll meet you outside. Really could use a drink and a chat.

What could she want to chat to me about? It seems that, lately, people only want 'a chat' with me if it's to have a go at me. Robyn wanted 'a chat' last week about my sickness. Lexi wanted 'a chat' about my mental health. Posey's already tried to have 'a chat' about my drinking which was the least fun conversation I've ever been involved in. I'm chatted out. My phone pings with a message as I look at it.

Posey, again.

Molly? Are you there lol? Are you hammered already??? *I don't even want to dignify that with a response. Although somewhere my brain is telling me that I'm offended because she's actually right. My phone beeps again. I must've done something that's really annoyed her.*

I'm heading into Soho now okay, I'll give you a call when I'm off the tube xxx

I fight off the urge to tell her not to bother, I actually do want to get out of here now. Paloma's had a sense of humour bypass and I'm out of drink vouchers anyway. Might as well let Posey splash out on a nice bottle of wine. Another pro of her recent promotion is that our fridge is always stocked with decent wines now and not the stomach-stripper stuff we used to have. Paloma has abandoned me and is chatting to Bar Goddess again. My legs are surprisingly wobbly as I head over to her.

'Hey, I'm going to go,' I say. 'Posey's coming to meet me.'

Paloma waits a beat before turning to face me, her face unreadable. My heart is hammering. I sometimes feel like she doesn't like me at all. Why do I feel like that? Is it the booze? It must be.

'Cool,' she says, calmly. 'Will you be all right on your own? You've had quite a bit to drink. Why don't you have some water?'

Something like outrage flares inside me. 'I've had the exact same amount as you!'

Paloma and Bar Goddess exchange a look.

'Sure you have.' There's a smirk on her mouth that I have a sudden urge to slap away. 'Just be safe, okay?'

I don't answer and find myself stumbling a little as I make my way out.

But maybe I'll have a little sit-down in the loos first. My head is spinning a bit. I probably should have eaten more than one prawn. Maybe Posey will get some nibbles as well. She's always telling me how important it is to line my stomach if I'm drinking. I splash some cold water over my face remembering too late that I'm wearing make-up. I watch my foundation go blotchy before my eyes in the mirror, like one of those optical illusion pictures. I don't really care though. I don't have the energy to redo it. Instead I drag myself into a cubicle and lock the door, pulling my feet up onto the toilet seat. I pull my phone out of my bag again. Three missed calls and a text. All from Posey. God, she really wants to talk to me. My heart starts to hammer again and my palms are clammy. Why is Posey so desperate to talk to me? It can't be anything good. She probably wants me to move out or something. That must be it. She can afford to live by herself now and why would she want a mess of a flatmate when she can afford her own space? Panic is hovering in the cubicle with me. Posey might be able to afford a place in London on her own, but I can't. And if she doesn't want to live with me anymore, I'll have to look for a houseshare. I can't face it. I can't move in with people I don't know. I'm terrible with people I don't know. Posey has known me for over ten years and we're used to each other's habits. I can't move into a house share where I have to put my name on my cheese. I'm thirty-two, not a student.

Okay, focus on facts. I don't know that this is what Posey wants to talk about. Breathe and focus on facts.

But I can't. The bad thoughts come too fast for me to challenge them. I'm hyperventilating. I cup my hands and breathe into them, letting the rhythm settle itself.

I'm just about to leave the cubicle when I hear the door to the loos open and stifled laughs, which I recognise instantly as Paloma's and Lexi's. I've suspected for some time that Paloma has a crush on Lexi, but I've never broached the subject with her. I decide to stay in my cubicle and eavesdrop. Which I know isn't a nice thing to do, but my curiosity wins out over my conscience most of the time anyway, so I stay put.

The laughing soon subsides and they continue a conversation which obviously started outside the toilets.

'Is she okay though? I do worry about her.' It's Lexi.

Someone turns on a tap.

'*I don't know.*' Paloma. '*She's been through a lot. I guess it's to be expected there will be cracks from time to time.*' *Another cubicle opens. I hear a lock sliding into place and the sound of someone peeing.*

'*She's so defensive.*' Lexi. '*I've tried to reach out to her a couple of times but I feel like she could bite my head off.*'

'*The thing about Molly is that she works backwards from assuming everyone hates her.*' *I knew they were talking about me. I freeze. And I could mean that almost literally. My insides are ice.* '*I guess it's some sort of emotional defence mechanism,*' *Paloma continues. Her voice is travelling, so I assume she was the one peeing. They must be pretty half cut not to check no one else is in the toilets. But Paloma assumes I've gone.*

'*Is she seeing anyone?*' *Lexi asks and for a second I think she's asking about my love life, but I quickly realise she means a therapist or something.*

Paloma pauses for a minute. A tap runs. '*I don't know.*' *She sighs.* '*We're not that close.*'

Then the roar of a hand-dryer, which almost makes me fall off the loo seat. And the door swinging shut behind them as they leave.

I stay sat in the cubicle, words pushing blood into my ears, making me dizzy and nauseous.

We're not that close.

We're not that close.

The betrayal hits me with such force I feel it physically.

How can she say that? Paloma is my work wife, my party buddy and the only other person I've confided in about Mum and how low it's made me. She's the person I turn to when the work side of my work/life balance is off-kilter. How can she say we're not close? How? I don't trust many people and Paloma's words feel like a slap in the face. And a huge reminder of why I keep my circle small. My face is damp and I realise I'm crying.

I stumble out of the cubicle and remember the drinks vouchers I found earlier. It takes me approximately ten seconds to get out of the loos, down the stairs and back to the basement bar. I hand the vouchers over to the now-bored-looking bartender.

'Same?' she asks.

'No. Can you make it vodka please? Neat.'

She shrugs the nonchalance only someone in their early twenties can truly master – why would she give a fuck – and pours out two shots in one glass. Then she looks at me and smiles before pouring another shot in the glass.

'Shh,' she says, raising her finger to her lips. 'I've been taking extra shots all night. It's probably half water the amount of times I refilled it from the tap.' We share a secret smile of understanding and she turns back to the bar, taking glasses from a dishwasher tucked away behind it and filling up the emptying shelves.

The vodka quickly warms the ice that has settled in my core and ignites fury.

Not that close? Not that fucking close?

I push my way through the people drunk enough to be

on the dance floor. They can fuck off, for a start. How dare they have the capability of enjoying their lives. Their laughs and the vibrations of their conversations are like arrows into my soul. Why can't I be like them? What is wrong with me? I'm planning to leave, I really am. But then I see Paloma and Lexi at a table with Zack. Their heads are bent in conversation. Talking about me. Paloma throws her head back and laughs. She looks like a wolf howling at the moon.

I rage over.

Fury and vodka fuel me.

I stab at Paloma with my finger.

She turns around and her face lights up. Briefly. Then it's a sun behind the clouds.

'Mols? I thought you'd gone?'

'I was leaving but then I went to the loos. Not that close, huh? If we're not that close then how do I know that you fancy her?' I jab my finger at Lexi this time.

'Molly . . .' Paloma stands and reaches a hand out to me.

'Oh get fucked, Paloma,' I say, already on my way to leave. I turn back only to throw one last spear at her. 'Snake.'

I stumble up the stairs and out of the pub, gulping in the air outside like I've been drowning. It's dark and cold and doing that awful not-quite-raining rain that still manages to soak you to your skin. I'm dizzy and feeling the effects of the alcohol now as I wind through clusters of people. My self-loathing follows me, faithful hound that it is. I've often thought my furious self-hatred is the only thing in my life that's displayed any loyalty. Paloma's words are echoing around my head and I can feel my phone vibrating in my pocket.

Not that close. Not that close.

The alcohol in my stomach is churning and I stumble into a pub on a corner, desperate to find a toilet so I can splash cold water on my face. But when I'm inside I find myself heading to the bar instead.

'Large Sauvignon Blanc,' I say to the bartender. 'With ice, please.'

He nods and I gulp the drink down the minute he sets it in front of me. I know it's going to hit my head quickly, but I don't care. All I care about is reaching that point of oblivion where I don't have to listen to what my brain is shouting at me. Paloma's words join the huge cacophony of voices constantly reminding me that I'm not enough. Not good enough.

I wipe my mouth with the back of my hand and pull out my phone. The display swims in front of my eyes. There are WhatsApp messages from Paloma. I don't want to talk to her or even see her name, so I block her. More tears threaten. *Not crying in a pub.*

Texts from Posey.

Posey! My true friend.

I'm meeting Posey.

Where is she?

Look at phone again. Write a reply.

There soon! Get a bottle xxx No vodka. Had too many. Lol.

Force my feet to go outside. Watch them. Right foot. Left foot. Right foot. Someone else's foot. In my way. Too late to stop it. And I'm hurtling towards the ground. Pain through knees and hands as I land on concrete. Tears won't stay back. Someone's arm. Someone's hand.

'Are you okay? Let me help you.'

A face. A man. Kind eyes. I nod. Yes, help me. Please help me. Someone help me.

And then nothing.

*

I practically run home, shame setting a fire beneath my feet.
I need to be back indoors, shut away in a place where I can
process these memories.

I'm crying with frustration by the time I get back to the
flat. As soon as I walk through the door, I can sense I'm
not alone. For a tiny fragment of a second, I expect Posey
to walk out of her bedroom, laughing like it's all been some
elaborate joke. But that doesn't happen. Obviously. There are
definitely sounds coming from her room though and when
I poke my head around the door, I see two women – a blonde
and a brunette – hard at work, cleaning.

'What the hell?' I'm shouting. Which I know is rude. But
why are there two women in my dead best friend's bedroom,
cleaning what could be a crime scene? And I need to be alone.
I've got so much I need to process. Why are they here? *Why*

are they fucking here? 'Why are you here? What are you doing?'

The blonde woman, who looks to be in her early forties, smiles at me as if I hadn't just yelled at her so loudly she dropped her duster.

'Oh hello, love,' she says in a strong East London accent. In fact, it's *so* East London, it sounds as if she's putting it on. Like she's a bit-part in *EastEnders*. 'You must be Molly. Jesse said you might be here.'

'What are you doing?' I ask again as if it's not obvious enough what they're doing. They're even wearing T-shirts with 'Keeley's Kleaning' emblazoned on the front. But I still want that clarification.

'Just giving the place a deep clean, hun.' The dark-haired woman speaks now. 'Jesse said it was fine to come in. He said he'd spoken to you.'

'Well, he definitely hasn't,' I huff.

'Don't worry,' says the blonde. 'We're almost done anyway, just need to run the hoover round and we'll be out of your hair.' She smiles again. I feel like I'm being gaslit.

I want to rip the Dyson out of her hands, but she said they're nearly finished. Have I really been gone that long? I stare at them as they continue to clean the last bits of Posey away before heading back out of the front door. This time I storm to the door at the side of the building that leads to the second-floor flat. I hammer on it, unrelenting, until a dishevelled Jesse opens up. His hair looks like he's brushed it with a balloon and he's wearing grey joggers and a greying T-shirt.

'What is it, Molly?' he says. His voice is weary rather than aggressive. He pulls his left hand over his face, his right holding the door open.

'What do you mean *what*?!' I'm shrill and ear-bleedy.

Jesse blinks slowly. 'What do you want?'

'Why are there two women cleaning Posey's room? She's not even been buried, Jesse, for fuck's sake. The police could have wanted to look at her room again or something. Jesus, half her *stuff* is still in there.'

He sighs, heavily. 'Molly. The police don't want to look at the room again, because it's not a crime scene. I called and checked it was okay before I booked Keeley in. I need the room cleaned because I need to rent it out as soon as possible.'

'*Rent. It. Out?*' Indignation isn't a tone that suits my voice particularly well. I sound too snotty, like I'm talking down to whoever's on the receiving end.

'Yes, Molly. Rent it out. In case you hadn't noticed, I'm not in the best financial shape of my life. Do you think I'd be living in my own property if I had a choice? I need the money from Posey's rent.' He sees the look on my face and his voice softens. 'Molly, I'm sorry, I know this is hard for you. It's not easy for me either. I'll make sure I get someone who I reckon you'll get on with. I'll try to anyway. Don't even know if anyone will want to rent a room someone died in.' He looks at me again, then half smiles. 'Although, if I put that "internet sensation Molly Monroe" lives there on the ad, I'll probably get a lot of offers.'

'Every time I start thinking you're a decent person under all your bullshit, you go and spoil it, Jesse. Do you know that?'

He shrugs. 'I don't care what you think of me, Molly. Just pay your rent on time or give your notice. And don't go annoying the cleaning girls, they're just doing their job.'

'Have your fucking notice,' I hiss as I walk away. Although I don't know why I'm saying it because I haven't got anywhere else to go and, even if I did, I can't afford a deposit. The thought of living with anyone other than Posey makes my heart ache and tears are stinging my eyes as I let myself back into the flat.

I sit miserably on my bed, waiting for the cleaners – sorry – Kleaners to finish up and leave. As I stare into space.

'How did I get here?' I ask the empty room before the tears come again.

*

It's another two hours before they actually leave. By this time I've already come to the conclusion that I need to speak to Patrick Goldman. Someone hurt Posey and he's the obvious suspect. In fact, now I think about it, that must be what she wanted to talk to me about the night she died. And if I hadn't been so sloppily drunk, I wouldn't have pissed her off and she'd still be alive now. I wipe tears away from my eyes with the sleeve of my jumper. I've been a terrible friend to Posey. It's little wonder she hadn't told me anything.

I wouldn't have told me anything.

I pad through to the living room and pick up Posey's laptop. I google Lulu's name again, but there's nothing new there. How could Posey possibly have found anything out when there is an absolute blackout online? I think again about DMing LeoTheLion from her account, but if they somehow know she's dead, I'll probably give them a heart attack. I don't want another death on my conscience. I'm tempted to open Twitter and find out what's being said about me today but manage to shut the computer down without hurting my own feelings. I sink back into the sofa, suddenly feeling exhausted with grief and frustration when I hear a knock at the door. I'm not in the mood to see or talk to anyone else after my confrontations with Oliver and Jesse, and briefly consider ignoring it. But whoever it is knocks again, harder this time, and I realise they're probably not going to go away. I look through the spy hole and see Patrick standing there, holding a bunch of lilies. What the fuck does he want? He's literally the last person I want to see at this moment in time, and certainly the last person I want alone in my flat with me. But it could also be the only time I will be able to talk to him alone. It's not like I can go and knock on *his* door and ask him if he was sleeping with Posey with Trudie and his kids there. My hands are trembling as I open the door.

'Molly.' I think for a moment that he's about to try to hug me, but instead he hands me the flowers. 'Sorry it's taken me a few days to pop by. I've not really known what to say to you.' I take the flowers.

'Thank you,' I say. 'Would you like to come in?'

He doesn't look like he wants to at all. Is that how a man who killed a woman in this house would act? But in the end, he nods.

'Yeah, let's be extremely British and have a cuppa while

174

we talk around our feelings instead of about them.' He gives me a weak smile.

Feelings? Interesting.

I stand back and let him into the flat. Then I watch him as he walks into the living room, giving Posey's room a really quick glance as he passes it. He doesn't wait for me to lead him through and I can tell he has definitely been inside before. He sits down on the sofa, although it's more of a perch than a flop.

'I'll just put these in water and make some tea,' I say. 'Do you take milk and sugar?'

'Just milk please, Molly.' He's painfully polite. Could he really be a killer? But, I guess murderers hardly walk around with a badge on their lapel. I plonk the flowers in the sink and make us both a tea. When I walk back through I see Patrick has stood up and is holding the photo of Posey and me on holiday that was in with her work stuff. I want to snatch it out of his hands.

'Here's your tea,' I say instead and hand him the mug. He sits back down on the sofa and I perch on the wingback chair.

'I just can't believe Posey's dead,' Patrick says. 'It doesn't seem possible.' He looks genuinely sad and I almost forget that I'm about to accuse him of murder.

'I didn't realise you were that close,' I say, watching his face for some sort of reaction. There's the tiniest of flinches but I can't tell if it's guilt, grief or maybe both.

'We spoke quite a lot,' Patrick says. 'I've had a couple of glasses of wine with her here on occasion.'

I bet you did.

'How does your wife feel about that?' I ask, but Patrick doesn't answer. He just looks into his tea as if he's trying to read his fortune. 'I know you were sleeping with her, Patrick.'

'What?' He makes a show of looking shocked, but it's not very convincing and even he seems to realise that. 'How did you find out?' he asks. 'Did Posey tell you? She said she wouldn't.'

My heart stings again slightly. 'No, it was actually Oliver. Her boss at *The Post*.'

Patrick nods. 'Right. Well, yes, we were in a relationship. I cared about her very much. In fact, I think I was falling in love with her.'

Love? I wasn't prepared for that. I've only just come to terms with the fact that they were sleeping together and now Patrick is telling me it was serious. God, Posey. Who even were you?

'So, what happened? Were you going to leave Trudie and the kids? Move in here with us?'

Patrick rubs his hands over his face. 'We hadn't talked about a future, not really. I wanted to but she just wanted to take things as they came.'

'I don't believe you. There's no way Posey would sleep with a married man and definitely not want him to leave his wife and family. What did you do? Hound her until she gave in? Or were you blackmailing her into sex?'

Patrick looks up at me and, for the first time since he arrived, I feel scared of him. His eyes look like he *could* possibly kill someone. 'What the fuck? No. That's not what happened at all. Posey made the first move on me, if you must know. She was absolutely gagging for it. Wanted it all the time. I even fucked her in my office once, over my desk and then up against the window. We've done it in most places in this flat too. She loved it. Couldn't get enough of me. Even gave me a key so I could sneak up on her while she was in the shower and stuff. Your friend was practically a nympho.' He looks smug as he tells me this. 'Yeah, I'm definitely going to miss that arse.'

'I think she was murdered.' The words are out of my mouth before I can stop them, almost like they want to shock Patrick as much as he shocked me. 'But that's not news to you, is it?'

'What the fuck are you talking about this time? She drowned in the bath.'

'I don't think that's true. And I think you know that. Did you hold her under the water? Did you drown her to keep her quiet about your affair? Did you strangle her? She had bruises all around her neck.' I'm amazed at how calm my voice is.

Patrick's, however, is not. 'You're fucking deluded,' he hisses. 'I would never have hurt that girl. *She* was the one who ended things with me.'

Wait. What? Surely that's another motive?

'Why? Why would she call things off with you if she was "gagging for it" all the time?'

A pained look crosses Patrick's face. 'She never really explained properly. Just told me that she was tired of being the other woman.' He shrugs, but I can sense his hurt. 'I think she actually had met someone else.'

'Why do you think that? How would you know that?'

'I've seen your landlord, that Jesse guy, leaving here a few times. I asked her about it but she told me it was none of my business. But she didn't deny it.'

'Posey and *Jesse*?' The thought of them together is even more ludicrous than the idea of her and Patrick. At least Patrick is smart and attractive if you like older men who dress primarily in Tom Ford and probably have regular mani-pedis. Jesse couldn't be more different. Jesse is a complete stereotype of a gym rat. And I'm pretty sure *he's* married too, but is having some sort of trial separation from his wife, which is why he's living upstairs. 'You seriously think she had something going on with Jesse?'

'I know, it didn't make sense to me either. He can barely string more than four words together. But like I say, I'd seen him coming out of here a few times. And I'd seen Posey, heading out too, glammed up, like she would be when we started seeing each other.'

'You were spying on her?'

'Molly, don't say it like that. I told you my feelings about Posey. I was insane with jealousy.'

'Well, there's your motive right there. *If I can't have her, then no one can.* It's just about the oldest reason in the book. The book where men kill women and get away with it.'

'I didn't kill her, Molly, I didn't. If you really think someone did this to her then maybe you should be talking to the police instead of throwing wild accusations around.' He puts his mug down on the coffee table. 'I get you're grieving, I get you've got your own stuff going on with that internet thing. But, Molly, maybe you need to think about getting some help. I'll see myself out.' He stomps out of the living room, slipping slightly on the polished floor. 'These floors are a fucking death trap,' he mutters before opening the front door and letting it slam behind him.

So it wasn't even just a one-off. It was a full-blown fling.

Posey and Patrick.

Patrick and Posey.

I can't work out what's disturbing me more, the fact that Posey slept with Patrick. Or the fact that she didn't tell me about it. Why wouldn't she tell me about it? Posey and I shared every detail about who we slept with, we'd done it since uni. I mean, there hasn't been a massive amount to report, on my side lately. Did Posey think that I was keeping things from her? Or did she think I'd judge her because Patrick is married. And a boring old cliche? But I'd never judge her. I never have, have I? I fast-forward through our decade-long friendship and come up with nothing.

Why wouldn't she tell me?

I look, again, at the holiday photo of us. Posey suddenly seems like a stranger.

I close the laptop and push it away from me, having seen more than enough, for now at least.

Posey and Patrick.

Patrick and Posey.

I wander into the kitchen and begin going through the cupboards, wishing again that I hadn't been so hasty with that bottle of Sancerre. I need something to take the edge off and help me process what I've discovered. All I can find is the half bottle of dusty Baileys we started drinking a few nights ago. How quickly everything can change. This isn't a revelation for me. I've felt this seismic shifting of the plates my life is built on before. I pour myself a large glug of the Baileys and down it, enjoying the way it burns my throat on the way down. I pour another and do the same before heading back to the living room with the dregs of the bottle.

Posey and Patrick.

Patrick and Posey.

Even dulled with alcohol, my mind can't escape from the sharp shock of discovering they'd been together. Posey couldn't bear cheating. Her real dad had left her and her mum when she was quite young, about seven I think, for another woman. Posey hated him for it, they didn't even speak. I remember her telling me about it not long after we'd met at university in Bristol. We were in her room, quite drunk on flavoured vodka we'd been drinking neat from a mug and a ceramic tumbler from the bathroom, designed to keep toothbrushes in.

'Cheating is unforgivable,' she'd declared during the late-night conversation about men and relationships. 'I'm pretty easy-going, but that's a non-negotiable. Cheaters are the worst kind of people. They're selfish. They have no idea of the amount of damage they do. Or, they just don't care.' She'd taken a huge swig of vodka at that point, I clearly remember her wincing as it went down. 'And then they just stroll off into their new lives. Why should they get to be happy when everyone they've hurt is devastated? Selfish and cowardly. I don't think anyone can be truly happy in a relationship built on pain and lies.'

How did someone with such strong views about adultery become the Other Woman? It's not like she didn't know Patrick was married with a family.

These things just happen. I never ever claimed to be perfect.

I don't want to listen to Posey's posthumous excuses right now, so I jam my earbuds in and download a guided meditation. It's while I'm breathing in for five and out for seven, while I'm hovering in a place between consciousness and a Baileys-induced slumber, that I think of something I learned from reading thrillers.

It's always the husband.

Always *someone's* husband.

Then I let myself fall into the darkness.

15

*

I wake up the next morning with an empty bottle of Baileys and a mild hangover. The conversation with Patrick rushes back to me. He thought there was something going on between Posey and Jesse. It seems as ludicrous this morning as it did last night. But, if I've learned anything over the last few days, it's that Posey had more than a few secrets. I need to speak to Jesse and there's no time like the present. I throw on some clothes, clean my teeth and head to his flat.

He answers the door within a few seconds of me knocking, like he's been waiting for me.

Maybe he has?

He's wearing his usual uniform of joggers and T-shirt. But, surprisingly, he's got a pair of glasses perched on his nose. I've never seen Jesse in glasses before and it makes me feel weirdly unsettled. How close we can live to someone and not know something as basic as whether or not they need specs to see. The thought makes me shiver.

'Molly, if this is about the room again, I've already told you. I need to rent it out as soon as possible. I'm not going over it with you again. If you've got a mate or whatever, or you can cover the whole rent, then we can talk about it. If not, then it's not up for discussion. I'm sorry. But you're not the only one with shit going on in your life.'

'Thanks for the speech,' I say. 'But that's not what I wanted to talk about, actually. Can I come in for a minute?' Jesse frowns at me, but more like he doesn't understand what I've said than I've made him angry. Then he shrugs and walks down his hallway, waving at me to follow behind.

His flat is a similar layout to ours but it's not as big even though it has two floors, one which I suspect is a loft conversion bedroom as there doesn't appear to be anywhere to sleep on the first floor. The similarity begins and ends with the layout though. While our flat is covered in soft furnishings, photos and knick-knacks Posey and I collected, Jesse's living space is sparse. He has a sofa and a TV and there's a large box he's using as a coffee table.

'Do you want something to drink?' he asks and I spot a half-empty bottle of whisky and a tumbler sitting on the makeshift coffee table. It's barely even 11am.

Interesting.

'No, thank you,' I say. 'I won't take up too much of your time. I just wanted to ask you a couple of things about Posey.' Jesse seems vaguely more interested in me now and peers at me through those surprise glasses before flopping down in an armchair that's actually just a massive beanbag and the only other piece of furniture in the room. He gestures for me to sit on the grey L-shape sofa. It smells weird. Like dog. And biscuit. It takes a second for my brain to register the smell as fake tan.

'What about her?' He reaches for his glass and takes a long gulp of the liquid, like it's apple juice.

'What was going on between the two of you?'

He looks more surprised by the question than Patrick did. And, even with the addition of the glasses, I don't think Jesse has the mental agility to pull off that kind of acting skill.

'Nothing,' he says, then, almost regretfully. 'Nothing at all.' He looks at me for a few beats before asking, 'Why? Someone said otherwise?' He's not suspicious or angry, like Patrick, just a bit stunned that I'm even asking.

'Patrick.' I gesture towards next door and Jesse nods, acknowledging who I'm talking about.

'He and Posey were shagging,' he tells me. Jesus, I really was the only person who didn't have a clue about the affair. 'If you want to talk to anyone about Posey, it's him.'

'So there was nothing going on between you? I know you've been to the flat a few times.' He doesn't ask me how I know, just sort of shrugs again.

'There was one night.'

WTAF?

'One night? You had sex?'

Jesse drops his head into his hands. 'It was a one-off. I'd gone round to check something in the flat. I can't even remember what it was now. Posey was clearly unhappy about something and I'd had a row with my ex about our kids. I ended up going over to the shop on the corner and getting us a couple of bottles of wine. We were drowning our sorrows.'

'What was Posey unhappy about?' I ask, bewildered.

'Something to do with work. Her boss was being a prick about a story she was trying to break. She didn't tell me exactly what but she was pretty pissed off with him.' That adds up with what Oliver has told me about Posey's reaction when he told her to drop the Lulu Lawrence story. 'It was just one of those things. A one-off. I didn't stay the night or anything like that. Posey made it clear it wasn't going to happen again.'

'But you wanted to?'

'I liked her. I enjoyed myself that night and hoped it could happen again but Posey told me she was seeing someone. At first I thought it was that dick from next door again but she assured me that was over. She reckoned she'd met someone through work and they were "giving things a go".' He does the quote marks with his fingers.

Work? Really? You were more professional than that, Posey.

'Do you know what his name was or anything?'

'I didn't exactly ask for all the details, Molly, I was quite upset if I'm being honest. I think she said he was called Josh. Something like that. Anyway, that was that.' He gives me a sly look. 'Maybe I shagged the wrong flatmate though. If that video of yours is anything to go by.'

'Right.' I stand up, making it clear that a boundary has been crossed and I'm ready to leave. 'Thanks for your help, Jesse, but I think I'll be going now.'

He shrugs again. Seriously, it's like a tic or something.

'Suit yourself. Offer's there if you're looking for a shoulder to cry on. Other body parts are available too.' He laughs at his own joke, but I'm stone-faced and he rolls his eyes at me. 'Fine. I'll see you out.' We walk in silence to the door and he opens it for me. Not entirely devoid of manners then. 'Molly.' His voice is serious now. 'I really am sorry about Posey. She was a good kid. Let me know if there's anything I can do, okay? I dunno, maybe I can keep the room empty for a month. Give you a chance to find someone or whatever?' It's probably the kindest thing he's ever said to me. Maybe he has a heart beating under all that muscle after all.

'Thanks, Jesse.' I give him a small smile now and head down the stairs.

Back in my own flat, once again I'm alone with a headful of news to process and absolutely no idea where to start with it all. Posey had confided in *Jesse* of all people about her frustration at work, not me. She'd even told him about the fling with Patrick and this new boyfriend. I'd never heard her mention anyone called Josh. Did she even work with a Josh? Although, that could just be something she'd said to get Jesse off her case. But Patrick said he thought she was seeing someone. And that he'd seen her going out all dressed up. Surely I'd have noticed if she'd actually been properly seeing someone? Surely she'd have told me?

But, then again, it seems that there was an awful lot that Posey hadn't told me.

Oliver's words come back to me.

Maybe I didn't know her at all.

Jesse also mentioned that Posey had been annoyed about something at work. This is news to me too. As far as I knew, Posey was still very much in the honeymoon period with her job after her promotion. I mean, that was how I thought things were until I spoke to Oliver. I make a tea and open Posey's laptop again, not sure what I'll find, but maybe something I missed. I'm just logging in when my phone starts ringing. The caller display flashes with Marilyn's name. She's finally returning my call.

'Hello,' I say, putting the phone onto speaker. 'Marilyn?'

'Is that Molly Monroe?' Her voice is quiet, almost a whisper, but I can still tell that she is well-spoken, most likely well-educated too. 'You said to call you?' She's so quiet, in fact, I can barely hear her and it makes me wonder if she's making this call furtively.

'Yes. Thank you for getting back to me.' I'm unsure of what to say next.

Just tell her the truth.

'I've got some sad news I'm afraid.' I think I hear a tiny intake of breath. 'I know that my friend Posey has been helping you with a story, but she sadly died a few days ago.'

Silence.

More silence.

I check the call is still connected. The timer is still going.

'What happened?' Marilyn finally asks, shakily, with too much breath.

'An accident,' I say. 'Well, that's what the police are saying anyway. I'm not so sure.'

'What do you mean?' Her voice is even shakier. 'You don't think Posey . . . hurt herself?'

'No! God no. But I don't think it was a cut and dry accident like the police seem to. I know she was investigating Lulu.' There's a sharp intake of breath when I say her name.

'You think it's connected?'

'I don't know,' I say. 'But I need to understand what her last days were about.' There's a really long pause and, if it wasn't for Marilyn breathing so heavily, I'd think she'd cut the call.

'She was a lovely young woman,' she says and I'm nodding even though she can't see me on the phone. 'She visited me here once. To talk about Lulu. Maybe you could come over too? I find it easier to talk to someone face to face. I can tell you everything I told Posey.'

So Posey visited Lulu Lawrence's family home? I wonder if there will be a point when the secrets stop coming. Or if the rest of my life will basically be me reeling from yet another revelation of Posey's.

'I'll come, thank you, that would be great.'

Maybe the only way to find out all of Posey's secrets is to walk in her shoes.

*

It takes just over two hours to get from Euston to Alderley Edge – with one change – and a further ten minutes in a taxi to the address in the village Marilyn gave me. We pull up outside a cottage, but not a small one, this cottage is impressive.

Detached and with a thatched roof. Well, it's impressive to my eyes anyway, I doubt Posey would've paused for a moment in slight awe, the way I am doing now. A small cough from the driver brings me out of my reverie and I pay and tip him, before taking a deep breath and walking up the pathway to the door of the Lawrence house. The door is painted white and there's no bell or smart camera, just a knocker which I gingerly clutch and rap twice.

The woman who answers the door is blonde and tiny, her collarbones are clearly visible and her cheekbones look sharp. But she's not the type of thin that shouts Pilates, tweakments and money – like Trudie Goldman – she's the type of thin that's caused by an ability to eat or keep still or rest. This type of thinness is becoming more recognisable to me. It's the kind caused by grief. It's the kind of thin Tina Porter has become. She's wearing a grey cashmere sweater and a pair of dark blue jeans that I suspect once were a skinny fit, but now hang off her hipbones. She has small diamond studs in her ears and a little silver M on a chain around her neck. Well, I say silver but it's more likely white gold or platinum. The Lawrences are not short of money. She looks around the age my mum would be now but then I realise that doesn't make sense as I'm seventeen years older than Lulu was when she disappeared. She should look much younger. Grief affects every atom of your being, not just your mind.

'Molly?' Marilyn's voice is small as well, almost as if it knows it's not being heard and is disappearing. If a voice could be a ghost, then Marilyn Lawrence's will haunt me forever.

'Yes,' I say, because what else can I say? 'Hi.'

Her face crumples with something that's almost, but not quite, relief and she opens the door wide to let me in.

'I'm so glad you came,' she says, with a tiny hint of a northern accent. 'How was your journey? Come into the lounge and sit down. Would you like a tea? You must be exhausted?' It's easy to tell Marilyn is a mother who hasn't had a child to look after for some time. She fusses me through to the living room and I accept her offer of a tea.

'Could I use your loo, please?' I ask her, suddenly becoming aware of the coffee I'd drunk on my train journey with no toilet break.

'Yes! Of course, it's just through here.' She leads me along a hallway, carpeted and painted a fashionable shade of grey so light it's almost white, to a small white door. 'This is the cloakroom, shall I take your coat?'

I thank her and hand my coat to her before stepping into the small, but pristine, cloakroom and doing what I need to do. As I'm washing my hands, I catch sight of myself in the mirror above the basin. I stare at myself in shock. At my protruding collarbones, my sharp cheekbones, the type of thinness caused by grief. How long have I looked like this? I hold my wrists under the cold water for a couple of moments, letting it bring me back into the moment and ground me. Then I dry my hands and take some deep breaths, readying myself to face another mirror of myself, Marilyn.

She's sat on her huge charcoal corner sofa when I get to the living room, her feet curled up under her, making her look even smaller.

'I've just brought in the milk and sugar for you,' she tells me. 'I wasn't sure how you take it.'

'Thank you,' I reply and pour some milk into my tea, this strange, strange ritual that feels both formal and comforting at the same time.

'I am so sorry to hear about Posey,' she says, an audible shake in her voice. 'She was such a lovely young woman. So much fight in her. Through all of this, she's the only one who has believed me. The only one who's helped.'

I can see she's fighting back tears, something she's probably become so accustomed to after a year of trying to get people to listen to her and not decide she's hysterical. She's become very good at it. I look around the room. There are more photos than I've seen before of Lulu – the girl who disappeared. She looks a lot like her mother, honey-blonde hair somewhere between curly and straight. Blue eyes that sparkle, even through the flatness of a photograph. It's sparkle that I have no doubt Marilyn once had too, but hers has been dulled by her pain. There are a few sweet pictures of the two of them together and several more of Lulu and Marilyn with a dark-haired man I assume must be Christopher.

'What about Lulu's dad?' I ask. 'Surely he isn't just ignoring what's going on?' Marilyn shakes her head and wipes her nose on the sleeve of her sweater.

'He thinks she's gone off somewhere. He's been abroad several times to try and find her, but no luck. He thinks I'm being hysterical about the police though. Says he's spoken to them several times and they haven't closed the case, that they're still looking for her.' She looks so confused and broken that I want to reach out and hold her. 'He says he hasn't given up but—' She sighs. 'The police think she's shut down and deleted all her own social media and Chris agrees with them.' I make a mental note to look more into Christopher Lawrence when I'm back on the train. Something about how Marilyn is talking about him niggles inside me.

'Did they get along?' The family look super close in the photos, but you can never tell what goes on behind closed doors. Even when you're behind those doors yourself, as I'm learning.

'Yes, but, I mean she was a teenager. She was happy and everything, but she was still a teenager. There were some days when we couldn't do anything right in her eyes.'

'But no big rows, no fallouts, nothing overly dramatic?'

Marilyn shakes her head again. 'Nothing. She was so normal it's almost boring.' She gives me a weak smile. 'She had a group of close friends, she didn't take drugs, she knew not to talk to strangers on social media. She was a smart girl. But when we first reported her missing the police tried to make out that we didn't know her at all. They seemed to assume she'd gone somewhere of her own accord and would turn up "when she was ready". But obviously she hasn't. And now she's over sixteen, they don't seem to care.'

'You spoke to Posey about social media, right? That each time you tried to start a group or campaign on any of the main platforms, it got shut down?'

'Every single time. I told Posey it was looking like a conspiracy and she agreed. She'd suggested we start some groups on the dark web, but I don't understand any of that. She was going to come up again and explain it to me. But then—' She breaks off, not wanting to talk about Posey's sudden death. But after a moment a tiny glimmer of hope appears in her eyes. 'Is that something you'd be able to do, Molly? Someone out there knows where she is. We just have to find a way of reaching them.'

The dark web. It's not something that's really used on a daily basis when you write about unicorns. Like Marilyn, I don't fully understand what it is or what it's for. And I've never even thought about finding out. That's why Posey was so good at all of this while I've just languished in the same job for years. But things can change. People can change. I look Marilyn in her eyes.

'I'll do whatever I can to help you,' I promise.

*

After we've finished our tea, Marilyn asks if I'd like to see Lulu's bedroom.

'Posey went and had a look while she was up here,' she says. 'I think it gave her a proper sense of Lulu and who she was.'

'Yes, as long as you're sure I wouldn't be intruding too much?'

Marilyn simply stands and offers me that watered-down smile again. 'Of course not, follow me.'

I follow her up an ornate staircase, catching a glimpse of a huge kitchen as we walk past it. A slither of green is visible beyond the bifold doors. Bloody hell, these rich people love their bifold doors. Meanwhile, Lulu's room looks like the pages of the magazine I may or may not still work for. She was fifteen when she disappeared, sixteen now, but the room looks like it's been made for someone much younger. There's a lot of pink, glittery things, a neon wall-sign with Lulu's name written in lights and a few cutesy-looking cushions scattered over the bed. If *Girl Chat* did interiors, this would be it. I wonder if this is something I can pitch. You know, if I still have a job.

'She wasn't street-tough like other girls her age,' Marilyn says, interrupting my thoughts. 'I think that's mostly my fault. She was so longed for and wanted that I probably treated her like a little girl for too long.'

'Is that what Christopher thinks?'

'He's mentioned it. We struggled to conceive Lulu and it just didn't happen again for us, so it's possible I overcompensated.'

'Does he think that's why she left?'

Marilyn grimaces slightly. 'It's a theory.'

Could Lulu have simply left home because she was feeling too smothered? It's not beyond the realms of possibility that she was fed up yet still innocent enough to be lured away by someone. That doesn't explain where she is now, though. And that's what Marilyn needs. Just to know, one way or the other.

'Thank you so much for talking to me today,' I tell her as we head back down the stairs. 'I'll do whatever I can to finish this for you. For Posey.' To my surprise, Marilyn wraps her arms around me and pulls me in close.

'Thank you,' she whispers into my hair and I swear she adds, 'be careful.' But her voice disappears into the wind as I step outside, readying myself for my journey back to London. I step onto the path leading from the cottage and bump straight into someone.

'Whoa there, missy,' the someone says, grabbing the wall of the house to steady himself. It's a man, wrapped up in a long woollen coat and carrying a battered leather bag. He stares at me for a moment and then looks up at Marilyn, who's still standing by the door. And then back at me. 'Who is this, Marilyn?' he asks her, his eyes not leaving mine.

'This is Molly,' she says. 'She's a journalist. She's just leaving.'

'A journalist—'

'She's going, Christopher, okay?' Marilyn storms back inside the house and I give Christopher a small smile. He doesn't return it and I feel his eyes still on me, even when I turn away and head into the night.

Later, on the train home, Jack texts me.

Hey M. Sorry for radio silence. You free tomorrow to learn the dark ways of the dark web?

16

@RIPWorld74: The conspiracy theorists are already hard at work. Although, I have to say, it DOES seem a bit weird. Maybe you're not all bonkers this time #MollyMonroe #MollyMurders

*

Jack and I speak later and arrange for him to come over the following afternoon and help me learn the basics of the dark web. Even just the name gives me the chills, but there's a spark of excitement there too. I'm now less convinced that Patrick had anything to do with Posey's death and more certain that whatever she found out about Lulu Lawrence is the reason she's dead. I fall asleep that night easily, tired from my long journey, but also feeling exhausted from using my brain for something other than battling my own anxiety. And when I wake in the morning, I realise I barely even thought about Twitter and what's being said about me yesterday. The sickening feeling of shame that's been my constant alongside the grief has lifted a little. I mean, it's still there, but it feels less like a concrete brick has been dropped on my chest.

I get out of bed, not quite with a spring in my step, but I don't have to drag myself out either.

Purpose, Molly. It's Mum's voice I hear this time. *It's because you've got a purpose.*

I almost smile as I fill the kettle and set it to boil for the first of my two morning teas. I settle with my tea and my laptop on the sofa, determined to learn what I can about Christopher Lawrence on the – what do I call it, the *light web*? – before Jack arrives. I may have only met the man briefly, but I didn't like the way he made me feel. And I don't think Marilyn was his biggest fan either. From what she said it was almost like he blamed his own wife for their daughter's disappearance.

There isn't a huge amount to discover about him online. He works as a lecturer, mainly at Manchester, sometimes in Sheffield. But he seems to have taken a sabbatical since Lulu's disappearance. That's all I learn from his LinkedIn. He has an Instagram account but it's locked and his Facebook isn't much more help; all I can see is his profile picture which – frankly – could be any white, slightly-balding middle-aged man. I can't even see his friends list, although I'm unsurprised that he has gone on a hard social media lockdown with his daughter missing. I sigh and search for Lulu while I'm on there, although I'm not shocked to find a teenage girl doesn't have a Facebook account. Even I find it cringe. I fruitlessly scroll through the other main social media sites for Lulu before coming back to Christopher Lawrence's LinkedIn page. I scour it again in case there is something I missed the first time. I'm about to slam the computer shut with frustration when I spot something in his 'education' section that I hadn't noticed before. It's only a small box, room for one establishment, and Christopher Lawrence's says St Andrews. Why is that ringing a bell in my brain? I think and think. Until it hits me. My mind, pickled by pop culture and gossip magazines, immediately jumps to Kate Middleton and Prince William. That's where they met. Nothing to do with the Lawrences at all. It's good to see that my own education hasn't been wasted. I sigh, annoyed at myself and my idiot brain, before closing the computer. I need to prepare myself for Jack's arrival and my forthcoming lesson on the mysterious dark web.

*

'So the first thing we need to do is download a VPN,' Jack is telling me as we huddle over my laptop.

'Sounds like something I could've downloaded in my throat after the other night,' I mutter darkly. Jack rolls his eyes at me. 'Okay, I can see you're dying for me to ask. What's a VPN?' He gives me a little smile. The geek.

'It stands for virtual private network and, in short, lets you browse the web anonymously. It also allows you to do things like encrypt your IP address.' His face is a bit excited while mine is blank and confused. 'Basically, it hides what you're up to online. And where you're up to it. So it's vital if you're about to go delving into the dark web.'

'Well that sounds exceptionally dodgy. Is it even legal?'

Jack nods happily. 'Oh completely. There are lots of benefits to staying low-key online that aren't at all nefarious.' I can't think of a single one, but I don't want Jack to think I'm an idiot so I nod knowingly as he explains. 'For example, they can protect you from hackers, which is always good if you shop online a lot. Super helpful if you're partial to an ASOS haul. They can give you access to stuff on streaming services outside of your location.' It's like he can read my mind.

'Why doesn't everyone have a VPN, then, if they're that useful?'

Jack shrugs with one shoulder. 'I suppose cost is an issue, most of them have a monthly fee and the free ones are notoriously crap. Also, living in the UK we have a relatively free internet – in theory. People in countries which restrict internet sites have more of a need for VPNs as they can bypass that stuff. I think a lot of people are frightened by them too. We've all had it ingrained into us that constant surveillance, all the CCTV et cetera, is for our own protection and we have nothing to fear if we're behaving ourselves.' I laugh darkly at this. 'Sorry,' Jack continues. 'That was insensitive of me.'

I wave him off. 'Don't worry. Being the scarlet woman of the internet is the last thing on my mind at the moment.' I'm surprised to realise I'm not totally lying.

He smiles. 'That's good to hear.' He reaches across the laptop keyboard and puts a hand on my arm. 'For what it's worth, I think you're remarkably strong and resilient,

Molly Monroe. You didn't tell me that when I found you weeping and wailing in Vauxhall.' He gives my arm a little squeeze.

'Oh no, I—'

'Don't even try to downplay it,' he tells me firmly. 'Just take the compliment. Now. Are we downloading this VPN or what?'

'Download away,' I tell him. 'I'll make us a tea.'

*

It takes a little while to get the VPN up and running, but I can see that Jack is in his element. I laugh and call him a nerd a few times, but basically leave him to it. I go to the normal web – which Jack has told me is called the 'clear web' – on my phone, managing to avoid Twitter and googling my own name, instead searching the Reddit thread for any new information on Lulu Lawrence. There is none. I wish I was more interested in technology, but there are some things that can't be feigned, and this is one for me. Eventually Jack calls me over.

'Molly, come here. Are you ready to enter the dark world of the dark web?'

I'm very much not. But. At the same time, I very much am.

'Kind of,' I say.

'Excellent. So, now the VPN is installed, we need to download a special browser.' He taps away for a few moments. 'A lot of sites on the dark web can only be accessed through the Tor browser. It's a double layer of anonymity, which is why this part of the net has a reputation for being a hotbed of illegal stuff. There we go, that's all installed.'

I take a look at my laptop. I'm not sure what I've been expecting but I'm a bit disappointed to see it still looks quite normal. And not very dark at all. It must be written all over my face because Jack lets out a bark of laughter.

'Yes, I felt the same,' he says. 'Sad it wasn't more obviously evil and that the keyboard didn't turn into a Ouija board. You'll notice some differences when you start searching though. It's incredibly slow, which is maddeningly frustrating now we're all used to fibre optic broadband on our phones.' He hands me the computer. 'There you go. That's basically it, now you just need to search like you would on the regular web. Just don't buy anything.'

'That's it?'

'Yup. Like I said, it's annoyingly slow and it cuts out and there are some things on there that will shock even someone as worldly as you. But yeah, that's it. Do you want me to stay?' I think of the evening stretched out in front of me with just the dark web for company and almost say yes. But, really, the less people who know what I'm doing, the better.

'No, it's fine. I'll text if I need any help. But thank you. I really appreciate the lesson.'

'Any chance you're going to tell me what this is about?'

I shake my head. 'Not yet. But hopefully soon.'

'Just remember, don't buy anything. I'll let myself out.' Jack gives the top of my head a quick kiss. 'I mean it, put your credit cards on ice if you have to. And be careful who you talk to. Whatever I said about not everything on there being nefarious, remember, there's usually a reason someone wants to be anonymous online. And it's rarely good.'

'Thank you,' I say again and watch as Jack disappears down the hall and back out into the real world, letting the front door click softly behind him.

*

Before I begin searching the newly unlocked dark side of the web for anything I can find about Lulu Lawrence, I check my phone to see if Marilyn has replied to me yet. She hasn't. I quickly tap out another text, asking her to call me back as soon as possible and if she knew anything about Posey using the dark web. I stick some bread in the toaster, I've barely been able to eat a thing over the past week, but I can't shake the image of the haunted thing which stared back out of Marilyn's cloakroom mirror at me. I slather the toast with butter, feeling slightly nauseous, and soft-boil two eggs. Dippy egg and soldiers had been my comfort food when I was little. My mum would always make them for me whenever I was sad. The soldiers cut into strips small enough for a child's hand, a little pinch of salt on the side on the plate, which I'm sure would cause heart failure in the mummy-community these days (yes, maybe I've spent a little too much time studying Trudie Goldman's Instagram). I'm not able to boil them to perfection like Mum could, and they're a bit more on the hard side than I'd like, but I eat them in front of the computer, feeling comforted nonetheless. Jack isn't wrong about the slowness of things on this side of the internet. I barely have the patience to wait while pages load up. But the wait is worth it. People on the clear web might not be talking about Lulu Lawrence, but people on the dark web certainly are. I go to the site named on the Reddit thread, TruthSeekers, go through a sign-up process and immediately see some of the same usernames thankful they haven't attempted to be imaginative about concealing their identity here. There isn't a huge amount of new information, more repetition of the gossip I already saw on Reddit, but it's much more recent, which sparks a bit of hope in me. She hasn't been forgotten. It isn't just me and Marilyn trying to work out where she is and what has happened to her. There's a bizarre sense of community here, but one I'm delighted to see. The girl who has been wiped out by legitimate mainstream and social media is still in people's thoughts. I scan through the various threads. So many theories. Some think Lulu ran away. Some think she was kidnapped. There's a lot of speculation that Christopher killed Lulu, backing up what Posey suspected.

I pick up my phone and call Marilyn. I might not have much for her in the way of new information, but at least I can fire up that little bit of hope inside her too.

But her phone goes through to voicemail again.

*

On Saturday morning there's a knock at the door. I'm still in bed, not quite asleep but not quite awake either. I'd been dreaming about Posey and kept trying to drift back into the same dream so I could see her again. I couldn't. Maybe

I should try one of those podcasts about lucid dreaming so I can control my dreams. I remember having a conversation with Posey about it a few months ago and she just howled with laughter.

'Molly. If people could choose and control their dreams, why would anyone ever be awake? We'd all be on a Greek island drinking free cocktails and having sex with Aidan Turner.' I'd laughed too, but now all I wanted to do was have a dream about her, no Greek islands or Aidan Turner, just Posey and the sofa. I wanted my mum too and had cried for about an hour between dozing.

I climb out of bed, not really caring about the whiff of unwashed that is lingering on my skin and hair. I open the door and am surprised to see Trudie Goldman standing there, looking as perfect as usual. She looks nervous though and has a bottle of wine in her hand. I'm confused. I don't think it's even 10am. Is this what having kids drives you to?

'Merry Christmas, Molly,' she says with a very small smile. Christmas? She's right. It's Christmas Day today. A wave of something like nausea rolls through me. It's my first Christmas without Posey. The first Christmas I won't be seeing Dad. I'll be sitting alone with just my own misery for company. The enormity of the realisation almost floors me and I have to grip the doorframe to stop my legs buckling. Luckily, Trudie doesn't seem to notice. She carries on talking.

'I have an apology to make to you. Can I come in for a second?' I look at the wine bottle in her hand and she lets out a small laugh. 'This is for you. To say sorry. Not to drink now.' She hands me the bottle. It's a red with an expensive-sounding name. Posey and her new wine connoisseur status would have been impressed.

'I suppose we could have a tea or coffee instead?' I say, now hoping I don't stink as much as I feel I do.

'That would be lovely. I can't stay too long anyway. Patrick's got the kids and I'm still breastfeeding the babies. I swear they feed every hour, on the hour, like they've been programmed. Even through the night. I've never been so tired.' She doesn't look tired but I imagine she's got some magic potion that banishes the eye bags and grey skin the rest of us get when sleep deprived.

I lead Trudie through to the living room and make us a cafetiere. I wouldn't usually bother but there is something about Trudie that makes me want to impress her. Maybe it's because she always looks impeccable and put-together, even with three kids under four, two of them newborns.

'So what was it you wanted to apologise for?' I ask her as I pour us both coffee. I've even got the matching mugs out that we generally only use when Posey's parents come over or something.

'I was extremely rude to you the other evening. Outside.'

'Right,' I say, nodding.

'I can't imagine how much of a shock it must've been for you. That day. The video and then finding Posey. The last thing you needed was me snapping at you too. I'm so ashamed of myself and haven't been able to stop thinking about it. I blame the tiredness.' She gives another tiny laugh.

'Apology accepted,' I say. 'Can I ask you something though?'

Trudie takes a swallow of coffee and nods. 'Yes, of course.'

'What did you mean there's just one slut living here now?'

Her blue eyes fill with tears instantly but she doesn't say anything.

'You knew about Posey and Patrick sleeping together?' I press her.

She wipes her eyes with the back of her hands, gives a barely perceptible nod. She even cries prettily. For God's sake. 'You knew too, I take it?'

I shake my head. 'Not until yesterday. Posey hadn't said anything about it to me at all. I only found out because her boss let it slip.'

'Hmm. Seems like it was one of the world's worst-kept secrets.' She sighs.

'How long have you known?' I ask, needing the details despite Trudie's clear pain.

'Pretty much since it began. Summer.' She stares at her feet. I notice she's wearing a pair of non-brand trainers. It's a little detail but it's something that doesn't sit quite right with the rest of Trudie's 'well-put-together' yummy-mummy-does-Christmas-Day outfit. 'He thought I didn't know,' she tells her shoes. 'But of course I did.' She scoffs. 'Before I was nothing but a glorified milk-machine that spends her days at baby yoga, baby fucking sensory and trying to make sure I don't look like I'm a crack-whore while doing it, I used to actually be smart.' She pauses, a frown. 'I still am smart. I've got the same legal MLitt from St Andrews as Patrick. It's where we met. Obvs.' She looks up at me. 'But now he seems to think he can fuck the neighbour and I won't realise it? Baby brain might be bad but it's not *that* fucking bad.' Her eyes are welling up again. 'Sorry, I keep swearing and I'm here to apologise.'

'It's okay,' I tell her. 'You obviously need someone to talk to.' I *do* feel sorry for Trudie, but I also want to know what else there is about Posey that I didn't know. I need to know if Patrick is really a potential murderer.

'They fucked in the kitchen once. While I was upstairs putting Lucy to bed and trying to not wake the twins up in the process. That's how I found out about it. Such a bloody trope too. I heard them over the bloody baby monitor.' She laughs, but it's mirthless. After everything I've heard about Posey over the past few days, I didn't think anything else would be able to shock me. I was wrong. She had sex with our married neighbour while his wife was in the house. Reading stories to her young children.

'Do you need a tissue?' I ask, but she shakes her head, using her cuff to mop up her spilling tears again.

'Patrick, the fucking idiot, apparently forgot all about it and I could hear every single thing. Every grunt and moan. Him laughing about me, up there reading to our daughter, knowing she needs to hear *What the Ladybird Heard* five times before she'll even consider falling asleep.'

'Does he know that you know?'

She shakes her head. 'No, but Posey did.' This surprises me and Trudie can obviously tell. 'We had a bit of a confrontation about it. God, I don't know why I'm telling you all this. I should go.'

Don't let her stop. Don't let her leave.

'No,' I say. 'Trudie, I know we don't know each other very

207

well but I'm not sure that Posey's death was an accident. I'm trying to work out what happened in the days before she died.' Trudie stares at me.

'What are you saying? You think she did it to herself?'

Keep it vague, Molly.

'I'm not sure. All I know is that some things don't add up. Please tell me what you know. Tell me what you mean by a confrontation.'

Trudie's eyes widen in horror. 'I was so angry, Molly. I came storming around the next morning. I was wild, all spitty and arched like a furious cat.' She shakes her head, ashamed. 'I asked her how long she'd been fucking my husband for. I called her a whore. We always blame the "other woman", don't we? Why *is* that? It should've been Patrick I grabbed by the throat.'

What?

'You grabbed Posey by the *throat?*' Have I got this all wrong? Could it have been Trudie who killed Posey? The scorned woman has as much motive as the cheating man to get rid of the bit on the side, right? Isn't that something we see in the news or is it just the stuff that happens in TV dramas and in middle-of-the-road thriller books?

'I was just so angry,' she says, avoiding my eyes. 'She told me she'd finished it, but he'd been moping around for days and when she said that, I knew it was because he was pining for her. He was in love with her and I'd just given fucking birth to his babies. I was full of rage and hormones.'

'Then what happened?'

'She told me that it wasn't because of that, it was because

he'd had his toy taken away and was sulking. My boobs were leaking and she tried to comfort me, tried to put her arm around me but I was so angry, I lashed out. I snapped something about not wanting her pity. I lunged for her before I even knew what I was doing.' She's full-scale sobbing now and I'd try to put my arm round her if she hadn't just told me she'd physically assaulted my friend. 'Posey was strong though. Very strong.' She half laughs, wiping her eyes again.

'Pilates.'

Trudie nods, knowingly. 'And then she held my arms at my side until I'd calmed down. I went home after that. I planned to confront Patrick but I couldn't bring myself to do it. Not if it really was over. Not with the twins feeding all the time. Not with the constant tiredness. I hoped it would go away.' Her eyes widen with fear again. 'Do you think she did this because of me? Because of what I said to her?'

I shake my head again. 'No. No, I don't. I think she was killed. And I think it might have been Patrick.'

*

Trudie doesn't say anything for an amount of time that feels immeasurable before finally saying, 'No. Patrick might be many things, trust me I've known him long enough to have seen some horrible sides to him. But he wouldn't kill anyone.'

'How can you be absolutely sure about that?'

'How can you be absolutely sure about her being killed?' She's got me there. 'Look, Molly, I need to get back to my family. The turkey won't roast itself. But, honestly, if you

209

think there's more to Posey's death than the police do, please don't drag Patrick into it. I'm just about keeping the balls in the air right now. It was over. He wouldn't risk his kids, his career. He's not perfect. But he's not a killer.' She stands up and wipes her eyes, taking a deep, karmic breath in. 'Anyway, I'd better get going. Enjoy the wine. And, I know it's too little too late. But I really am sorry about Posey.'

I follow her down the hallway and close the door behind her.

What do I make of all of that? Trudie attacking Posey? Her knowing about the affair the whole time? And Posey? She may well have called things off but she was still sleeping with him for months. And she'd not only confided in Oliver, but she told Trudie too.

I traipse back into the lounge where my laptop is still lying with the Lulu Lawrence research I'd been doing on it. But I can't even bring myself to open it. Maybe I was way off. It seems like I barely even knew Posey at all. Maybe Oliver was right.

I'm about to go and pour myself a glass of wine and fuck all this off when Trudie's words make alarm bells go off in my brain. Kate and William. They weren't the only couple to meet there, were they?

I used to actually be smart. I still am smart. I've got the same legal MLitt from St Andrews as Patrick. It's where we met.

I'm grabbing my laptop and pulling up Christopher Lawrence's LinkedIn page before I even register what I'm doing. I was right. St Andrews too. It *probably* is pure coincidence that Christopher Lawrence went to the same university as the Goldmans. Christopher's page doesn't even say which years he attended, but one thing I remember Posey parroting over and over to me when she had her teeth into a good story is 'that there is no such thing as coincidence'. She was never wrong. Well, rarely. So Posey was looking into the puzzling and complete disappearance of a teenage girl, while having an affair with our married neighbour who happened, along with his wife, to attend the same university as the dad of the missing girl. And then Posey dies in mysterious – sorry, police, but I know what I know – circumstances. There's definitely something about the situation which is beyond pure coincidence. I pick up my phone and scroll through to Marilyn's number and hit the call button. I expect her to answer immediately after yesterday, thinking I have news, but it goes through to voicemail again. I leave a message.

'Hi, Marilyn, it's Molly. Um, merry Christmas. I just wanted to know if Christopher knows someone called Patrick Goldman from university? Give me a call back when you can.'

I text her the same thing, watching as my phone makes the little swoosh sound and the message is marked as delivered.

I'm still sitting and staring at the computer, trying to work out what all this means when my phone rings.

It's Marilyn Lawrence's number.

'Marilyn. Does Christopher know someone called Patrick Goldman?' I say when I answer the phone. But it isn't Marilyn who replies.

'Hello, Molly. This *is* Christopher.'

I gasp.

'I'm calling to ask you, politely, to stop contacting my wife.'

'But, I—'

'She's been through a lot, having everything raked up by your friend, so I'd really appreciate it if you could just respect my wishes and leave us alone.'

'I just thought—'

'Please stop. My wife is unwell and this constant hounding from you and your friend is making things worse. Our daughter isn't missing. Do you understand that? There is no story here. Please leave us alone.'

I try to say something, anything to keep him on the line, feeling the one strong link I still have to Posey being wrenched out of my hands. But before I can even open my mouth, the line goes dead. I try to call back, but it rings out. One minute later, my phone beeps with a text. From Marilyn's phone.

I mean it. Stay the fuck away. Or else.

I drop my phone, my hands trembling.

Christopher Lawrence just threatened me.

17

*

I wake up the next morning, still feeling shaken after the call
and nasty text from Christopher. I think about the things
being said about him on TruthSeekers too. Could they be on
to something? A lot of them think that he had something to
do with Lulu going missing and I definitely didn't get good
vibes from him. Not when I bumped into him and not on the
phone either. I need to look more into Christopher and his
potential link with Patrick Goldman. If Christopher won't
tell me then the only other person who can give me answers
is Patrick. I shudder at the thought of talking to a possible
murderer again. But I need to get answers. I need to take
a leaf out of Posey's book and try to meet him in a public
place.

I make myself my morning tea and settle down in front of the TV. I switch on the news for the first time in days, wondering what I've missed while I've been hunkered down. There's a breaking news story and I'm surprised to see that the reporter is live from Alderley Edge. Wrapping the throw around my shoulders, I turn the sound up and lean in closer. The road she's in looks a lot like the road where the Lawrences live.

'The two bodies were discovered in the early hours of this morning after neighbours complained of hearing a "heated argument" coming from a property in the street. Police arrived and found the bodies of a man and a woman inside the property. They're not looking for anyone else in relation to the deaths.'

It's too much of a coincidence. I stare at the screen, unable to hear anything else the reporter is saying because the blood is rushing through my ears too loudly.

This is my fault.

I might not be a news reporter but I know enough about news rhetoric to understand that the deaths are a suspected murder-suicide. I think back to the threatening text Christopher sent me last night.

This is definitely my fault.

Posey suspected Christopher killed Lulu. And then she died. Now Christopher knew another journalist was close to finding out the truth so this time he killed his wife and then himself to keep the secret. I sink back into the sofa. I need to get the full story. I pick up my phone and call Oliver at *The Post*.

'Oliver Valentine.' He answers right away.

'It's Molly.' I hear Oliver sigh. 'Oliver, I've just seen the news. It's Marilyn and Christopher, isn't it?'

'Molly. Merry Christmas. And you know I can't tell you that.'

'Yes, you can! For all intents and purposes I'm a freelancer working on this. Of course you can tell me. I'll find out anyway. I'll call the police and tell them I'm a journalist.'

'You sound just like her sometimes, you know that?' Oliver doesn't sound so angry with me anymore and I beam down the phone.

'So what can you tell me?'

'Not much more than what's on the news right now, to be honest with you. Details are sparse. No cause of death has been officially given yet.'

'But they're treating it as a murder-suicide?'

'Yep, it looks that way. Police don't suspect there's a third party involved.'

'So Christopher killed Marilyn and then took his own life?' There's a long pause and I can almost hear Oliver's brain ticking over, wondering what to say.

'No, Molly,' he says eventually. 'Christopher was strangled. It was Marilyn who killed *him*.'

I hang up the phone before collapsing back down on the sofa again. I can't breathe and try to focus.

One thing you can see, two things you can smell, three things you can hear.

Marilyn.

Marilyn killed Christopher. And then took her own life.

But why? If she thought there was any chance of Lulu coming home, why would she kill herself? It doesn't make any sense. Unless she knew that Lulu was never coming home.

Did she?

Did Posey know this too?

Things still aren't quite knitting together. There's something I'm missing. But what? I pick up her laptop again and go through each folder carefully, but nothing stands out to me.

'What have I missed, Posey? What is it?' I wait, hoping to hear her voice steering me in the right way. But it doesn't come. Great. She chooses now to finally shut up. I stand up and pace around the living room, trying to pull everything together. What doesn't make sense? I pick up my phone and open my email app, ignoring the deluge of unread mails, searching for Posey's final message to me.

I want you to know that I've put together a file. It's in The Place. Just in case anything happens to me.

A file. She says 'a file', not numerous files.

Maybe I was wrong about The Place. Maybe she meant something else. Could there be a physical file hidden away somewhere? I pace around a bit more, thinking and thinking.

Where, where, where?

And then I remember something, a conversation with Posey months and months ago.

'What would be the worst thing about dying?' Posey had asked.

It was a Saturday mid-morning and we were both nursing hangovers. I'd been sprawled on the sofa while Posey had made herself a nest on the floor from an oversized bean bag and some cushions. We were sharing the remains of a pizza we'd had delivered the night before.

'Um, probably being dead,' I'd replied.

'But you wouldn't really know you were dead, would you?' Posey countered. 'I'd miss ham and pineapple on pizza.'

'But you wouldn't know you didn't have ham and pineapple on pizza.'

We both considered this in silence for a moment.

'If I die,' Posey said, 'I need you to do something for me.'

'Urgh, do you have to be so morbid? I'm trying to watch *Selling Sunset* without an existential crisis catching me off guard.'

But Posey was insistent. 'No, Molly. This is important. I need you to promise me something.'

'*Okay*. What?'

'If I die and my mum comes over to go through my stuff, make sure you move the shoebox under my bed.'

'Ha. Okay.'

'I mean it. It's the one place I can't have her looking.' She was peeking at me over a cushion at this point. 'If something happened to me, my mum would be in absolute bits. The last thing she would need is being faced with evidence of my sex life. As far as she's concerned, I'm still a virgin. We cannot shatter that illusion.'

This made me laugh, despite my aching head and dry throat.

'Pose, I'm almost certain your mum doesn't think you're a virgin.'

Posey smiled enigmatically. 'Whatever. I pretend she

does and she pretends I am. It's an unspoken rule. So, you promise?'

'Posey Porter, I solemnly swear that if anything happens to you, I will spare your mother the indignity of having to sort through your dildo box.'

Posey laughed. 'See. This is what best friends are for.'

'Yes. We have best friends to clear out our sex drawers in the event of our death.' I'd thrown a piece of stuffed crust at her head then.

I dash into my bedroom, my heart thumping out a techno rhythm in my chest. This must be it. I haul the shoebox of sex toys out from under my bed where I'd shoved it on the day Tina visited. This must be The Place. It has to be. The one place where she wouldn't want anyone else but me to look, in the event of her death. The heavy clump of feelings that has been settled deep in my gut seems to move to my throat as I think back to that flippant conversation, our casual attitude towards death. God, if only we knew.

'Please let me be right. Please let me be right,' I whisper to myself.

I take a deep breath and lift the lid off the shoebox. And I am right! Because there, nestled in between a trio of anal trainers and a rechargeable clitoral suction vibe is a phone. This must be what Posey meant when she said she'd put together a file. Of course she didn't mean a literal, physical file. It's not the dark ages. I could kick myself for not under-standing she meant a digital file. I gingerly edge the phone out of the box with my fingertips, trying not to touch anything else. My hands are trembling as I pull the handset out. It's not

218

Posey's iPhone – the latest model, which Tina took away with her. It's an older one. Suddenly I'm certain that this phone will have all the evidence I need to convince DI Wolfe and DS Freeman that Posey's death wasn't accidental.

That someone killed her.

And that it has something to do with the Lawrence family and Patrick Goldman.

I take the phone into the living area and sit down on the sofa. I need a few moments to ground myself before I turn it on. I have no idea what might be on it, but I know it won't be a fun read. Should I make myself a tea first? My mum always told me that tea is a grounding drink. I have to say I agree with her. I pad through to the kitchen and pull a mug out of the cupboard, clicking the kettle on as I pass it. Even the ritual of selecting a teabag, pouring the boiled water over it and adding the milk makes me feel calmer. It's almost comforting in its predictability.

Once I've let the tea brew – two minutes is optimal – I take the teabag out and carry the mug back to the sofa. I warm my hands on the mug until they start to sting. Then I pick the handset up and turn it on.

It takes a couple of minutes to fire up and I hope it's charged. I don't want to root around in Posey's sex box trying to find a lead that fits the phone. I'm pleased to see the battery icon indicating the phone has some charge. I'm less pleased to see that Posey has facial recognition installed. I fling the phone down on the sofa with a yelp of frustration. Tears are burning the backs of my eyes again. I thought I was getting somewhere. I thought this was the answer. But, as usual, I'm wrong. I don't know why I keep letting myself think I'm good enough or smart enough to figure any of this out. I should know by now that this kind of thinking only ever leads to disappointment. Because I'm not good enough. I'm not clever enough. And every person who has sat with me and tried to convince me that these thoughts are intrusive and not true is a fucking idiot. But not as much of a fucking idiot as me. A stupid, fucking deluded idiot. I sink down into the sofa, as low as I can go. And I let the tears come, knowing there's every chance that they will never stop.

18

*

I sob on the sofa for what feels like hours. I miss calls from Jack and Robyn. How can I have been so stupid? Of course I'm never going to be able to prove that Posey was killed. The police think I'm just some drunken idiot who was stupid enough to get caught on camera. The whole world thinks I'm a stupid slut. Even Jack is probably only being nice to me because he feels sorry for me. I'm pretty sure Robyn is calling to tell me I don't have a job anymore. Which is a good thing. I'm not a journalist. Posey was the journalist. She was the clever one who could figure stuff like this out. She was the one with all the contacts. I bet she'd be able to get a phone unlocked easily. This thought makes me cry even more, all the shame and self-pity I've been trying hard to keep at bay finally crashing over me like a tsunami. I want to drink. I want to drink and drink and drink so I don't feel any of this anymore. I don't care what I promised Posey. Posey's dead. It doesn't make any difference to her what I do.

I stomp into the kitchen, wiping my tears as I go. There must be something in here. I root through the cupboards pulling out old packets of cereal, tins we've had since the turn of the century, and bags and bags of more bags.

'Where is all the fucking booze?' I scream at nothing.

I swear a bit more until I'm brought back to the present by ringing. It's the landline again. I stand up with a hiccup, hoping against hope that it's Dad. Hoping that he wants to see me after all.

It's not Dad, it's Tina. I don't want to answer, but she's the only person in the world who probably feels worse than I do. So I do.

'Hey Molly, love.' Her voice feels like a balm. 'How are you doing over there?'

'Not bad,' I lie. 'How are you?'

'I'm okay,' she lies back. 'I just wanted to let you know that Posey's body has been released now. She's at the funeral parlour in Wandsworth. It means we can start making plans for the funeral now. I wanted to keep you in the loop. I hope you don't mind? We're looking at next week.' It feels so soon. Too soon. Too soon to say goodbye.

'Okay,' I say back. 'Just let me know day and time, if I can do anything.'

'I will. You're such a sweetheart, Molly. You're so strong.'

We say goodbye and I cry again.

This is real.

This is really happening.

I must cry myself to sleep because I wake up and it's night. Posey's secret phone looks at me mockingly from the other side of the sofa. I miserably pull myself up, looking for my own phone which I find squashed down between the cushions. There must be some way I can get into it. Posey wouldn't give up. A photo of Posey maybe? I pull up Google on my phone but a quick search tells me a photo won't work because facial recognition uses 3D technology and photos are flat. I need Posey's face. Which is basically impossible because she's dead and lying in a fridge at a funeral parlour. I squeal with frustration again and throw myself facedown on the sofa. I must knock my head a little because suddenly, magically, I have an idea. And it's actually a good one.

I pick my phone back up and send Jack a text.

Would you come with me to the chapel of rest tomorrow?

Jack's reply comes quickly.

If that's what you need me to do then of course I will.

After that I text Tina to ask if it's okay to visit Posey for a final time.

Yes darling, absolutely. She looks so peaceful. I've spent a lot of time with her today, just holding her hand. You need to give the funeral parlour a call and arrange a time so they can get her ready for you.

I try not to focus on what 'getting her ready for me' might entail as I call the funeral director. A man with a very sooth-ing voice answers and agrees for me to come in at noon the following day. I wonder if he'd had special training to make his voice sound so warm and comforting. The exact opposite of a doctor's receptionist.

*

It's just before noon now and Jack had met me at the bus stop on Upper Richmond Road. My heart gave a little jump of pleasure when I saw him waiting for me. It's so weird how, in just a few days, he's become the only person I feel I can turn to.

'Are you sure you want to do this?' Jack asks, his voice cutting across my thoughts. He's wearing dark jeans, a plain black sweater and a parka. His eyes look slightly bloodshot, like he hasn't had enough sleep. I feel a pang of guilt. I hope it's not because of me.

'I need to,' I tell him. Although I haven't told him exactly why. I'm not sure it would put me in the best light, confessing I need to use Posey's dead face to unlock a secret phone I discovered stashed in with her vibrators.

He nods, once. 'Okay. I get that. Do you want me to come in with you, at least?'

I shake my head. 'It's fine. Not my first rodeo.' I give him a weak smile, which he returns, equally weakly. There's not a lot of bright-side thinking that can be eked out of a visit to a funeral parlour.

The funeral home is nestled between a solicitor's office and a small newsagents. The window display is very discreet, just a sombre placard with Wilson & Son since 1887 etched onto it.

We walk into the main reception together, Jack's hand a reassuring presence on the top part of my arm. The receptionist is the guy I spoke to on the phone yesterday. He doesn't look old enough, or world-weary enough, to be working in such a morbid place.

'I'm Molly,' I say. 'I'm here to see Posey Porter? I think we spoke earlier.' If he knows who I am from the video and media, he has the good grace not to show any hint of it on his face. Will I always think this about everyone I ever meet? For the rest of my life?

'Sure, I'm sorry for your loss. Would you like to follow me and I'll take you to see Posey.'

'I'll wait here?' Jack says; the undertaker guy nods at him. They exchange weak smiles and that's how it will be now whenever anyone mentions Posey. Just lots of exchanging of weak smiles and people sorry for my loss. I follow the undertaker through a carpeted corridor lined with shelves of urns and various lumps of shiny marble.

'She's just through here.' He gestures at a door with a sign saying 'Chapel' on it. 'Take your time. I'll be waiting back in the front when you're ready.' He gives me a little half nod, half bow and steps back for me to go and see the dead body of my best friend.

I've done this before, but even so, seeing Posey laid out in front of me like this almost physically winds me. She looks like a doll of Posey. Her skin has a waxy, unnatural shine from whatever's been used to embalm her. She's got make-up on to disguise how death has sucked all colour from her. Her eyes are closed and, I don't know how and I don't want to, her lips have been pulled into a small smile. Last time I did this, I'd been encouraged. Lots of people had told me how peaceful they'd found the experience. How it was a chance to say a final goodbye. How it just looked like their loved one was asleep. I didn't feel any of that then and I don't feel it now. I hate it. Posey's fake smile looks like a smirk. I'm expecting her to leap up any second and laugh her head off at my terror. Her hands are placed neatly in her lap and I take one of them. It's heavy and cold.

'Oh Pose,' I say, my voice strangled. 'What happened?' I suddenly feel overwhelmed by the sadness of it all. More than anything I want to tell my best friend about the horror of the last few days. I want to hold her hand and tell her about the livestream, about the Twitter witch hunt, about the horrible, horrible articles online. I want to tell her about finding her, just lying there dead and bloated in the bath and how no one will listen to me because I know, I *know* that there's no way she did this to herself. I want to tell her how much I love her and miss her. And I also want to shout at her for keeping so much of her life from me.

So I do.

I hold her hand and I talk and shout and cry until there are no words left and then the tears come instead.

Finally, when my eyes have cried themselves raw, I place her hand back in position and do what I came here to do. Tentatively, feeling like I'm about to unleash something awful into the world, I take her phone out of my bag.

'I'm so sorry, Posey,' I say as I hold it in front of her face. For a moment nothing happens and I think whoever has painted this death mask on her has made her so unrecognisable, she can't even unlock her own phone. But then the screen glows into life and I let out a huge, relieved breath. 'I hope what I'm looking for is on here,' I tell her, sternly. 'You'd better not have put me through this for nothing.'

There's a small bench, which I suppose is for those so grief-stricken they cannot stand, and I perch on the edge of it, scrolling frantically through the phone before it turns itself back off. I don't want to have to do this more than once. I go to the Settings app and turn off facial recognition and passcode. Just to check I've done it properly, I let it fall into sleep mode and then I shake it. Her home screen lights up in front of me. I sigh with relief again.

'I'm going to find out what happened to you,' I promise Posey before I leave. 'I'm going to finish your story.'

I walk solemnly back into the reception where Jack is fiddling on his phone and the funeral guy is clicking away at his computer. I get a weird feeling, like I've walked into a room where people have been talking about me and immediately try to act like they were doing something else. I guess this is another feeling I'm going to have to live with until someone develops the software to erase viral videos from people's actual minds.

'All done?' the undertaker asks. 'You can see her any time before the funeral. Just call ahead and we can make sure she's ready for you.'

I smile, weakly of course, at him. 'Yes, thank you. I won't be back though. But, thank you. She looks very peaceful.' It's a total lie, but I'm beginning to realise that a lot of the language around death skims the truth, skates over it like blades across ice.

And we all just smile weakly at each other, knowing we're all, actually, just full of shit.

*

My heart is hammering all the way back to my flat. I don't want Jack here when I go through the phone. I don't want him to see this sneaky side of me. A side of me that only went to visit my best friend in the chapel of rest because I needed her face. We walk back to the bus stop in silence.

'Look. I think I need to be on my own for a bit. After that, you know?' I say.

Jack looks me in the eye, weighing up whether this is a good idea. 'You sure?'

I nod. Firm. I'm sure. 'I need a bit of space to process it all.'

He returns my nod. 'Fair. Let me at least see you home though. Make sure you make it there in one piece.'

'Make sure I don't stop at a bar on the way, you mean?'

He breaks eye contact with me and I know I'm right.

'I'm not going to. I promise. But you've heard of Deliveroo, right? You know that they can bring as much white wine as I can drink to my very doorstep, should I require it.'

Jack frowns. 'Are you sure you should be alone?'

'Relax. I'm sure. But yes, you can walk me home if it makes you feel like a hero. Just don't try to come in for a cup of tea or anything.'

He grins. 'No danger. I've had your tea. You can keep it.'

Miraculously the bus arrives quickly and we sit side by side on the upper deck. I let my head rest against the window, the coolness of the glass soothing. We don't say anything as the bus makes its stop-start journey to Clapham Junction where we get off. We wander along the street to Lavender Rise in silence. The good kind of silence. Which is just as well because my mind is fizzing with a strange combination of fear and anticipation over what I'm going to find on this secret phone of Posey's. When we get to my door, he watches me put the key in the lock and turn it.

'Can you go now?' I laugh. 'You're making me feel bad for not inviting you in.'

'No, no. Don't you feel bad, Molly Monroe. You do your thing. I'll just make my way back to the dangerous streets of Fulham alone and undefended. Don't you worry.'

I turn and smile at him. 'Thanks. For today. I really don't think I could have done that totally by myself.' Awkwardly, and cringing at the memory of trying to kiss him just days earlier, I throw my arms around him. The need for human contact suddenly overwhelming.

He hugs me back. 'My pleasure. Well, not exactly a pleasure. You know what I mean. And listen, if you need me at all, later. Or whatever. Just shout, okay? I'm very good at sofa-sleeping should a lady not want to be alone.'

'Noted. Speak soon.'

He gives a little half salute before turning and heading back the way we came. I very nearly call him back, but part of me is still cringing from the pathetic pass I made at him. And the rest of me knows that Posey's secrets are something I need to face alone. I watch his retreating figure until he disappears from view. Then I step inside the flat, pulling the door shut behind me and clicking the latch so it's locked. I reach up and turn the deadlock at the top too. I don't usually lock myself in. Locks make me feel trapped rather than safe. But that was before I found Posey, likely murdered, in her own room.

I walk through to the kitchen and make a tea, readying myself to face whatever I'm about to find on this phone.

It's only then that I have something tug at my brain, wanting my attention.

Didn't Jack say he lives in Vauxhall?

*

I don't understand what this means. Jack definitely told me he'd found me wandering around in Vauxhall that night. And it wasn't just me he told, he told the police the same thing when they were asking me about Posey. Lying to me is one thing, but lying to the police. There must be a simple explanation, but I can't for the life of me think of one. Maybe I misheard and he didn't actually say Fulham at all? My mind *has* been a bit all over the place.

With trembling hands, I switch Posey's second phone back on.

It doesn't look like it's going to give me all the answers I need. It just looks like a normal, if slightly bare, smartphone. It's not covered with social media apps, sleep apps, news apps, dating apps and all the other rubbish we fill our phones and lives up with. There's no WhatsApp. No email.

But there is a file. And it's labelled Molly. This is what she meant. This is what she meant me to see.

But I also notice that she's had a load of missed calls from Marilyn Lawrence. And there are three voicemails Posey hasn't listened to as well. She must've used this phone to communicate with Marilyn. I feel uneasy as I tap the voicemail app, unsure how I feel about listening in on a message sent from one dead woman to another.

Just do it, Molly.

So I do.

And then I have all my answers.

19

*

It's Marilyn's voice.

'I didn't mean to do it, I really didn't. I love Lulu. I love her more than life, but—' Marilyn pauses and takes in a deep breath. 'You don't have children, do you, Posey? So why would I expect you to understand? The love you have for a child is like nothing else. Nothing compares. Romantic love is all very exciting and sexy and passionate. But it fades and soon you're just two old farts floating around in the same four walls, getting on each other's nerves. I know Christopher was sleeping with other women. I know he and Patrick did it all the time on their 'trips'. I don't blame him. We still love each other, but it's not the same. And it doesn't even come close to the love a parent has for their child. That's what pure, unconditional love looks like.'

There's another pause and I realise the voicemail has played out. I fumble with the phone as I try to play the next one. I finally manage to coordinate my fingers. The second voicemail starts with Marilyn sighing. I hear what sounds like a cork being pulled out of a bottle and the slugging of liquid into a glass. Then come some wet noises as she drinks whatever she poured herself and licks her lips.

'She was too good for this world, Lulu,' Marilyn eventually continues. 'Too good and too sweet. And every day I found myself looking at more and more headlines about what she had to look forward to in her life. I don't know how you journalists do it, I really don't. There must be something inside you that isn't quite right. Because how can you just keep writing, what's essentially the same story, over and over again and it not break you? Woman is murdered. Woman is missing. Woman is raped. And that's on top of all the other shit we have to deal with. The unwanted groping. The everyday sexism. The fucking pay gap. The domestic workload. The emotional labour. Everything is on your shoulders when you're a woman.' Another long pull of what I assume is wine. 'Do you know how many wonderful women I've watched be rubbed out from the moment they come of age? Eventually it all gets to them. They start out as these fabulous bright young things, ready to go out and do anything, to fight for the world. But, bit by bit, that same world grinds us down. And we don't shine anymore. So we Brasso ourselves up a bit. Post on social media pretending we're having a ball, when we're dying inside. Look at Trudie Goldman. I was in awe of her at university. I couldn't believe someone like her would even consider letting me into her inner circle. She was a force of nature once upon a time. So smart. So funny. She had the world at her feet. Look at her now. She sits at home all day, nothing more than a milk machine, while her husband gets all the glory. I never thought I'd pity Trudie. But the moment she shackled herself to Patrick, she began to lose her spark. And she just sits there, knowing her husband is fucking the pretty neighbour because what else can she do?'

The recording goes silent and I wonder if that's it but there's some scrambling about and the click of a lighter, a deep breath, a long exhale. Marilyn's a smoker.

'There's nothing she can do because she threw her lot in with Patrick. She could've had the career, her own money in the bank. But she didn't. So she can't leave because where would she go and with what money? Patrick would cut her off in an instant if she took the kids and – make no mistake, he's powerful – he'd make sure she never saw them again. So there she stays. With her children, her brilliant mind festering away, while Patrick blazes all the trails. But hey, at least she's got bifold doors and that gorgeous extension to show off on bloody Instagram.' She gives a snort. 'I could barely watch us all fade away but it was Trudie who faded the most.'

The second voicemail ends and I click play on the third and final one.

'Women can't have it all, Posey, you know that, right? It's a lie. We can have bits of things, if we're lucky. But ultimately we'll all be abused in some form or another. I know, you're waiting for me to get to the point. Why I did it. Well, as you know we were at a Christmas market. Lulu always loved Christmas. She believed in Father Christmas until she was twelve. She still hung a stocking out, even as a teenager, she didn't believe in him anymore, but she was happy to play along with the story. I loved that. But last year it was different. She'd become sullen and withdrawn, she wanted to spend less and less time with me and more talking to friends online. I was losing her. I was losing her and she was about to get sucked up into a world that would use her and break her, steal her shine. There was a grotto at the market and I joked about her sitting on Santa's lap. The look the old man in the fake beard gave her sealed it. It was disgusting. Like he was appraising how fresh a cut of meat was. That was my baby. My baby.'

Another delay as Marilyn fights off tears. She sounds snotty when she manages to compose herself enough to start talking again.

'I wished for a boy when I found out I was pregnant. I wished so hard for a boy. I knew I wouldn't cope if I had a daughter, this innocent life that I'd one day have to hand over to a man's world. I cried for weeks after she was born. Christopher said it was postnatal depression but it was beyond that. I took pills but it was terminal. And I loved her. I loved her so much, Posey. Do you understand? That's why I had to kill her. To keep her safe.'

I pause the recording, stunned at what I've just heard.

Marilyn killed Lulu.

Not Christopher.

Not an unknown assailant.

Her own mother.

She loved her sweet, innocent daughter so much that the only way she could think of saving her from a world that would grind her down was to kill her. I need a drink myself to be able to listen to the rest of this. I walk through to the kitchen and find a bottle of vodka tucked away in a cupboard. That will do. I pour myself an over-generous measure and bring the glass to my lips.

Don't do it, Molly. Stay strong. Keep a clear head.

I stare longingly at the liquid. It was alcohol that started this whole thing. Comments from social media ping into my head like notifications.

Drunk whore

She was asking for it being that pissed and alone

Molly Monroe is an absolute mess

Slut

Instead of pouring it down my throat and letting it numb everything, I pour it down the plughole. At least it'll give the pipes a good clean, if nothing else. I send the rest of the bottle down too. Better to keep temptation out of reach entirely. I pour myself a glass of water and down that before going back to the living room and pressing play on the last part of the voicemail.

'We went home after that. I felt like everywhere I looked there were eyes on my daughter. Eyes of monsters who wanted to touch her and taste her and feel her and break her. I drank a bottle of wine. Christopher and Lulu watched some reality shit on the TV. I took some pills to help me sleep. That's all I can remember. I woke up the next morning and I was in Lulu's bed. She was next to me. Dead.'

The recording suddenly stops and I stare at the phone in horror.

'No,' I say out loud. 'That can't be it. I need more.' I stare at the phone in desperation before I realise that the battery has died. It's just out of juice. I race through to my room, scrabbling around in the mess of wires knotted together at the side of my bed, until I find a charger. I plug the phone in and wait, tapping my toes impatiently on the floor while it gets enough power to turn back on. It feels like several lifetimes until it finally glows with life. My fingers are fat and uncoordinated as I find the last voicemail and hit play again.

'I didn't understand what was going on at first,' she's saying now. 'I thought she was asleep and I tried to wake her up. "Wakey wakey, sweetheart." But there was nothing. Her eyes were open. Her lips were blue. And then I began to remember the night before. I'd stumbled to bed drunk and woozy on pills. Christopher was already in bed and he looked at me like I disgusted him. I've no doubt I probably do. I slurred something about sleeping in the spare room but went through to Lulu's room instead. She looked so lovely asleep. Like an angel. Like a little girl again. And I couldn't bear it anymore.'

A deep shudder of a breath, and then,

'I held a pillow over her face. She didn't even struggle. Didn't even cry. Always such a good girl. When I realised what I'd done, I screamed and screamed. Thank goodness our cottage is detached. The neighbours would definitely have called the police. I was screaming absolute murder.' She laughs, darkly. 'Christopher came running in and everything is sort of a blur after that. He sat on the floor for ages, just sobbing. I tried to explain, but he wouldn't listen, kept saying that he always knew I'd do something like this, that he should have protected her. From me! The irony of it. Eventually, he got his head together and promised me that we'd work it out. No one would need to know. He'd keep me out of prison. He told me he loved me. I thought I'd maybe been wrong about unconditional love. We came up with the story of her going missing but we weren't ready for the amount of attention it generated. I couldn't cope, so Christopher told the police we'd made a mistake, that she'd left of her own accord. Patrick came up, they came up with a plan to keep it out of the papers and news sites. It wasn't hard for him, being the hot-shot lawyer he is. Patrick promised he could shut down anything on the internet with a few strongly worded emails. The doctor gave me some different pills, stronger ones for my trauma.

'And then I forgot. I forgot what I did, Posey. I didn't know where my baby was and there was nothing apart from this aching chasm where there should have been a child's love. Christopher says it was the shock and grief hitting me at once, I totally blocked it out. I started setting up groups on social media. Patrick was having to work like a cart-horse chasing me around the net, trying to shut me up. And then I emailed you, Posey.

'And you listened. The truth has been coming back slowly over the last few days. So I really, really need you to stop looking into the case now, okay?

'Because Patrick will do whatever it takes to keep Christopher and I out of the news.'

The voicemail ends and my hands are shaking. It was Marilyn. Marilyn had killed her own child and Patrick killed Posey to shut her up. And whatever happened in Alderley Edge last night was Marilyn's final attempt to control the narrative. But she must've forgotten she'd left this voicemail for Posey. Forgot her confession. Poor Marilyn. I can't even begin to imagine what a horrible, dangerous place the world was through her eyes. So horrible she couldn't bear to see her own daughter grow up in it. And so horrible she thought the only way out for her was to die, and take the man she loved with her. I can't feel angry with her. She was clearly a very unwell and troubled woman. But there's still one person I can be angry at.

Patrick Goldman.

The murderer living right next door.

My anger quickly shifts to ice-cold fear.

The fear flushes any thoughts of being brave out of my system.

There's a message on my phone from Jack.

Been trying to call you but nothing connecting. Worried about you. On my way over to make sure you're okay.

Jack is on his way over.

Jack will know what to do.

20

@LucyLocs80: WORST CHRISTMAS PARTY EVER!
#MollyMonroe #bodyinthebath

*

It was Marilyn.

Marilyn killed Lulu.

And then she killed her husband and herself.

I don't know what to do and sit, shocked to my core. Could Marilyn somehow be involved with Posey's death too? But that still doesn't make sense. Posey thought it was me who came into the flat that night. Why? She didn't have to answer the door. Whoever it was let themselves in. She clearly wasn't expecting anyone so this person must've had a key. There's no reason that Marilyn would have a key to our flat. And why would she need to when she said herself that Patrick would do anything to keep her safe. A scorned ex-lover with a career and reputation to protect.

Posey's phone is still in my hand and I open the file called Molly, more than a little terrified about what I'm going to find buried in here. There's a document inside and its title freezes my blood in my veins.

IF I GO MISSING

It seems to be a downloadable form that Posey has filled in. All the details of her life and the people in it, in case something happens to her. Why would she do this and go to such lengths to keep it hidden if she wasn't scared? My heart is hammering as I read on.

If I Go Missing PLEASE GIVE THIS FORM TO THE POLICE
FULL LEGAL NAME: Posey Alessandra Porter
Nicknames or pet names: PeePee, Pose, Nosey
RACE: Caucasian
DATE OF BIRTH: 14 April 1991
HEIGHT: 5 feet 6 inches
APPROX WEIGHT: 9 stone 10lbs
GENDER: Female
HAIR COLOUR: Dark brown
EYE COLOUR: Brown
IDENTIFYING SCARS OR TATTOOS AND PLACEMENT:
Serpent tattoo on spine
PIERCINGS: I have two piercings on each lobe and a belly button piercing. I don't wear any other jewellery on a daily basis.
PRESCRIBED MEDICATIONS: None
ALLERGIES: Avocado. I know, right? Very un-millennial.

NOTES ON MENTAL AND/OR PHYSICAL HEALTH:
Nothing exciting to report here. I am physically and mentally healthy. Occasional stress due to the nature of my job, but I have no history of depression or any other mental illness. Recently my boss has referred me to the wellbeing officer in HR on the basis he was concerned about my emotional wellbeing. I fully dispute this.

—

PHONE NUMBER: 077934 889773
ADDRESS: Flat 2, Lavender Rise, Lavender Hill, SW11 3AA
MEMBERS OF HOUSEHOLD AND RELATIONSHIP:
I live with my best friend, Molly Nicole Monroe. We have known each other since we both did our journalism degrees together at City University. She works for a magazine called *Girl Chat*, which is for preteens. Her number is 079986 09078. She is in my phone as my ICE contact too.
(Recent photo)

—

PLACE OF EMPLOYMENT: I work as an investigative journalist for *The Post*. I was recently promoted. My boss is Oliver Valentine. I'm sure you've heard of him.

—

CLOSE WORK FRIEND: I don't really have any close work friends. Not everyone has been very impressed with how quickly I got my promotions. The person I'm closest to would be Oliver. At least I thought I was.

—

RELATIONSHIP STATUS: I'm single. Officially. But I've recently started dating a man called Josh. At the time of writing this, it is very early days and no one knows about us. Not even Molly. He is 32.

—

OTHER RELATIONSHIPS
MOTHER: Tina Porter. School teacher.
BIOLOGICAL FATHER: Julian Porter. Journalist.
SIBLINGS: Three younger half-siblings, all under the age of ten.
(Recent photos of all)

—

OTHERS

Name: Patrick Goldman (recent photo)
He is our next-door neighbour. I've known him for the two years I've lived here. I'd been having a sexual relationship with him for nine months until I called it off recently. He's

married to Trudie. They have three children. He is a lawyer. I called off our relationship partly because of how things are developing with Josh and partly because of his family. I don't want to be that woman. He had a key to the flat from when we were sleeping together. He has returned it but I am not convinced that he wouldn't have made a copy. As I write this I am planning to talk to our landlord about having our locks changed.

—

Name: Jesse Keyes (recent photo)
Jesse is our landlord. Yes, we found it hilarious that his surname is Keyes. I had a one-night stand with him recently. He's also currently living in the flat above ours, but I'm not sure that's official. Jesse recently found out that I'd been sleeping with Patrick and wasn't very happy about it. He has been threatening to throw me and Molly out of the flat, but I've threatened to tell HMRC about his various rental properties that he's not paying tax on. Jesse says that he is in love with me. The feeling isn't mutual. He was angry when I told him I didn't want to see him again. I told him I had met someone though and he seemed to accept this.

—

Name: Oliver Valentine (recent photo)
Oliver is my boss at *The Post*. We have recently clashed over a story I was working on that he refused to run. Oliver has

been a long-term friend and colleague and I was stunned when he fobbed off my discoveries about the Lulu Lawrence case, even though I was gathering a lot of evidence to back up what I'd discovered. Against my will, Oliver referred me to HR. I was furious. He made me feel like I was being a stereotypical 'hysterical' woman instead of a professional who was doing things by the book. Oliver has never treated me like this prior to this story so I've been shocked by his behaviour.

—

Name: Josh Jackson (recent photo)
He is the man I have just started dating and I'm hoping I have a future with. Like I said, it is early days but I really believe this is the man I am going to marry. I met him through work and he has been helping me navigate the Lulu Lawrence story.

—

Name: Molly Monroe
As I've already mentioned, Molly is my flatmate and best friend. She will be the person who gives you this file. Molly knows me better than anyone in the world so please listen to anything she tells you.

—

Name: Marilyn Lawrence (recent photo)
I have been in regular contact with Marilyn Lawrence, the mother of Lulu Lawrence, a schoolgirl who went missing last year. But then was found. Except she wasn't. Marilyn has spoken to me in depth about how her husband has been shutting her down every time she has tried to talk to the authorities about Lulu. He has told people that she is mentally ill. Marilyn is distraught. She says she has no idea where her daughter is and is becoming more and more frustrated because no one is listening to her or taking her seriously.

—

Name: Christopher Lawrence (recent photo)
I believe that Christopher is responsible for the death of his daughter, Lulu Lawrence, and has had help covering this up. I've been told several times by different sources that Lulu didn't go missing at all. Christopher made the initial report, but then withdrew it, saying it had been a mix-up and Lulu was safe and well, living with a relative. No one could confirm this version of events and I wasn't able to trace any living relatives. Marilyn has contradicted this. She has repeatedly tried to tell police and the media that Lulu is still missing. I believe Christopher has been gaslighting his wife, telling her that she is mentally unstable and undermining her to police and journalists.

21

*

The first thing I notice is that the 'recent photo' Posey has used of me is not a very flattering one at all. It's one she's taken from my Facebook page that I should've deleted but clearly haven't got around to yet with all the *stuff*. I'm all gums and fine lines. Looking at it depresses me. When did I get so old? My forehead is showing how my face generally settles into an expression that would be called Resting Bitch Face and the line between my eyebrows suggests I spend a lot of my time frowning. Neither of these are appealing looks. I'm smiling, but it looks so forced that it's actually grotesque. I am suddenly filled with a huge rage towards both Posey and my own face. Why didn't she use a nice one of me, taken with a filter that makes me look younger, prettier? What makes me angriest is that, out of my once slim face, I see my mother staring back at me.

Staring and judging.

'Why this pic, Posey?' I shout into the emptiness, tears burning my sinuses where I hold them back, trying to focus on my anger instead. I know where I am with anger. Disappointment. Shame.

Self-pity, essentially.

Because that's what you look like, says my mother's voice in my head. I understand she probably has a point here. If Posey had used one of the photos I post on social media, no one would recognise me. Unless it was a screengrab from the Twitter video. I suddenly have to gulp down a huge pang of sadness. Posey doesn't know anything about that video. Two weeks ago, she would've been the one I'd be talking to about it. She'd be trying to console me while I wailed about how much of a fuck-up my life has been since my mum passed away. She'd listen with the patience of a saint while I blamed everyone else for the poor decisions I made. She'd pour me a wine, tell me that none of this was my fault, that anyone judging me was really just projecting onto me. She'd assure me that I wasn't a slut. That I couldn't be one, because it's just a word used to control female enjoyment of sex. And we'd end up getting into a feminist discussion and setting the world to rights. She'd help me turn my tears, my shame, my horrible, omnipresent self-loathing into something fierce, something to be reckoned with. She'd never let me sit here feeling sorry for myself, letting all the hatred I have for myself win. But, of course, this will never happen.

'What the fuck am I going to do without you, Pose?' I ask her empty bedroom. 'Who will put me back together now?'

I let the tears fall now.

They are softer than I expect, somehow. Tears of shame feel like crying acid. They hurt the inside of your face and scar the outside of it forever. But these are new tears. It turns out tears of grief are still painful. They still feel like someone is reaching into your core, pulling out everything that makes you vulnerable and leaving it on the outside for everyone to see. They still leave you spent, emotionally, physically. But I'm stunned at how they also feel like I'm being washed from the inside out. Grief is the cost of love, according to cliché, and I suddenly realise why this is new to me. I've never allowed myself to grieve, because I've never allowed myself to love, not really. Because, not that deep down, I don't consider myself to be lovable. But Posey loved me. She did. She didn't use this horrible photo of me to hurt me or make me feel bad.

She used it because it's what I look like.

It really is as simple as that.

And I cry and cry, letting out my love for her, until I feel totally scooped out.

The second thing I notice is Posey's references to this 'Josh' person. And what leaves me absolutely staggered is Josh. Not because I'm shocked that she's been keeping secrets from me. I can only imagine how I'd have reacted if she'd told me she was seeing someone. It wouldn't have been pretty. That's all I know. But it's not that. It's the photo. Because the photo Posey has posted of Josh – her new boyfriend – is very obviously, a photo of Jack.

Jack who is currently on his way over.

I need to get out of here.

I pull on my trainers, grab my phone and my keys and shrug myself into my coat. I don't know where I'm going, but I know I can't be here when Jack arrives. I don't know who this man is. Could he be dangerous? Could he be the one who killed Posey? I don't know anything about him after all. I've let him into my life because I've been grieving and lonely. I've taken him completely on face value.

I'm a complete idiot.

I let the front door click shut behind me and I pull my hood up, protecting myself against the wind and rain, but also in case I run into Jack as I make my escape. I daren't go to the train station, in case he's there. Instead, I turn the other way, walking swiftly past the closing shops, until I reach a pub which Posey and I used to go to most Sundays to read the papers, drink red wine and have a roast dinner. I'll be safe here until I can work out what to do next. Where to go.

I order a Diet Coke and sit down, taking my phone out of my pocket. There must be some answers on here. But I don't know exactly what I'm looking for. I open my banking app, something I tend to avoid, to see if there are any clues from that night. Jack already told me that he paid for the Uber from Vauxhall to here. But I obviously got to Vauxhall from Soho somehow. It's a horror show. I mean, more than usual. I often find myself wondering if there's someone who looks at my bank statements and just shakes their head in utter despair. Actually, they're more likely to laugh and wonder what the fuck is this girl doing? I put my financial incompetency to the back of my mind and try to focus on the transactions from that night.

I'm well into my overdraft. Almost two grand, in fact. I've just never really got around to paying it off since I left uni. Unlike a lot of the people I studied with, I didn't have rich parents to give me an allowance each month. I didn't have anyone to support me or buy me a flat. I'm student-loaned up to the max and, realistically, I know there's probably no way I'll pay it off in my lifetime. Writing for a preteen magazine doesn't exactly pay well. I seem to be in more debt every single month, not less. I even opted out of the company pension scheme because I just couldn't afford the amount of money they would be taking. Anyway, none of this seemed to bother me the other night, it would seem. Looking at my bank account, I'd been spending like I'd just won the EuroMillions and didn't have a care in the world. Despite the free drinks and subsidised bar at the hell hole where the Christmas party was held, I still managed racking up a bar bill of over £100. Wow. I must've been buying drinks for the entire editorial staff. I skim through the rest of the outgoings. I spent a similarly stupid amount of money in a bar on Glasshouse Street. When was I there? I don't remember being there. I have a sudden surge of adrenaline. Someone must've cloned my card! The buzz doesn't last long though as, on closer inspection, it turns out I used Apple Pay. And my phone is very much still with me. There are about five transactions all from the bar. I'm guessing I was buying rounds of Jägerbombs or something like that.

But for who? Who was I with?

I quickly tap out a text to Paloma.

Did we go to a bar after the party?

Her reply comes quickly.

Molly. Babe. How are you? I've been so worried. You've not replied to any of my messages!

I'm okay. I'll fill you in asap but I really need to know if you and I went anywhere else?

No babe, you left without me. You still don't remember? You were really pissed at me.

Yes, I remember that.

We're not that close.

I miserably turn my attention back to my banking app. After the bar, I seem to have headed to another pub where I was supposed to meet Posey. There's only one transaction here though for £18.99, which I assume is a bottle of wine. The next transaction confuses me as around half an hour later I spend £86 in a place called The Zen Bar which I've never even heard of. I open the Safari app and type 'Zen Bar London' into Google. Apparently, it's a bar all the way over in South Kensington and not the sort of place I'd go to. The website shows glossy people drinking expensive drinks while wearing expensive clothes. Why would I be there? And who did I think I was, spending such a ridiculous amount of money there? The time of the transaction is just after 11pm, shortly before the time stamp on that video. I keep clicking through the images. Until something clicks inside me. The exterior is distinctive. Very grey. Very flat. I grimace and open my Twitter page, ignoring the notifications, clicking straight on the video.

70k shares.

I ignore the ongoing dialogue, telling me exactly what kind of slut I am.

The video is grainy, but not CCTV grainy. For the first time since last week I'm grateful for the wonderful camera technology of current iPhones. I zoom in to the image of me on the screen. The image of me, down on my knees, my dress riding so high up my thighs a glimpse of my knickers is visible.

At least you're still wearing them, says Mum-In-My-Head.

'Shut up,' I tell her.

Past my thighs, the outside of the bar is visible. It's grey. The same sort of teal-tinted grey as the exterior of Zen.

Okay. Well, now I've located the scene of the crime. That's something. But there's nothing that even hints at who the man is. *Could* it have been Jack? The only bit of him that can be seen is his jeans. Yes, even *that* bit of him isn't visible as it's in my mouth, his hands on my head.

An average fit. Darkish blue. Like ninety per cent of men out in London.

A text notification makes me jump. It's Paloma again.

M? Are you alright??

I'd better reply. She might be able to help.

Yeah I'm okay. Just overwhelmed by everything. According to my Apple Pay, I was in South Ken that night. I have no idea where else I might have been. Any idea???

Check your location history on your phone, babe.

My WHAT?

Location history, M. Tells you where your phone's been. It's tucked away in Settings, under the Privacy tab.

Molly? You still there? Did you find it?

Paloma's messages barely register as I'm already fumbling with my phone, trying to get to the Settings app. A tug of frustration almost makes me howl out loud. How does everyone know this stuff apart from me? What is *wrong* with me? The frustration makes way for a wave of pain that twists my heart. I want my mum. I want her to hold me close to her chest and stroke my hair, telling me that there's nothing wrong with me, it's the world that's wrong. And I'm crying again, because I know there's no way that it's going to happen. And now there's no Posey here to help me either. I'm spiralling faster than I can claw it back. I need to focus on something. I take some deep breaths as I scroll through Settings until I eventually find the Location History option. I'm sure my heart stops beating as I scroll through the various locations my phone has saved. Home, work, the bar at Bond Street, the basement pub in Soho, then various other bars in Soho, South Kensington, a kebab shop near Clapham Junction station and home.

But that can't be right. I hold the phone closer to my eyes as if that will somehow let me see something that is not there.

The truth, however, is staring me in the face.

I wasn't in Vauxhall that night.

I didn't go there at all.

22

*

I definitely have to get farther away from here. Jack lied to me. Is his name even Jack? He lied about buying me a kebab. He lied about finding me near his home in Vauxhall. What else is he lying about? He knew Posey. Maybe she'd even given him Patrick's key. Was he in the flat that night Posey died?

I grab my phone, stuff my feet into my shoes and run out of the door, the bartender giving me a quizzical look as I go. It's getting dark now and I don't know where I'm going to go. The police? I think of how humiliated I felt the last time I spoke to them and know I can't face that. Not yet.

Where can I go?

Who can I trust?

I look at my phone again and see another text, this time from Robyn.

Hi Molly. I've been trying to get hold of you. Nothing to do with work, I just want to make sure you're okay. Please call me. xx

Robyn? Could I? It would have been completely unheard of a week or so ago, but my life has turned completely upside down in that time. And it's not like I have anyone else.

Before I can talk myself out of it, I call her.

'Molly? Is that you? Thank God, I've been so worried. We all have.' Robyn sounds genuinely pleased that I've called. 'Molly? Say something!'

'Sorry, hi,' I manage. 'I'm sorry. I've had a bit of a shock. Sorry.'

'Molly, stop apologising. Do you want to talk about it? Are you okay?'

'No I'm not really very okay,' I hear myself saying, the words out before I can stop them. My voice is trembling. What is this? Cold? Fear? All of the above?

'What is it? What's happened?' I don't even know where to begin. Finding Posey's body, her investigation into Lulu or what I've just discovered about Jack . . . Josh . . . whatever his name is. Instead of explaining, all I can do is sob quietly down the phone as I walk. Once again I'm pleased I live in London where no one feels the need to ask me if I'm all right. 'Oh God, Molly. Where are you?' Robyn asks. I can't answer her. 'Do you want me to come over?'

I manage to say, through my tears, that I'm not at home and that I can't go back there. I probably sound stupidly dramatic, but Robyn is calm, soothing.

'Molly. I want you to get in a cab and come to mine, okay. Can you do that?'

'I can't af—'

'I'll pay for it, don't worry about that. Just get to me as quickly as you can, okay? We can sort whatever this is out.' Her kindness makes me cry even more and I'm such a mess she has to text me her address because I know there's no way I'll remember it.

I flag down a taxi and give him the address in West London. The driver doesn't ask me any questions and I sob softly to myself in the back.

23

*

It takes almost an hour to crawl through the traffic to Robyn's townhouse near Lancaster Gate. She's waiting on the doorstep for me and pulls me into a huge hug after paying the driver.

Inside she makes me a tea, heaps in the sugar as I ask her to and then sits with me as I tell her my story. And she listens. She doesn't laugh when I tell her that I believe Posey was murdered. She doesn't cross her arms or make a face or suggest I've let my imagination run away with me. She doesn't bring up the video and tell me that my perspective can't be trusted because I'm just a drunk and a slut. She doesn't say anything until I get to the end of the story.

'So Marilyn killed Lulu? Then Christopher? Then herself?

And you think Patrick killed Posey because she was about to find out the truth?'

'Yes,' I explain again, 'but it also could have been Jack. He was there that night and his real name is Josh and Posey thought he was her boyfriend. But he's lied to me about everything so he could easily have lied to her too.'

Robyn is agog. 'Who's Jack?'

So I go back to the beginning and tell her about waking up that morning and Jack was in my bed, but we were fully clothed and how he told me he'd found me wandering around Vauxhall.

'But I wasn't even there!' I say, waving my phone at her. 'Paloma showed me how I can find out on my phone where I've been and I wasn't there! He lied.'

'But what has Jack, or Josh, got to do with Lulu Lawrence?'

That's where I run out of steam. I can't link them together at all.

Robyn is musing. 'So we need to find out if there is some link between the Lawrences and Patrick? Or this Jack/Josh person? Something solid?' She pulls out a laptop. Hers is even more expensive than Posey's.

Robyn sits close to me on the sofa and she starts the type of frantic searching I was doing just moments before on my phone. But after an hour, she still hasn't found anything. She lets me lie down on the sofa and even though I'm painfully aware of the oddness of the situation, I'm so exhausted I do. She pulls a throw over me and continues her search while I doze, my mind still whirring away in the background, unable to still itself.

I'm not sure how much time passes before I'm startled awake by Robyn's voice.

'Molly! Look. Look at this.'

And I could kiss her because there, right there on her laptop, is Trudie Goldman's Facebook page. Clever Robyn has been trawling Trudie's social media trying to find something that could help us. What she's found is pure gold – a photo, hidden in the depths of almost fifteen years of albums and pictures. It's an old picture, a photo of a photo that's been uploaded. A photo of a student party, many years ago, in an album called St Andrews. Trudie is at the centre of the photo, but to the left of the frame, barely visible is another woman. A woman tagged Marilyn Fisher. I think back to my conversation with Marilyn and the voicemails on Posey's phone. She said something about Trudie being the golden girl at university, so it's no big surprise to see her in the picture. What I'm staring at is another man, again in the background, not looking at the camera and laughing. But there's no mistaking his bright blue eyes and laid-back posture.

Oliver.

'That's Posey's boss.' I make Robyn jump because my voice is so shrill. 'Oliver Valentine.'

'Fuck.'

'This can't be coincidence. There's no way?'

'No,' Robyn agrees. 'It can't be. But why would Oliver not mention he knew them all? Did Posey know?'

'I think I need to pay Oliver another visit,' I say.

'Is that safe?'

I consider this for a few moments. Is it? 'I'll go to *The Post* again in the morning. There's not much he can do to me in a glass box in the middle of an open-plan office.'

'I can come with you?' Robyn offers.

'Thanks, but he's more likely to talk if he doesn't think he's being ambushed. I'll be fine. I need to go back to the flat and get Posey's phone and laptop, but then I'll come straight back here.'

Robyn nods. 'Okay, that sounds sensible. But Molly, for God's sake, turn off location services on your phone before you do anything.'

'Actually, I think I should keep them on and give you access? You know. Just in case.'

Robyn smiles. 'That's a much better idea.' She makes a more serious face. 'I've made up the spare room for you. I don't think you should be going back to your flat until we get to the bottom of this.'

'Won't your husband mind?'

Robyn looks away from me. Stares at the window for a moment. 'We're actually separating for a while. To see how it goes.' I don't know what to say so I stay silent. 'Anyway, don't worry about that. You've got enough on your plate.'

'I'm sorry,' I say.

Robyn reaches over and squeezes my arm.

'Well, I'm not. We've been making each other miserable for years. It's actually a relief.' She lets out a loud sigh. 'Right. I think I'm about ready for something a bit stronger than tea. Fancy a glass?'

I nod and Robyn heads to the kitchen, returning with two glasses of red wine and some crisps in a bowl.

We spend the rest of the evening watching some bad reality show and planning what I'll say to Oliver tomorrow. Eventually Robyn shows me to the spare room, which is more like a hotel suite, and I sleep like the dead.

*

I'm waiting by the doors of the office for Oliver to arrive this time. I don't want another showdown with the receptionists or security for that matter. He sees me as he's strolling up the road, bag slung over his shoulder and reusable coffee cup in hand. I'm greeted with an eyeroll and a hint of a smile.

'Hello again,' he says. 'You're becoming a regular fixture here. Should I get you a pass made up?'

'No,' I say. 'I just have a few more questions that I think you can help with. Won't take long.'

Oliver sighs. 'Molly, I've told you everything I know. I don't know how much more help I can be.'

'Really?'

'What?'

'You've really told me everything you know?'

'Yes.' He's confused.

'You haven't mentioned that you know Patrick and Trudie Goldman. Or that you knew Lulu's parents too. Totally neglected to mention that you know them all from uni.'

Oliver's face drops.

'Okay,' he says, resigned. 'You'd better come in.' I follow

him through the doors and he signs me in at the desk. 'Do you want this?' He offers me his coffee. 'It's crappy machine stuff otherwise.'

'You really think I'm going to drink anything you give me?' I say. 'With people you know and work with dropping dead around you?'

Oliver's laugh is grim. 'Well, suit yourself. But I didn't know I was going to see you today, did I? And I'd hardly poison myself. And no one has died by poisoning, as far as I know, have they?'

I narrow my eyes at him. 'I don't think this is the time for flippancy, Oliver.'

We reach the top of the escalators and I follow him into the office, to his glass box. There are a few raised eyebrows, as staff recognise me from my previous visits. I wonder if they know who I am.

'Does anyone called Josh work here?' I ask.

Oliver turns and looks at me, puzzled. 'Nope. Why?'

I take up what I'm now beginning to consider 'my' seat. Oliver plonks himself behind his desk.

'Marilyn killed Lulu,' I tell him. No point in wasting any more time.

Oliver looks weary. 'Molly, you're beginning to sound more and more like Posey. I know you've had a tough time and it's understandable. But I really think you need to talk to someone. A professional. This level of obsession isn't healthy.'

'I've got her recorded confession.' The words land exactly as I hoped they would. Oliver's jaw is flapping somewhere near his knees.

'How?' he manages to ask, eventually. But I'm not going to be railroaded by him. I'm telling this *my* way.

'Posey was apparently dating someone called Josh who she met at work,' I say to Oliver's blank face. Ha. You didn't know everything about her after all, did you?

'Definitely no Joshes here. And I discourage workplace relationships anyway. Too much shit to clean up when it inevitably hits the fan.' He has a point, although I know the ban would've made it even more appealing to Posey and her anti-authoritarian streak.

'Any Jacks?'

'Not on *The Post*.' He taps a few keys on his computer. 'Are you going to tell me about Marilyn's confession or what?'

'I will. But you can start by telling me why I saw you lurking in a seventeen-year-old photo in the depths of Trudie Goldman's Facebook.'

'Okay.' He leans back in his chair and I feel like it's story time at infant school. 'Yes, I went to St Andrews and I knew them. Not extremely well. I was reading English and they were all doing some sort of law course. But Marilyn dropped out in the second year and Christopher ended up switching at some point. I'm not sure what to. But I knew Patrick from halls in the first year. We were neighbours.'

'And you stayed in touch?'

'On and off. Mostly off. Our paths went in different directions as you can see. But, we'd meet up, maybe once a year for a pint. Send Christmas cards, that sort of thing.'

'Why didn't you mention you knew them when I first came to you? You have to admit it looks pretty dodgy.'

'Honestly, Molly? I just didn't want to muddy the water. I know you think that Patrick has something to do with Posey's death, but I don't think you're right. He's a bit of a shit, but I really don't think he's got it in him to kill someone.'

'Right. And not covering the Lulu Lawrence story? Did that have anything to do with Patrick?'

'Patrick's a very powerful lawyer. If he wants something hushed up, it gets hushed up. That's not something I can control. If I get an email from our legal team telling me to leave something, that's what I do.'

'So much for the freedom of the press.'

'This isn't new information for you, Molly. You know how it works.'

'I do and it's so fucking frustrating!' I slam my hand on the desk and Oliver's eyes widen. I don't think he's heard me raise my voice, let alone swear before.

Although, he *has* seen me giving a blow job.

Life is strange.

I take a breath and compose myself. 'Marilyn told Posey that Patrick would do anything to protect her. Why would she say that?'

'Do some maths, Molly.'

'Excuse me?'

'How long ago did you say that Facebook photo was posted?'

'Like sixteen or seventeen years ago?'

'Right. And how old would Lulu Lawrence be now?' His words sink in.

'Lulu was Patrick's daughter?'

'Correct. He and Marilyn were a thing at uni. Well, in the first year anyway. But when she got pregnant, he didn't want to know. That's when she dropped out.'

'And Christopher switched courses?'

'Yep. He didn't like how Patrick was treating Marilyn. Chris had always had a thing for her himself. They married when Marilyn was pregnant. I guess she didn't want to be on her own with a baby and Chris agreed to raise the kid as his own. It all looked like it would work out. Until after graduation and Patrick and Trudie got together and moved to London.'

'Marilyn didn't take it well?'

'She had some sort of mental breakdown. Chris said she'd been struggling with low mood since the birth but she just completely lost it when Patch and Trudie became a thing.'

'We don't say "lost it", Oliver. We say "had a mental health crisis",' I tell him.

'Whatever. She was unhinged. She had treatment and took a load of pills but it always seemed to creep back in. And then it went into overdrive like a year ago.'

'What happened a year ago? Apart from Lulu disappearing? What triggered it?' Oliver doesn't answer but I'm talking more to myself at this point anyway. 'The twins. She found out Trudie was pregnant again? Or more to the point, was expecting twin boys.'

'I'd put money on it,' Oliver says.

'Do you think Marilyn was threatening him? That she'd tell the world that he abandoned his first daughter unless he helped cover it up?'

'Could be. Or maybe he just wanted to protect her.

Marilyn was always so vulnerable and I think Patrick, in his wise middle age, regretted how he treated her. He wanted to make things better between them.'

I laugh. 'Oh don't make him out to be a saint, Oliver. He was still cheating on his wife. Lying to Posey. Probably *murdered* Posey.'

'I didn't say he was a saint. He's human. He's done some shitty, shitty things but I don't believe murder is one of them. I just don't.'

'But he's got double motive – keeping the affair quiet, and keeping the truth about Lulu covered up. Posey had given him a key so he had opportunity. And if he drowned her while she was in the bath, then he had means. Oliver, we have to do something with this. I've got all the evidence we need at home. I've got Marilyn's confession. We can run the story, at least the stuff about what happened to Lulu Lawrence. It's the biggest story in years. You can give Posey a posthumous byline. It would be incredible!' Oliver is looking at me. I know from what Posey has told me that he's a sucker for a good story so having the biggest scoop of the year, no, decade is more than just a little appealing. 'You'd win an award. All the awards!' I add, not knowing how true this is but firing myself up with my words. 'Imagine it. You'd be a hero.' I'm on my feet now, placing my hands on Oliver's desk. There's a spark in his eyes and for a second, I think he's going to be the person Posey knew he could be. I think he's going to throw caution to the wind. But then his eyes land on the photo on his desk. His own kids and partner. He sighs. It's heavy and loaded with finality.

'I need my job, Molly.' And then, 'I'm sorry.'

I want to storm out of the office, but I'm too defeated so I slink away, once again trying to merge in with my surroundings. Outside, I flag down a black cab and give him my address in Clapham. I call Robyn from inside the car.

'He wasn't having any of it,' I tell her.

'Oh Molly, I'm sorry. But don't give up. I'm in the office but I'll head home soon. Meet me there?'

'Yeah, I'm just popping back to the flat to grab some things and then I'll head to yours.'

'We'll work something out. It's not over. Far from it. We'll talk about what to do next later, okay?'

'Okay,' I say, a small smile managing to break out on my miserable face. Robyn's enthusiasm and belief in me not being a total fuck-up remind me of Posey.

'Call me when you're on your way?'

'I will. See you soon.'

'See you soon.'

24

@JackDanielS: Y'all watch way too many true life dramas. Police said death isn't suspicious. #MollyMonroe #bodyinthe-bath

*

I spend the rest of the journey writing up Posey's story on my phone. If Oliver won't print it there will be someone who will. There has to be. Then I have an idea. Do I really need the backing of a publication to get the story out? When I have my own social media following, which is now in the tens of thousands? And it's not like I'm making outlandish claims. I might not have the proof that Patrick killed Posey but I can back up every other aspect of the story.

When I've hurriedly written the story, amazed at how quickly it trips off my fingertips, I open the App Store and reinstall Twitter.

I take several screenshots of my work.

And then I post them.

The truth about missing teenager Lulu Lawrence and the people who don't want you to know about it

So I know many of you, most of you, are only following me because you've seen the slew of videos, GIFS and memes that have become part of internet culture over the past few days. Most of you are here to hate-follow me, to call me some extremely misogynistic names for getting drunk enough to give oral sex to a stranger and being stupid enough to have it live-streamed. Which is, if you're still laughing at it, an actual sexual assault. I didn't know who the man was. I don't even remember it happening. And I certainly didn't know, let alone consent to it being live-streamed. And then shared thousands and thousands of times. Every single one of you have seen the most humiliating moment of my life. And most of you have found it funny. Some of you have slid into my DMs suggesting I practise my oral techniques on your penises. Many have sent me pictures of their penises. Note – this is also sexual assault so please stop doing this. But I'm not writing this about me or for me. This is the first time I've had 45 thousand followers and, while not for a reason I'm very proud of, your number can help me tell a very important story. You may have seen in the news recently that a young woman was found dead in a bath in Battersea. She was a journalist – a brilliant one – but her death didn't make the headlines. A few lines on a few news sites when she and the story she was investigating deserve so much more. The police aren't interested in the truth so here it is.

Lulu Lawrence went missing at a Christmas market in Manchester last December. Her worried parents, Marilyn and Christopher, reported the sixteen-year-old's disappearance to the police force covering their home village of Alderley Edge and the force in Manchester. A nationwide manhunt began for the pretty blonde until a few days later when it was called off. Lulu wasn't missing at all. She'd left home of her own accord, something a sixteen-year-old is entitled to do, and the case was closed.

That was the official account, but the truth is something much darker and is probably linked to three people dying as it was uncovered. My late friend, Posey Porter, a senior reporter at national disgrace *The Post*, tried and tried to get bosses to listen to her as she dug deep into Lulu's life and discovered she hadn't left home. And she hadn't gone missing at all. Because she died at home the night she went to the Christmas market. Murdered by one of the people who was supposed to love and protect her. Posey believed it was Christopher Lawrence who had killed his daughter, but the truth is that she died at the hands of her mother, Marilyn. Esteemed lawyer, Patrick Goldman was Lulu's real father and he helped his former lover cover up her crime and dictated what the papers and internet could write about Lulu. The bodies of a man and woman recently found in a house in a 'Cheshire suburb' were those of Christopher and Marilyn. A murder-suicide. But unlike the usual story of a man killing his wife before taking his own life, this was the other way around. Marilyn murdered her husband and then killed herself. You may think there is such a thing as freedom of the press in this country, but the truth is bitterly the opposite. Like so many other things, it's the rich and powerful pulling the strings, printing smoke-and-mirror stories, distracting you from what is going on in front of your eyes, but you're unable to see. Do you really think the story of a drunken thirty-two-year-old woman performing a sex act on a London street is more newsworthy than the murder and cover-up of a young girl? It's not, is it? But this is what our media want you to believe. They don't want you to know what's really going on. Posey was on her way to finding out the truth and reporting it, one way or another, as I know she would have, but she mysteriously died the same night I was too drunk to even get myself home safely. The police have said her death was a 'tragic accident' but an email Posey sent to me the night before I found her body in her bath told me that she was afraid and that she knew what had happened to Lulu Lawrence. I took this to the police and they ignored me. I did my own investigation. I found the truth. I've been called everything from a deluded drunken slut to a fucking lunatic, despite evidence, in attempts to discredit me. But this, followers, this is the truth.

#TheyDontWantYouToKnow

25

*

I fumble as I try to ram the key into the lock, desperate to be in and out of my flat as quickly as possible. I just need to grab the laptop and phone and get back to Robyn's. But as soon as I step through the door and slip my shoes off, I can feel something is wrong. Something is off in the flat and, for once, it's not the bins.

Don't be silly, Molly, you're imagining it because you're scared. Just go and grab the laptop and phone, then get out. You can leave the front door open.

Too late. The door slams shut behind me, making me jump.

Pull yourself together.

I breathe slowly in through my nose and slowly out through

my mouth. It calms my thundering heartbeat a little, but I can't shake the feeling that there is someone – or something – else here with me. I shake the thought out of my head and scurry into the living room, planning to grab what I need and bolt. But I was right. I'm not alone.

'Hi, Molly.' The voice comes from behind me. I know who it is before I turn and face him. Blue eyes burning holes into my flesh.

'Patrick . . . how . . . ?'

'How did I get in? Well. As you know by now, Posey and me were a little more than friends for a while. She gave me a key.'

'You should have given it back,' I stutter, my eyes frantically scanning the room for the devices.

'Well, I did. But I also took a copy. Just in case. You never know when keys are going to come in handy. Bit disappointed in Posey actually. She was a smart girl, in some ways, I thought she would've had the locks changed. But I guess she was distracted. Are you looking for something?' He's smiling and it's then I realise he's holding a laptop under his arm, the same laptop I came here to retrieve, Posey's laptop. 'I *did* knock first. Actually, I was hoping to see you.' His smile is sinister now. A big, greedy crocodile grin. 'I saw your article on Twitter. It's already got a lot of traffic, Molly. For something that isn't true.' He says the words in such a matter-of-fact way that I wonder if he actually believes his own lies. Could he be that unhinged? Why am I wondering that? This man murdered Posey. He's as unhinged as they come.

'But it *is* true, you know it's true.' I know I should probably be trying to keep him sweet and just get out of here as fast as I can, but the words are tumbling out of my mouth and I don't seem to have any control over them. 'You might have been able to silence Posey and Lulu and Marilyn and probably loads of other women I don't know about. But you don't get to silence me, Patrick. Because it's already out there. It's already published. You're too late. Whatever you think you're going to do to me to shut me up, you can't. It's done.' I sound a lot braver than I feel. Sweat is pooling everywhere on my body that sweat can pool. The calm, controlled breathing has left the building too.

'No, no, Molly. And I thought you were supposed to be a journalist? I thought you were meant to know about law. It's only true if you can *prove* it's true.'

'I can. I have evidence.'

'Yes. I assume you mean this.' He holds up Posey's laptop. 'And this.' Her phone. He then drops them onto the wooden floor before stamping viciously on them both. Patrick didn't bother taking his shoes off when he let himself in. A little shriek of dismay comes out of my mouth as shards of plastic and Apple innards fire across the floor. 'Now you don't have any evidence, Molly. And without evidence, the little *essay* that you posted on social media, is nothing more than the completely non-credible rantings of a drunken little slag.' He's managed to take three or four paces towards me during his speech and is close enough to shout the last two words directly into my face. His teeth haven't been cleaned since his last coffee and my nose tries to recoil from his breath. 'A drunken little slut who is going to need to lawyer up quite quickly because I am going to bring the mother of all libel cases to you. Do you understand?'

I don't say anything.

'DO YOU UNDERSTAND?' He screams it at my face this time. I feel spittle. This time *I* recoil. But I nod too, scared now. I know what this man is capable of.

'Good girl,' he says, satisfied. 'I guess we're even now anyway.'

'What do you mean?'

'We have come full circle,' Patrick says. He laughs and it drips with cruelty. How did you ever find this man attractive, Posey?

'You killed her,' I say. 'She worked it out, like I did. She knew that you'd helped Christopher Lawrence cover up Lulu's death and you killed her. To keep her quiet.'

Patrick shakes his head and looks at me from under his furrowed brow. It's condescending.

'I didn't kill her. I wanted her to keep quiet, yes, but I didn't kill her.' He kicks the broken bits of laptop and phone to one side and sits down on the armchair. 'Why would I want her dead? She was much more useful alive. Not to mention excellent in bed. Much easier to control and keep an eye on when I was fucking her.'

I scowl at him, the hatred I feel making the tips of my fingers tingle. 'You weren't fucking her though, were you? She ditched you. And that was even before figuring out what a psychopath you are. She found someone else, didn't she? Someone better and you couldn't handle it. Just admit what you did.'

He looks at me again, considering me.

'I'm not a murderer, Molly. Whatever you might think of me. I hoped a video of you humiliating yourself in front of the entire world would be enough to keep Posey quiet.' He laughs. 'I thought she'd realise then what I'm capable of. But she never got to see your movie debut, did she? It's really quite sad.'

What? WHAT?

'You?' The magnitude of what he's saying makes me dizzy and I stumble back until I'm sitting on the sofa. 'That was you.' Patrick's the man in the video. My stomach rolls and roils and I clutch my hands over my mouth, bile threatening to pour out of me.

He laughs at me. 'Oh, don't worry, little Molly, it wasn't me you were *servicing.*' He puts an emphasis on the word that makes my skin feel like insects are burrowing into me. 'But I was the cameraman, yes. Unfortunately, I'm not as au fait with modern technology as I should be and rather than just recording a TikTok to send to Posey, I set it live. Careless.' He tilts his head to one side as he continues to appraise me. 'It was a work colleague who you were enjoying yourself so much with, by the way. I'm sure that's been playing on your mind. Jeremy. Nice lad. More than happy to take up the challenge of getting you in a compromising position, Molly. Not that you were much of a challenge though. I can arrange a get-together if you like? That would be nice, wouldn't it? Quite the meet-cute.'

'I was drunk,' I say to the floor. 'It was assault. He assaulted me. *You* assaulted me.'

Patrick shrugs as if he couldn't care one way or another. 'Who's going to believe you though, Molly? Actually, my mistake worked out quite well for me as it turns out. Because now I need you to disappear. You need to stop drawing attention to me. To a story which is well beyond your journalism pay grade and fuck off.'

'I'm not going to do that,' I say.

'It's really not up for discussion, Molly. We can either do this the easy way, or the hard way.'

'What's the hard way?' I ask, although I'm already sure I know the answer.

'I said I'm not a murderer and that's true. So far. But if you don't agree to go away and fucking stay away, then I'll have to make you disappear. And, like I said, your little video nasty and that incoherent piece of drivel you wrote about Lulu Lawrence have made it easy for me. A woman shamed. A woman clearly not in control of her mind or her actions. You've set the narrative up perfectly, Molly. No one would even question it if you took your own life.' He smiles and it's eerie, like the corners of his mouth are being pulled upwards against his will. 'I've even picked the perfect spot. We're due a really cold snap in the next day or so. I thought the Serpentine would be nice for you? A proper Ophelia death. What do you think?'

'You're going to kill me?'

'I don't want to, Molly, but I don't think you're going to go away quietly like I want you to. Are you?'

I don't reply. I'm trying to work out if I can outrun him to the front door. He's several steps behind me and at least fifteen years older. But he's in good shape. The odds aren't great.

'I mean, the best thing you can probably do is kill yourself. It would be understandable in the circumstances. Your life is over anyway. You realise that, don't you? You'll never work again.' He's walking towards where I'm sitting, each step bringing my imminent death closer. 'So, what do you think, Molly? He reaches into his pocket and pulls out a syringe filled with a clear liquid. 'I came prepared. Just in case you put up a fight.'

'What's that?'

'Enough insulin to kill you. Having a diabetic wife has finally come in useful. It would be a nice gentle death too, Molly. You'd just drift away peacefully.' He taps the needle and holds it out to me. 'Tempted? Even a little? It would be the end to all your suffering, Molly. All that pain would be gone.' He perches on the arm of the chair, offering the syringe to me like a gift. 'I know you've had a hard time, Molly. Posey told me all about your mum. And your drinking problem. That you can't get a proper job or hold down a relationship. She told me how you were suicidal at university.'

Posey.

Posey, how could you?

She betrayed me. All those things she knew about me, the pain I shared with her, she shared with him. Hot tears spill out of my eyes and Patrick's words start to make sense. He's right. I've thought about it before. I've thought about it recently. What have I got to live for? I mean, really? I mess everything up. No one would miss me.

'Think about it, Molly. It would be so easy. Just a tiny little scratch and it's all over. Who would even miss you? You're an embarrassment, your dad would probably be pleased.'

Dad. My dad would miss me. I might be an embarrassment now, but he'd miss me. He's already buried his wife. I can't let him bury his daughter too. I just can't.

'Fuck off, Patrick,' I say, shoving his hand away from me and standing up.

He stands too. 'That's a shame. I hoped you'd be willing to do it yourself, but I guess I'm going to have to get hands-on with you after all.' He moves towards me. But I'm faster, sliding right past him on the polished floorboards in my socks. A frantic ice dancer, skating for her life. He makes a grab for me as I pass him, ripping a chunk of hair from my head. The pain propels me forward.

'You killed her!' I scream. 'You killed Posey.' I turn and hurl myself down the hallway, towards the front door, where I crash straight into another body.

I look up.

It's Jack.

*

'Jack! You need to help me. Patrick's here. He killed Posey. And he's trying to kill me. I need to get out of here. I need to get out of here now.'

I look up at Jack. He has a firm hold of me. I try to pull away from him and get to the door, but he holds me tight. Why won't he let me go? And then I remember that I don't know who this man is at all. How did he even know I was here? My blood runs cold as I remember Robyn's advice to turn the location services off my phone. How I didn't do it.

Jack.

'Let go of me!' I'm clawing him and biting him, thrashing to get out of his grip, but he's strong.

'Molly, calm down, please.' But I'm not listening.

'You. You're a liar. You're not even called Jack.' He looks at me, stunned, and I take the chance to slip out of his hands and towards the door. I just need to get outside. Then I can run.

'Molly,' Jack calls as I make my break for it. 'Wait I'm not—'

I don't hear the rest of the sentence though. The front door is within reach, but I *can't* reach it because my left foot is sliding on the wooden floor and the floor is rising up to meet my face. I try to put my hands out to break the fall, but I'm not fast enough. My head hits the floor. The last thing I hear is the crack of bone on wood.

The descent into darkness is welcome.

26

*

*

I open my eyes, groggy, the familiar feeling of having had too much to drink feels like home now. I wonder if I'm stuck in some eternal loop of passing out and waking up feeling awful, again and again, for the rest of time. But as my eyes begin to focus I notice, not without a flicker of surprise, that I'm not on my bathroom floor. I'm in a bed. It's soft and white and smells clean. That's how my brain registers it's not my own bed. And then I remember.

Jack.

I really have come full circle.

I can't remember how I got here but I remember Jack being there seconds before I was sucked into darkness. Did he kidnap me? Are he and Patrick holding me hostage somewhere? In a basement? In *Patrick's* basement?

I do a mental scan of my body. My limbs are all able to move. I don't appear to be bound or gagged or anything like that. I'm no professional kidnapper myself, but I'm pretty sure it's a basic rule that, when you snatch someone, you should really have them tied up so they can't escape. And gagged, so they can't scream the name of their kidnapper as they run. I wonder if I should scream, but my mouth is so dry, I very much doubt I could manage more than a croak. Again, not a professional, but I've never heard of police being alerted to a woman held hostage in a basement by a series of croaks. The other thing is, weirdly, I don't actually feel any sense of jeopardy. I don't *feel* scared. Not that my gut is any more trustworthy than the man who brought me here.

'You do realise you're saying all this out loud, don't you?' That voice.

Jack.

I try to scream for real as I pull myself into a sitting position where I see him sat in a green plastic chair by my side. He looks almost relieved to see me awake and moving. The room I'm in is alarmingly white and I can hear distant chatter and some beeping. There's a flat-screen TV on the wall opposite. Tea- and coffee-making facilities on a modern dresser to my right. There's a door next to the TV which is slightly ajar.

I can see it leads through to an en suite bathroom. There's a big window, with an orchid so pink I question its realness, on the sill. It's all so clean and lovely, I could be in a hotel.

Or.

Hospital.

I feel panic rising in my chest when I spot a canula in my hand and try to pull it out. It hurts too much though and I let out a squeal of pain.

'Take it easy, Molly,' Kidnapper Jack says as he reaches for a button somewhere above my head and pushes it.

Two seconds later, a nurse comes rushing into the room. Not kidnapped then. Dramatic bitch.

'Ah, Miss Monroe.' Her voice feels loud and intrusive in the quiet white room. 'We've been waiting for you to come round.' She smiles cheerfully, giving Jack a wink, and pours me a glass of water from a jug next to my bed. 'Here, have some of this. I bet you're mad thirsty.' She's right and I gratefully gulp the water down. I need to hydrate my addled brain. 'And how're you feeling?' There's a hint of something in her voice, perhaps West Country or Cornwall.

'Um . . . confused,' I say, truthfully. It's the one emotion I can firmly put a label on. 'I need to—' I gesture at the bathroom with my head, keeping a wary eye on Jack. I need to get away from him.

'Oh! Of course, let me help you.' She holds out her hands and helps me to my feet. I gingerly try to swing my legs off the bed, fully expecting them to be weak. But they're not. Not at all.

I walk barefoot into the small bathroom, clutching the

nurse's arm. She lets go of me and I close the door behind me, quickly locking it too. I need to get my thoughts in order. Is Jack here to finish off Patrick's work?

There's no mistake that this is much more than a run-of-the-mill NHS hospital. There are Elemis products in the shower. The loo roll is folded into a little point with a gold sticker holding it down. It could almost be a hotel. I sit on the loo, pee, wipe (after a small battle with the sticker which my right thumbnail loses) and flush. I wash my hands with Elemis soap. Then use a bit of the Elemis hand cream. Ooh, it's really thick and luxurious. My hands drink it in within seconds. I splash cold water on my face and hold my wrists under the faucet for a moment. What's going on? What do I know is true?

I'm in what appears to be an expensive private hospital.

I'm being watched by a potential kidnapper.

Last night I was almost killed by our next-door neighbour who I think killed my best friend.

Her boyfriend could be here to finish me off.

Nope.

Nothing makes any sense.

There's a gentle knocking at the door. 'Molly, come out. I need to talk to you.' Jack's voice cuts through the door. 'Come out and let me explain everything.'

'Where am I?'

'You're in the en suite. It's much more comfy in the main room.'

'Funny. You know what I mean.'

'You're in a private hospital. You had a nasty bump on the

285

head last night. Don't you remember? You slipped on your flooring trying to get away from Patrick Goldman.'

Is that what happened? My brain tries to piece together the events of the night before. I remember Patrick being in the flat. I remember discovering that Jack's been lying to me. Is he lying now?

'I have coffee here. It's not instant,' he says.

He's trying to lure me out like a I'm a traumatised dog and he's an RSPCA officer. He'll probably lasso me round the neck and drive me off to the pound if I go out there. Is that what they do?

'You've been lying to me,' I say, pathetically.

'Yes. And I'm sorry and I want to tell you the truth.'

I scoff. 'You don't know the meaning of the word.' I sound overly dramatic against Jack/Josh's soft, coaxing tones. Like a harried wife in a kitchen-sink drama.

'You'd be surprised.' There's a sigh, followed by a soft thud against the door and then a sliding sound, like fabric moving against the paintwork. I imagine Jack/Josh has slumped to the floor now, his back against the door. I take the same position in the bathroom.

'What's your real name?' I ask. It's a fair enough question.

'Joshua,' says Jack.

'Why did you lie to me? Why did you tell me your name is Jack? Why did you tell me you live in Vauxhall? What were you doing at my flat last night?'

'Come out and let me explain, Molly. Please. You're safe here. If you really feel scared of me, you can just push a button and a nurse will appear. Like a genie.' He has a point.

I tentatively get to my feet and unlock the door. Jack scrambles up from the floor and backs away from me, holding his palms out so I can see he doesn't have anything in them to harm me with.

I walk the long way round to the bed, not taking my eyes off him for one second.

I sit cross-legged on the bed, holding the nurse buzzer thing close to my chest.

'Start at the beginning.'

He nods once and takes a deep breath. 'Right, so, my full name is Joshua Jackson.' He waits for this to sink in.

'Oh. Like on *Daw*—'

'Yes, like on *Dawson's Creek*. Stop laughing.'

I can't help it though. I've always been oddly fascinated with people who share a name with someone famous. 'It could be worse,' I say. 'It could be Michael.'

'That's my dad's name. He's had a harder time than me.' I have to concentrate very hard to stop myself laughing.

'So, what should I call you?'

'Whatever you like, Molly. You certainly had a few choice suggestions last night.'

'I think you'll always be Jack to me,' I say, slowly. 'But why did you lie?'

'So, as you know now, I knew Posey. I was involved with Posey. Romantically.' He takes another deep breath. 'This is all going to sound a bit mad.'

'Jack. In the last week, I've had a sex tape go viral, my best friend has been murdered and no one believes me. The police think I'm insane. I found out that my now-dead best friend has uncovered something *extremely* dodgy, that has cost her her life. I've also found out about her affair with our neighbour and our landlord. Oh. And you. So, please. I think I can cope with things sounding "a bit mad".'

He raises his eyebrows and nods. 'Yes. Sorry. I didn't mean to patronise you.'

'It's fine. Continue.'

'So, you're probably wondering why you're here.'

'It's definitely on my list of questions, yes.'

'Like I said, this is a private hospital. You're here to make sure your bump on the head isn't serious and to keep you safe.'

'Safe from what?'

He takes a deep breath. 'Well, you've uncovered everything that Posey did. And, we want to make sure you don't end up being hurt. Especially as you've made everything public. But the good news is, we've made arrests. You won't be here long.'

'Who is "we" and why are you making arrests? Or let me guess, you aren't really an IT expert.'

'I am. Sort of. But not in the way I let you believe. I work undercover for a government agency which keeps an eye on the dark web. Amongst other things.' He tilts his head to one side. 'We've been trying to find out the truth about Lulu Lawrence. And Marilyn. And Posey. But you did it all. And on your own. You're a hero.' I wait, not quite knowing what to say, more used to being brushed off and ignored. 'We've arrested Patrick. You were right. It was a disgusting attempt to cover up the truth about that poor girl. Posey had worked it out too. But we weren't quick enough. It cost her her life.'

'And I cost Posey hers,' I whisper. Jack reaches for my hand, but I pull it away before he can touch me.

'No, Molly. You finished her story. The one she didn't get to tell. You did her proud.' His words are little comfort to me though. 'We've also charged Patrick with sexual assault, voyeurism, bribery, perverting the course of justice and the disclosure of sexual imagery without consent. He'll appear in court this morning. I believe he's planning to plead guilty.'

'Right,' I say, an intrusive image of Trudie and her children flashing into my mind.

'It means you won't have to give evidence,' Jack tells me. 'We're also working on getting the video removed completely from the internet. Sometimes even the internet can be chip paper, Molly.'

I'm silent. There is so much to take in. Then I remember something else.

'You loved her. Posey. You were a couple.'

Jack looks sadly down at his hands. 'Yes, I did. And yes, we were. It was very early days and I shouldn't have been romantically involved with her, but it was sort of hard not to fall in love with her.'

I smile sadly. 'That's one thing I can understand in all this mess.'

'I sort of virtually "bumped into" her while she was researching Lulu and was worried she was going to piss someone off. When I realised my plan to get her to drop the story wasn't going to work, I decided to help her. I completely underestimated her.'

'You tricked your way into her life?' I'm not shocked by

his admission. Men trick their way into women's lives and beds all the time. At least Jack's reason for doing so was a worthy one.

'Yes. At first. But then. Well, it became more.'

I nod, again, not surprised. People fell in love with Posey all the time. She was just one of those people. And, of course, she would have loved him back. They were a match in every possible way. Brilliant minds, dazzling looks. They would have made quite the couple. What a waste. But then a memory pops into my head from a time that feels equally a million years ago and a few days. Of waking up in bed and discovering Jack beside me. Of his smile. And of the quiet clicking of the front door closing when I came out of the shower.

The sound I thought was Posey leaving for work.

And then the slip-up when Jack told me he lived in Fulham, not Vauxhall where he apparently 'found me'.

'You were there. You were there that night.'

Jack sighs. 'I didn't have anything to do with Posey dying, Molly, I promise you. I wouldn't hurt a hair on that girl's head.'

'Why were you there? That morning? Why were you in bed with me? Why didn't you leave when you said you were leaving?'

He looks at me, puzzled.

'I heard you!' I continue. 'I heard you leaving. I thought you'd already gone, but when I got out of the shower, I heard the front door close. I assumed it was Posey leaving for work, but it was you, wasn't it? You already knew she was dead.'

Jack shakes his head. 'No. I'd left. When you went to take a shower, I knocked on her door but she didn't answer. We'd argued the day before. About Lulu. She refused to drop it and I called her stubborn and infuriating. She hung up on me and wouldn't answer her phone so I came over later to talk to her. But when I arrived, you were there, drunk out of your brain. Incoherent. Crying your eyes out.'

'Okay, so you were telling the truth about that bit, at least.'

'Yes. And I couldn't leave you like that. I tried knocking on Posey's door to help but she didn't answer. I mean, I could hardly just burst in when we'd been rowing. I thought I'd let her cool off and speak to her in the morning. I thought she was sulking. So I put you to bed while you told me your life story. You fell asleep and I was going to stay a little while, to make sure you didn't fall out of bed or choke on your vomit or something. But I ended up falling asleep too.'

'But why did you tell me your name is Jack? And that you lived in Vauxhall?'

He sighs, rubbing a hand over his face. 'I panicked, I suppose. I obviously didn't know Posey was dead and that you were blackout drunk. I was thinking about you talking about me later, telling her about a bloke called Josh who'd spent the night in your bed. I suppose I didn't want her getting the wrong idea.'

I nod, even though his words sting a little. 'So if it wasn't you who left the flat, who was it?'

'I'm not sure we'll ever know,' Jack says. 'I mean, Patrick had a key, so it could've been him.'

'Maybe he came round in the morning to make sure he hadn't left anything incriminating in Posey's room,' I muse.

'That question was put to him, but he's denied it.'

'It doesn't make sense though. If he's pleading guilty, why won't he admit it? He had a key *and* I saw him lurking around outside in the morning.'

Jack sighs heavily. 'The only thing he won't admit to is killing Posey. Says he didn't touch her. Wasn't there that night. Wasn't there that morning.'

'What? But it *was* him. He did it.' I feel panicky, like I'm losing my tenuous grip on reality. 'Why is he saying it wasn't him?' A memory comes back to me from the previous night. Patrick spitting fury, more than ready to shut me up for good. 'He came to the flat to kill me,' I say. 'It's not like he's not capable of it. He told me as much.'

Jack nods. 'He was desperate. To get Posey's evidence. To discredit you.'

'To silence me.' I look up at Jack. 'He explained how he'd already laid the groundwork for *my* disappearance.' My head feels like it's about to spin off my shoulders. Images from the awful video claw their way into my mind. Me, on my knees on a London street. My dress riding up my thighs. A man I can't see in front of me, his hands on my head. Another man filming, laughing. The humiliation hits me with a fresh force and I let my head drop into my hands. I don't want Jack to see me like this, burning up with shame.

Jack is nodding. 'Yes. You're really lucky no one hurt you, Molly.'

I can't keep the indignation out of my voice. 'No one

hurt me? No. One. Hurt. Me? I'm sorry. Was it you who had *the* most humiliating experience of your life posted on social media? Was it *you* who had to sit and watch it with your boss, while everyone else in your office already knew? Did you have to have a conversation with your *dad* about it?' I draw a breath. 'But I suppose it's different for men, isn't it? It's all a big laugh and boys will be boys. You don't even know shame. Not on the same level as women.'

Jack nods. 'That's why they did *that*. The video. The shame it caused.' He shuffles slightly closer to me on the chair. 'There are a number of reasons women might go missing and the police wouldn't look into it right away.' He lets this sink in for a moment.

'So, you're saying that if something happened to me after the video went viral and I disappeared, it wouldn't be taken seriously?'

He sighs again. 'It's not that they wouldn't take it *seriously*. They just might not prioritise looking for you. It would be an easy assumption that after a trauma like that, you'd probably make yourself disappear.'

Each one of his words is a wrecking ball to my nervous system. My fault. My. Fault. I think back to how worthless I felt and how – passing though the moment was – I wondered if my life would be easier if it was over.

'I shouldn't have let myself get so drunk,' I say, miserably.

'Stop that,' Jack says. 'This isn't on you. It's not on *you* not to get drunk. And, in all honesty, I wouldn't be surprised if you were helped along on your way a bit anyhow.'

'You think I was drugged?'

293

'It's completely likely. Have you ever had blackouts like that before?'

I think for a minute and shake my head. 'No. I mean, I know I've been a mess for . . . a while. But I usually have *some* recollection of what I've done and where I've been.'

Jack nods to himself, as if I'm confirming his suspicions.

*

There's a knock on the door that makes me jump up like a startled deer.

'Who's that?' I whisper to Jack.

He doesn't answer me, just opens the door. It's DI Wolfe.

'Jackson.' He nods at Jack, then turns to me. 'Hello, Molly,' he says. He's not wearing his usual non-uniform-police police suit. Instead, he's got on a pair of jeans and a slightly rumpled Ralph Lauren polo shirt. He looks like someone's dad. He looks like *my* dad. 'How are you doing?'

'Are you joking?' I ask. 'How do you think I'm doing? I've been humiliated, discredited, ignored. I've been viral on social media for most of this week. And because of this video, the police ignored me and thought I was being dramatic when I tried to tell them my flatmate had been killed.'

Wolfe at least has the decency to look slightly pained by my words.

'Yes,' he says, looking at his shoes, which are Converse high tops. I bet he smells like a mid-life crisis. 'Look, Molly, I owe you an apology. I'm sorry. Truly.' He looks it. And I can't believe for one moment that apologising is something

Wolfe does easily. It feels unusual, being on the moral high ground, for once. Not as good as I thought.

'It's okay,' I say.

'And I owe you a "thank you" too. Your gonzo reporting, while it probably broke the journalistic code in a thousand different ways, solved a crime. Well, several actually. And look,' he drops a pile of newspapers I didn't notice he was carrying on the bed-table thing in front of me, 'you're famous.' He coughs, embarrassed. 'Again.'

The Twitter post, I'd forgotten all about it. I spread the papers out in front of me. The headlines make me gasp.

Molly Monroe Saves the Day

From drunken zero to superhero

Molly Monroe is now doing the police's job for them

The mystery of Lulu Lawrence
solved – by a viral TikTok

Top City Lawyer Arrested in Lulu Lawrence Case

I flick through the reports and am surprised to see myself being spoken about positively in both red-tops and the more serious papers.

'Wow,' I say, tears threatening to spill down my cheeks. There are photos of Lulu, Marilyn and Christopher, and of Patrick being led away in handcuffs.

'You're a hero, Mols,' Jack says, giving my arm a squeeze. I skim as many of the reports as I can, but I can't find what I'm looking for. 'It doesn't say anything about Posey?' I glance up at Wolfe and his eyes look sad for a second.

'He hasn't been charged with Posey's murder,' he tells me. 'I'm sorry, Molly. I know that's why you started all this. I know it's not what you want to hear.' I stare at him, my mouth opens, but words don't come.

'But . . . he has a key,' I eventually manage to stutter. 'He told me, Posey gave him a key. He told me.'

Wolfe nods. 'Yes, we found it. But it wasn't him, Molly. He couldn't have done it. He has a watertight alibi.'

And then I realise.

Of course he does.

Because while someone let themselves into our flat and killed my best friend, Patrick was in Central London, filming me as I humiliated myself with a 'stranger'. Filming me, but accidentally starting a live stream.

The timestamps are his alibi.

My video is his alibi.

'He must've got someone else to do it for him,' I say, but even I can hear the fight has left me. However Patrick Goldman pulled off killing Posey, he's going to get away with it.

'He's being charged with a litany of crimes, Molly, including what he did to you. But we just can't pin this on him. There's nothing apart from circumstantial evidence to say Posey's death was anything other than the very sad accident we said it was. I'm sorry.'

I sink back against the pillows, feeling like everything has been sucked out of me. I feel totally empty.

'Fuck.' It's all I manage to say.

Jack swoops to my side. 'Molly, please don't let this get you down. Please. Look at what you've done. You finished Posey's investigation. You found out what happened to Lulu. You're amazing.'

'Yes,' Wolfe says. 'You really should be proud of yourself. You've done some excellent work here. I know it's hard but please try not to tie yourself in knots about Posey. You did your best.'

'But you think I'm wrong. You don't think she was killed.'

'I didn't say that,' Wolfe says. 'I said there's no evidence. It's not the same thing.'

'So, you *do* think she was killed?'

'What I think doesn't matter. What the CPS thinks matters. And there's just not enough evidence to keep investigating. I'm so sorry. I really am.' The three of us sit in silence for a few moments, processing Wolfe's words. Eventually, he takes a deep breath. 'I'll leave you to it. I'm sure there's lots here for you to take in, Molly. But please, give me a call if you need anything. I mean it this time. I won't fob you off.' He gives us a small smile, before letting himself out. We're left alone and just stare at the door for a few moments. Then Jack turns to me and I suddenly see the strain all of this has taken on him. His face isn't the beautiful, untroubled face I've always seen it as. His eyes are tired. Tired and extremely sad.

'Are you okay?' he asks.

'Not really, you?'

'Not at all, actually.' He sinks down onto the bed, suddenly exhausted. 'I really loved her, you know.'

'Me too. It was impossible not to.'

Jack looks at me and smiles a smile dripping in sadness.

'She didn't tell me about you,' I say. 'I don't know why. I wish she had. Why don't you fill me in on everything? I'd love to know.' I pat the bed next to me. 'Come on, story time.'

Jack heaves himself up until he's propped up on the pillows next to me.

'I promised I'd keep her safe,' he whispers. 'I promised her and I let her down.'

I lean my head on his shoulder. 'It's a pretty non-exclusive club,' I say. 'But tell me. Tell me from the beginning.'

*

I let my eyes fall shut as Jack begins the story of him and Posey. My head is still pounding, but a nurse slipped in earlier with some tiny pills in a paper cup.

'Take these, petal. You had a really nasty knock. It'll take the edge off.' I feel them begin to carry me away, out of pain as Jack talks.

'It was accidental, how we met,' he's saying. 'I was looking into Lulu Lawrence after seeing some horrible rumours on that dark web forum.' I feel him shudder next to me. 'She thought she was being really stealth, but she was actually leaving a trail of mess all over the net. Both sides of it. I messaged her. Not very nicely to begin with. I sent her a threat, hoping it would scare her off.' He gives a dark laugh.

'But it did the exact opposite?' I *did* know Posey. And I know that she wouldn't be scared off by someone behind a keyboard threatening her. It would have made her even more certain there was a good story and more determined to dig out the truth.

'Yep, the exact opposite. It was like I lit a fuse in her.' He smiles at this memory of Posey, her tenacity. 'So I decided to try a different tack and befriended her. On Reddit.'

'You're LeoTheLion?'

He nods. 'I wanted to tell her why she should leave the Lulu story, that I thought she could be putting herself in danger. But it was impossible to do that without telling her who I am and what I knew.' He smiles again. 'That woman was absolutely relentless. She wore me down in the end and I agreed to meet her and tell her everything I knew, as long as it was off the record. I'd lose my job if it was found out I'd been spilling secrets. And that's best-case scenario. I could go to prison.' He sighs now. This is something still weighing heavily on him, but I don't ask. I let him talk about Posey. 'I arranged to meet her in a bar near Waterloo. It was a busy place, she insisted on that. We were both holding copies of *The Anglian Times* so we could recognise each other. Posey, rightly, said we needed something obscure because too many people would be reading *Metro* or whatever. She was smart in ways I wasn't. What she didn't know is that I wouldn't need her to be holding anything to recognise her. I'd done a full search on her already. I knew she was the most beautiful woman I'd ever seen. She was even more beautiful in real life. That zest for life poured out of her. But I think

I was already a bit in love with her before that night. Not very professional of me, but what could I do? I walked up to her and asked her if she was Posey Porter – like I didn't know – she waved her copy of *Anglian Times* at me and said, "Leo the Lion, I presume."

'"My name's Josh," I replied. I don't even know why I gave her my *real* real name. It just sort of slipped out. I guess she really was a great journalist. I knew then that I was in trouble. I asked what she wanted to drink, but she said she already had some water. I went to the bar and got water for myself and, because I hadn't eaten since lunch, some salt and vinegar crisps. I opened them and split the packet down the middle, putting it on the table.'

'Ah, universal pub language for "these are for you too".' Jack grins at me.

'That's exactly what Posey said. Later, like days later, she told me all about how I passed her Pub Snack Test.' The mention of Posey's Pub Snack Test makes me laugh. She basically had this theory that you could tell exactly what sort of a person you were drinking with based on what bar snacks they chose.

'It's quite simple and yet to be proven wrong,' she had told me one evening, back when we were both poor students, trying to make the cheapest bottle of house white last an entire evening. 'For example, olives hint at potential for pretentiousness. Anything scampi flavoured indicates lack of respect for companions. Those things reek. Nuts suggest possible ulterior motives. Think about it. They're not easy to share without a certain amount of finger proximity. This is someone who wants to touch you. Obviously, if they don't offer them up for sharing then they're just a bit of a dick. Crisps are a good choice, and salt and vinegar, the ideal flavour. Ready salted is the missionary position of the crisp world while cheese and onion follow the same theory as scampi. Anything outside of the Big Three flavours is too risky and demonstrates an individual only concerned with their own pleasure. Certainly not someone you should be considering having sex with.'

I imagine her running through her theory in her head, mentally awarding Jack a full five stars. She would have fancied him already, probably from the moment he turned his back and she watched him walk to the bar, but this would've sealed it.

'Things got quite flirty almost right away,' Jack's now saying. 'I reiterated that what I told her had to be off the record. She held up two fingers and said, "Guide's honour." I told her that it only counts if it's three fingers and, honestly, the look she gave me. I couldn't breathe for a bit. But I managed to pull myself together and tell her about Lulu, the stuff you found out by yourself, the media blackout, that she wasn't in touch with her friends, that Marilyn was still looking for her.'

My mind wanders to Marilyn, who'd seemed desperate and grief-stricken when I'd met her. I don't believe she harmed Lulu out of maliciousness. She was broken and very unwell and no one gave her the help she needed. I think of Patrick, how he was so desperate to keep his part in Lulu's story quiet that he pulled strings and blackmailed people, under the pretence of helping Marilyn. If he'd wanted to help her, save her, he would've made sure she had professional help for whatever mental condition she was suffering from, had been suffering from for most of her life. It was tragic. No one needed to die.

Jack carries on, telling me how he and Posey ended up spending most of the night at the bar. How she'd gone to get the next round of drinks and had come back with a huge pink piña colada for him, complete with a pink straw, a paper flamingo, an umbrella and a pineapple garnish.

'She got the pinkest, most outrageously girlie drink she could find, thinking she'd embarrass me. But she didn't. She was impressed when I proudly drank it, even though there were some laddish types around giving me looks.' Another one of Posey's self-reviewed personality tests. And another box ticked for Jack. She would've been smitten after that.

'I was smitten after that,' Jack says, like he's read my mind. 'I was desperate to see her again. To keep seeing her. To kiss her. But she told me she was involved with someone and she needed to end it properly. She told me it needed to end anyway, but she was adamant she had to do that before she'd take things further with me.'

'Patrick,' I say.

'Patrick,' Jack confirms.

'Did she know about his involvement with Marilyn and Lulu?' I ask, but Jack shrugs.

'I don't know. But I can't imagine something like that slipping past her. I like to think she broke things off with him because of me, but if she was starting to have suspicions about him, that could have had something to do with it too. As much as I my ego doesn't want it to be true.' He gives me a half smile. 'She did it the next night and after that we spent as much time together as we could. I don't know why she didn't tell you. I guess she was respecting the fact that I shouldn't be involved with someone with a conflict of interest. I'm sure she would've told you if she could.'

I feel a stab of hurt. 'I wouldn't have said anything.' I sound petulant.

'I know that now,' Jack tells me, nudging my shoulder gently. 'But I didn't know anything about you back then. I didn't know that you're cut from the same cloth as Posey. I didn't know that you are also the most incredible woman. I didn't know that you were in danger too. I might not have been able to keep Posey safe, but I promise you, Molly Monroe, I will not let you down.' His words are like a lullaby as the pills the nurse gave me kick in a little more, pulling me into a place where I feel fuzzy and warm.

And safe.

27

*

Nine months later

It's strange seeing my dad again after all this time. He looks like an older version of himself. Which, I suppose, is exactly what he is. It's just weird to see a face you once knew so well, suddenly old. I notice how he winces slightly as he pulls out the chair opposite me and sits. He's as grey as a goat.

'Old age,' he gruffs, eyeing me. 'I thought I told you not to come here anyway?'

'You did,' I agree. 'But you also accepted the visiting order, so I assumed that you wanted to see me really.'

He shrugs. 'I don't want you around here. Around these people.' He gestures at the other inmates dotted around the visiting room, a half-snarl on his face. 'The things I've had to hear them say about you. I wanted to protect you from that.'

'Thanks, Dad.'

'So, what was so important that you just had to come and see me?'

I pull the book from my bag and proudly slide it across the table to him.

'Look,' I say, unable to keep the smile out of my voice. 'I've been published.'

'Something smutty, is it?' someone shouts, having seen me pass the book to Dad. 'Worth a read if it's anything like the videos you make.'

'I will break your fucking neck,' Dad shouts back, earning him a warning look from the guard nearest us. 'Fucking lags,' he hisses. 'I'm sorry, Mols. That's why I didn't want you to come here. You shouldn't have to hear that.'

It's almost funny. 'Believe me, I've heard a lot worse than that. I'm actually pretty un-shockable these days.' A half truth.

Fact: I'm not completely un-shockable.

What I've passed to Dad is a copy of my book, *The Girl in the Video*. I had been approached by a publisher and asked if I'd be interested in writing my story. The book has been out for only a week, but it's selling pretty well, by all accounts. I don't really care about that though, holding my own book in my hands is enough. Being able to give this to Dad is enough. More than enough. I beam at him, like I've just passed him his first grandchild.

'What's it about then, this *Girl in the Video*?'

'It's about me. A memoir. And the truth.'

Dad nods slowly, as if he doesn't understand. He was never much of a reader, from what I can remember. Although you'd think he'd make an effort to pick up a book now he has all this time on his hands. 'Suppose I make an appearance in it then?'

It's a funny thing, when you tell people you've written a book, one of the most common things they ask you is 'Am I in it?' which, I think, says quite a bit about the human ego.

'One or two.' I smile.

He gives me an awkward smile back and we sit there for a minute or two, half-grinning at each other.

'I'm actually here with some news,' I finally manage.

'Not pregnant, are you?' He looks suspiciously at my belly.

It's such a ridiculous notion I almost laugh. 'God, no,' I say. 'I'm actually leaving for a bit. I'm going to travel for a little while. So, I guess this is a goodbye. Of sorts. For a while.'

He cocks his head to the side as if I'm something wildly exotic that needs careful examination. After a moment or two he nods again. Just the once. 'Good,' he says. 'Could never bear the thought of you stuck in that miserable flat in that miserable job.' I look at his hands. These big bear hands that used to tickle me and hold me and protect me. Hands that also inflicted unimaginable harm. They don't look as big as the hands in my memories. They are older hands that worry the skin on each other.

'Coming from a man serving life?'

'I don't regret what I did, Mols,' he says, the tone changing rapidly. 'I'd do it again. In a heartbeat.' My sense of justice is obviously something I inherited from my dad.

'I know,' I say. 'I'm sorry I've been angry at you for so long.'

'I don't blame you. I'd be pretty angry with me too.'

'Not because of what you did. But because you left me by myself.'

'Oh, Mols. You were at uni. A grown-up.'

'It didn't mean I didn't still need at least one parent around.' I sound petulant.

He hangs his head so suddenly it's as if someone snapped his neck. 'I know that now. That's the one thing I'd do differently. I'd wait a few more years.' A couple of beats pass between us before he almost whispers, 'I'm sorry.' This time I reach my hand out and put it over his. 'David . . . that monster hurt your mother, Molly. He was the reason she . . . she . . .' He doesn't need to say anything more.

My dad killed a man.

I wish I could say that he didn't mean to do it or that it was a tragic accident, but I would be lying. He fully intended to harm David Ayers on the day he beat him into a coma. He didn't blink when David died in hospital and the attempted murder charge he was being held on became a murder charge. He refused a lawyer and pleaded guilty, telling the court that they had blood on their hands too. According to newspaper reports at the time, this didn't sit well with the judge, who handed him a twenty-five-year sentence. The judge had said that not only was Dad's crime appallingly violent, but the amount of time he'd been waiting to carry it out was frightening. He said that Dad had not only ripped apart the lives of David's family, but also that of his own daughter. He also said that Dad's apparent lack of remorse was bordering on psychopathic. But I'd like to know what the judge would have done if he was in Dad's position. If he'd been let down by the police – over and over again. If his beloved wife had died because of them. If he'd been left to bring up a grieving young girl alone. None of this was reported in the newspapers. It's the reason I decided to become a journalist. I thought I'd be able to find the truth and write it. I was very naïve back then.

I was the one who'd found Mum. I was only twelve, but it's not the kind of thing that slips your mind. She was on her bed though, not in the bath. Her eyes were the same as Posey's and I thought dead people always closed their eyes before they died. I didn't know she was dead and I lay down next to her, telling her about school that day. I chattered away to her about how I didn't like my lunch so much that day and could I have cheese and ham but no salad in my sandwiches the next day, because the salad goes all floppy by lunchtime. And then I just lay there, looking up at the ceiling, as she was, assuming we were in some kind of shared reverie. The memory is a video on pause until our neighbour, whose name I can't remember, comes in. Then there was shrieking and lights were turned on because it was dark outside by then and two police came and asked me things and the neighbour was crying. And then Dad was there cuddling me, saying, 'I thought you were both gone' over and over again.

David, a man my dad once employed in his kitchen-fitting business, had become obsessed with Mum. He'd been helping with our new kitchen but kept turning up at our house once the job was finished or if Dad was working elsewhere. Once, David was in the house when I came home from school. He'd always been nice to me but this day he snarled at me like a beast and told me to 'scram'. It was only later I found out that he'd attacked Mum when she'd rejected him. And he wouldn't leave her alone even after that, telling my dad they'd been having an affair, that Mum had been pregnant with his baby and a bunch of other lies. Dad didn't believe a word of it and they reported Ayers to the police. But nothing was done, the police decided the matter was 'domestic' and Ayers harassed my mum until she was a ball of pure anxiety. We're not sure if she meant to overdose on the sleeping tablets that took her life or if she was just trying to get a break from the constant fear she was living with. She didn't leave a note. Dad and I agree that it was an accident, but one that could've been prevented if the police had taken the complaints about harassment seriously. Only Dad took it much worse than I realised and, seven years later when I'd left for university, he tracked Ayers down and battered him. Dad had planned on beating Ayers to death and had waited for me to leave home to do it.

'I'm glad you've left that job though. I'm happy about your book,' Dad eventually says, breaking our shared silence. 'It's good to see some of the fight back in you, Molly.'

'I've been so scared for so long,' I say. 'Scared of making a wrong move. Scared of losing even more. I tried to live my life without making any ripples and look.' I laugh, darkly. 'It all came crashing down anyway.'

My dad's blue eyes shine sadly at me. 'Let me tell you one thing I've learned, mostly the hard way, shit stuff is going to happen to you, no matter what. You can hide away at home all day, not making ripples, not taking chances. But.

The bad stuff will keep happening. Not one person on this planet lives a completely charmed life. We lose loved ones, there will be wars, there will be suffering.'

'This is a horrible pep talk, you know that, right?'

'Shh. I haven't finished. The bad stuff will keep coming, Molly, no matter what you do. But the good stuff, the moments that take your breath away, the moments when you can't see anything bad because you're so dazzled by happiness, those moments you've got to work for. Do you understand what I'm saying?'

I nod. 'Shit happens so balance it out?'

'Shit happens so balance it out.' He smiles. And then his face turns serious again. 'Just to clarify, this isn't balancing it out.' He gestures around the visiting hall. 'This wasn't part of the plan.'

'I know, Dad,' I say. 'I know.'

He smiles at me and it's a full-face smile this time.

'I'm proud of you, Mols,' he says. 'I know I'm not the greatest role model and I'm an even worse dad, but look at you. Look at what you've achieved in spite of it all. You've never given yourself enough credit.'

My heart aches when we say goodbye. I don't know when I'll see him again but I promise to write.

'Just don't put anything about our prison-break scheme in the letters,' he calls over his shoulder as he's herded back to the cells with the other inmates. 'They *read* them.'

I shake my head at him, but return his full smile. He'll be okay. He's still got his sense of humour.

My flight leaves later today, but there's one more stop I need to make before heading to the airport.

*

It's been a while since I've visited her grave. A wave of guilt washes over me as I realise it's probably going to be a long time before I do it again. I lay down the bunch of sunflowers, her favourite, and squat awkwardly by the headstone.

'Hi, Mum,' I say as I run my fingers over the smooth marble, feeling the indentations where her name is embossed in gold. 'I'm sorry I haven't been to see you for a while. Things have been . . . tough . . . weird. But they're okay now. I think. I hope.' I pick up some dried-up flowers, crunching the dead leaves and petals in my fingers. 'Patrick is in jail. He pleaded guilty to all the charges. I don't remember them all, but he's been sentenced to fifteen years. So that's something. And I didn't have to give evidence.'

I'd written a victim statement though; about the abject shame I'd felt when the video went viral. About the abuse I suffered on social media. About the trauma counselling I've been having weekly and the long-lasting impact his actions have had on my mental health. It was the hardest thing I've ever had to write. Apart from the eulogy at Posey's funeral, that is.

It's very definitely summer now. The trees are blazes of green glory and, the sun is high and alone in the sky.

'So. I have some news. I'm leaving for a while. It feels like the right time now to see what the rest of the world has to offer. I've got a deal for a second book. And I'm using the money from the advance to buy a ticket to Hydra.' I pause, never feeling comfortable talking to empty space. Even with no one else here I feel the prickles of self-consciousness rise. 'It's a Greek island,' I add because the silence feels awkward. Then I laugh at myself, fully aware of how ridiculous I am. 'It was all bohemian artists and stuff in the Sixties,' I tell her, as if she wouldn't have known. 'Maybe I'm hoping some of that creativity is still living there and will rub off on me.'

I sigh as a small gust of wind blows around me, making me shiver. 'I couldn't stay in the flat after what happened there. Anyway, Jesse has put it on the market. I can't imagine it will be easy to sell. House of Horrors and all that. Although some people like that kind of thing, don't they?'

I'm not a believer in ghosts. But if I were, I'd say that the ghost of Posey will forever haunt that place, although I'm hoping that some of what I've done since her death will help her to rest in peace.

'Anyway, I'm not going forever. Just for a year or so to start with. Then I'll see how I go. I've got a good advance from my publisher so I should be okay out there for a while.'

I sigh again, not sure what else to say.

'I miss you. Every day. I always will.'

I place a copy of my book down next to the sunflowers, knowing the inscription will go unread and the pages will get ruined by the rain due in the next few days. If the winds don't carry it away before that. Or the rats discover it and use it for bedding. I try to ignore the voice in my head telling me that's all it's good for. I guess that's something I still need to work on. Like my second book, I'm a work in progress. And. And this is okay.

I kiss the tips of my fingers and gently transfer the kiss to the marble headstone.

'I love you, Mum.'

And then I turn and walk away, towards a smiling figure in a car waiting patiently by the cemetery gates for me.

'Ready?' Jack asks me as I strap myself in beside him.

'As I'll ever be.' I take a deep breath.

'I'm going to miss you, Molly Monroe.'

'I'm going to miss you too . . . Joshua Jackson.' I gently hum the *Dawson's Creek* theme song.

'Actually. Not that much.'

We both relax into easy silence as Jack drives us out of the city and onto the motorway towards the airport.

*

My flight is from Heathrow to Athens. I then have to take a train to Piraeus and finally a ferry to Hydra. I've chosen Hydra because of its creative history. A place that was inspirational for Leonard Cohen seems like a pretty good place for me to write in. Jack hangs around with me at the airport before I check in.

'Need to make sure you actually get on the plane.' He grins as we nurse airport beers, waiting for my gate to be called.

'You can still come?' I say but he shakes his head.

'I'll come for a holiday, I promise. Oh, I almost forgot

to give you this.' He hands me a gift bag and I look at him, puzzled.

'I thought we agreed not to do goodbye gifts, it's not goodbye, remember?'

'It's actually from Jesse,' Jack says. 'He's sad he didn't get to give it to you himself, but he wanted to wish you well and apologise for being a bullshit landlord and selling your home.'

I roll my eyes but take the bag and stuff it into my hand luggage. 'A bit too little, too late, but whatever.'

I try not to cry when I go to check in and leave Jack, waving at me. But it's *not* goodbye. I'll be back – and hopefully healed – one day.

*

The journey is long and sweaty, but when I step off the ferry in Hydra I feel a freedom I've never felt before.

'Here for a holiday?' an old man with a ruddy, sun-loved face asks as he steps down alongside me.

'Of sorts,' I reply. He chuckles.

'Well, let me tell you a thing. You'll love it. And when, if, you leave, throw some coins into the harbour. It's an old superstition that will ensure you come back here one day.' He pats my arm and saunters off. Which is an impressive gait for a man of his advanced years.

I look at my new surroundings, my lungs aching from breathing in the fresh sea air during the hour and a half ferry ride. It's an impossibly pretty island. Tiny, white houses speckle the mountains and dazzle against the blue skies. The kind of blue that defines the colour. I wonder if I've ever truly seen blue before this moment. Chatter from Hydra Port, the island's only town, and an almost tuneless ringing of bells, which still manages to be beautiful, makes up the soundtrack. The air smells like salt and donkeys and promise.

As I take in this moment, I can never imagine standing in a queue six-people deep, to get on a train underground again. It seems a totally ludicrous suggestion. I read that Leonard Cohen once said of Hydra, 'Nothing offends the eye.' He would've been talking of Sixties Hydra, but it's still true. The island is untouched by modernisation. It remains free of resorts or chain hotels.

It's perfect.

'Molly!'

I hear my name and let my gaze roam over the handful of people waiting near the moored ferry for the passengers to disembark. She's waving and looks smaller than she ever did in London. I wind my way through the small crowd of bodies and towards her.

'Molly.' She says my name again and enfolds me in a huge embrace. I worry about how I smell after the hours on planes, trains and water-mobiles. 'It's so good to see you.' She lets me go and holds me at arm's length, taking me in. 'It's so good to see you.' I nod my agreement, a smile as warm as the Greek sun spreading across my face.

'Hi, Robyn.'

She chatters away to me as she helps me with my bags, telling me all about the apartment she's rented us for the next few months. It's a fifteen-minute walk from the port and is exactly what I hoped an apartment in Hydra would look like, whitewashed bricks, some type of flower sprouting from every crack. Inside it's tiled and cool and I flop onto a modern L-shape sofa that looks comically out of place in the old building.

'Drink?' Robyn asks. I nod and she disappears into the kitchenette while I scrabble around in my bag, looking for my phone. I promised to text Jack as soon as I got here so he knows I'm safe and haven't managed to get myself kidnapped or detained en route.

'What's that?' Robyn hands me a glass of ice-cold water, she's pointing at the gift bag Jack gave me.

'Oh. A present from Jesse apparently. He's sorry about selling the flat and generally making my time living there horrible.' I laugh. Robyn laughs too.

'Open it,' she says. 'I want to know what gift he thinks could possibly make up for being an A-grade twat.'

I pull the bag open. There's a bon voyage card with no envelope, which means he probably stole it from the corner shop. He's scribbled the word 'sorry' in it.

There's also a bottle of wine.

A bottle of Twin Oaks Sauvignon Blanc.

It was him.

28

*

Posey

I press send on the email and slam my laptop shut. I want to catch Molly and make amends with her before she goes to bed. I hate falling out with her and I need to be a more supportive friend. I should be finding out why she's going so badly off the rails at the moment. I've been too involved in this Lulu Lawrence stuff and haven't paid her much attention. I know Molly and I know this is her way of crying for help. And I'm the only person she's got.

I throw my bedroom door open, just as I hear her footsteps in the hallway. It's dark, but I can just about see her outline.

'Molly! Come on, I'll make you a coffee. Let's sit down and have a chat. I'm sorry. I don't care about the stupid dress.' I reach to click the light on at the wall outside my room, but there's suddenly a hand around my wrist, gripping me hard, pulling me back into my room.

'Yeah. You're right. We do need to have a chat. But let's do it in here.'

It's not Molly, I know that even before he speaks. Before he drags me into my room, throwing me down on the bed.

'What are you doing here?' I ask. 'You're not meant to just let yourself in without notice!'

'I told you. I always keep a key for emergencies. And I consider this an emergency. Have a drink with me, Posey.'

'Jesse, you've had enough already. Go home. And leave your key. You know you're not meant to do this. I'll call the police.' But he's not listening to me. He's lurching towards where I landed on the bed, there's a bottle of wine in his right hand. It's the same bottle we shared the time we had sex. I search his eyes for the Jesse I know, but they're expressionless. I've seen the same look in Molly's eyes when she's having an alcohol-blackout. He's beyond drunk and I feel prickles of fear poking at me. 'Jesse, come on. Go upstairs and sleep it off. You're going to feel terrible in the morning. But we can talk tomorrow, okay? I promise.' He turns to me and I'm relieved to see his eyes have come to life again. The relief is short-lived though as it registers that he's looking at me with contempt.

'Why don't you want me? I'm in love with you, Posey. I've been in love with you since the day you and Molly came to see the flat.' He sags against the pillows and I can't help but feel sorry for him. He looks utterly defeated now.

'Jesse. I'm sorry. I really am. I just don't feel that way about you. But you're a really good friend.' I don't know what to say to soften the blow. 'You cheered me up so many times over the last year. And you've helped us out loads. I *do* appreciate that.'

'Why did you sleep with me?'

'I . . . I don't know. I shouldn't have. I didn't realise you felt like this. I wasn't trying to lead you on.'

He snorts. Snot comes out of his nose and I'm physically repulsed by him. I need him to get out of here.

'Do you love that dickhead next door? Is it because he's rich? Is it because he's married?' He sounds so forlorn and I start to feel bad again. But I shake the feeling away. I should be able to say no to this man, without it turning into this.

'I don't love him either, Jesse. I don't. It's been over with him for weeks as well.'

'You used us both?'

'It wasn't like that. It wasn't. Please, go home. We'll talk tomorrow.' I'm tired now. I want him to leave so I can go to bed. 'Please, Jesse. It's been a really long day and I just want to go to sleep.' I'm not prepared for it when he starts to cry. Real, shuddering sobs like a little boy. I'm not great with crying people. Especially when I'm the cause of the tears. I go to my bathroom and grab a handful of sheets of loo roll. Then I go back to where he's still sobbing on my bed. 'Here you go, Jesse, stop crying. It's okay.' I scoot up next to him and gently put my arm on his. He takes the tissue and blows his nose.

'You really want me to go home?'

'I think you need to go home and sober up, Jess.'

He looks sadly at the bottle of wine. 'Will you please

just have one drink with me? Just one for old times' sake and then I promise I'll go. Please, Posey.'

I sigh. I want him to leave so badly that I'll even swallow down a glass of wine I don't want.

'Okay,' I tell him. 'Wait here. I'll go and get some glasses.'

I get two wine glasses from the kitchen. When I get back, Jesse seems calmer. Well, he's stopped crying at least. He pours us each a glass from the bottle.

'Thank you,' he says quietly.

'Just one drink, okay?' I take a long gulp of the wine. It's every bit as awful as I remember it being. He's definitely more of a lager lout than wine connoisseur. The wine goes to my head much quicker than it should. I haven't eaten anything all day though so it's not surprising. I was planning on getting something with Molly but obviously that didn't go to plan. But still, I feel much wobblier than I should after one glass. Even if I did down it on an empty stomach. Jesse is watching me, intently. I need space away from him. 'I'm going to get some water,' I try to say, but my words are as thick as blood in my mouth. I attempt to stand up, but my legs don't want to and the last thing I see is the floor crashing up towards me. Or me crashing towards it.

'Jesse,' I try to say. 'What have you done?'

I somehow know they're going to be my last words.

I have so much more to say.

A Letter from Katy Brent

Thank you so much for choosing to read *The Murder After the Night Before*. I hope you enjoyed it! If you did and would like to be the first to know about my new releases, you can sign up to my mailing list below.

Sign up here! https://signup.harpercollins.co.uk/join/6n7/signup-hq-katybrent

I hope you loved *The Murder After the Night Before* and if you did I would be so grateful if you would leave a review. I always love to hear what readers thought, and it helps new readers discover my books too.

Thanks,
Katy

How to Kill Men and Get Away With It

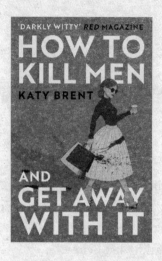

Meet Kitty Collins.
FRIEND. LOVER. KILLER.

He was following me. That guy from the nightclub who
wouldn't leave me alone.
I hadn't intended to kill him of course. But I wasn't
displeased when I did and, despite the mess I made,
I appeared to get away with it.
That's where my addiction started . . .
I've got a taste for revenge and quite frankly, **I'm killing it.**

**A deliciously dark, hilariously twisted story about
friendship, love, and murder. Fans of *My Sister the Serial
Killer*, *How to Kill Your Family* and Killing Eve will love
this wickedly clever novel!**

Acknowledgements

Wow, I can't believe I'm actually writing another one of these. I feel so honoured. There are so many people I want to thank, if it takes a village to raise a child then it takes a city to get a book to publication. So forgive me if there's anyone I miss out.

First off I want to thank the amazing editors who helped bring Molly Monroe's story to life. Belinda Toor and Audrey Linton, I don't have the words to tell you how much I have appreciated your insights and guidance. This book would be nothing without you both and I will be eternally grateful. You both know how nervous I've been about the Tricky Second Novel and have guided me through the process with patience and kindness. Thank you.

My wonderful agent, Euan Thorneycroft, I'm honoured to have you on my team. Thank you for un-muddying the waters for me and your endless patience with my endless questions. Here's to more books and more road trips.

Massive thanks to everyone at HQ and HarperCollins who have made my dreams come true with both this book and How To Kill Men. Emma Pickard, Natasha Gill, Jo

Kite, Komal Patel, Caroline Lakeman, Thomas Wright and everyone else who has been involved. I couldn't have asked for a better publishing experience and that's down to you guys.

Big thanks to Graham Bartlett for talking me through the police procedural bits and bobs which Molly had to deal with. Crime writers, I cannot recommend Graham enough if you need guidance and advice in this area.

One of the best things about being a writer is the wonderful writing community and I am lucky enough to have met and connected with some brilliantly amazing people over the past year. Special thanks to Amy Beashel for the sprints, the chats, the reassurances and just massive love and support. It means so much. Also huge thank yous to Jesse Sutanto and Laurie Elizabeth Flynn – the writers really are all so nice here. Sarah Clarke, Charlotte Levin and Ruth Kelly for your support and insights into the biz. And Rob Dinsdale, just thank you for everything.

Sadly, while I was writing this book, I lost someone close to me who I loved very much. This experience made writing Molly's grief a much more visceral experience than I'd anticipated. But it also helped me process something that made absolutely no sense at all. Cherith Nicholl, this one's for you doll. I love you and cannot imagine a world without your light in it. Sleep well, beautiful girl.

My ever loving and supportive friends and sisters, thank you always for the fun, the laughs, the love. You all rock.

My mum, Carla, thank you as always for your love, support and dog-sitting. I love you very much and *literally* wouldn't be here without you.

And my darling children, Seb and Sophia, thank you for just being who you are unapologetically. I love you always and forever.

Lastly, and definitely not leastly (it's a word now, okay) thank you to every reader, blogger, reviewer and bookseller who has got behind me and supported both of my books. You make dreams come true, you really do, and I can never ever thank you enough.

Dear Reader,

We hope you enjoyed reading this book. If you did, we'd be so appreciative if you left a review. It really helps us and the author to bring more books like this to you.

Here at HQ Digital we are dedicated to publishing fiction that will keep you turning the pages into the early hours. Don't want to miss a thing? To find out more about our books, promotions, discover exclusive content and enter competitions you can keep in touch in the following ways:

JOIN OUR COMMUNITY:

Sign up to our new email newsletter: http://smarturl.it/SignUpHQ

Read our new blog www.hqstories.co.uk

🐦 https://twitter.com/HQStories

📘 www.facebook.com/HQStories

BUDDING WRITER?

We're also looking for authors to join the HQ Digital family!

Find out more here:

https://www.hqstories.co.uk/want-to-write-for-us/

Thanks for reading, from the HQ Digital team